Praise for *Dreams of Di*

"I love Patricia McKillips's novels, but even more, I am pa her brilliant short stories—those coruscating jewels that are both remarkable for their language, their power, their wit, and their depth. She writes pure fantasy and historical fantasy with equal ease. More, more please."
—Jane Yolen, author of *Briar Rose, Sister Emily's Lightship, The Devil's Arithmetic,* and *Sister Light, Sister Dark*

★"McKillip (*Wonders of the Invisible World*), winner of the World Fantasy Award for Lifetime Achievement, collects nine dazzling shorter pieces (both originals and reprints) in this outstanding collection. The brief, creepy "Weird" opens the volume, merging an oddly romantic picnic in a bathroom and a mysterious threat outside into something that exists in a darkly beautiful interstitial place. The longest piece, "Something Rich and Strange," which appeared originally as a standalone novella in Brian Froud's Faerielands series, is an ecological fairy tale that contains the most gorgeous of McKillip's prose ("her blind stare of pearl and wormwood")—and the weakest of her plots, but even weaker McKillip is well worth reading. The newer stories also shine. "Mer" is a small gem about a nameless witch, a fishing village, and a mermaid statue. "Edith and Henry Go Motoring" features a toll bridge that leads travelers on an unexpected journey. Beyond the short fiction, the volume finishes with an essay on writing high fantasy, and an appreciation of McKillip's work by renowned fantasist Peter S. Beagle. Fans of exquisite prose and ethereal fantasy will need to own this."
—*Publishers Weekly,* starred review

"Some authors we read for their characters and their plots, others for the beauty of their language. I read Pat McKillip for all three. She's gifted beyond compare, a national treasure who should be cherished

by all lovers of literature, and *Dreams of Distant Shores* is a perfect example of why I hold her in such high esteem."
—Charles de Lint, author of *The Onion Girl* and *The Riddle of the Wren*

"Ever since finding and loving *The Riddle-Master of Hed* many years ago, I have read everything Patricia McKillip has written. You should too. Start with this book!"
—Garth Nix, author of *Sabriel* and the Keys to the Kingdom series

"Anyone about to open this book is a very lucky person indeed. You are about to encounter mysteries, monsters, jewels, songs, witches, a treasure chest of story. Here are magic worlds, places of enchantment, and a wonderful, lyrical voice to guide you through them."
—Lisa Goldstein, author of *The Red Magician* and *The Uncertain Places*

Praise for the Patricia A. McKillip story collection
Wonders of the Invisible World

"McKillip's is the first name that comes to mind when I'm asked whom I read myself."
—Peter S. Beagle, author, *The Last Unicorn, The Line Between,* and *Sleight of Hand*

"Endlessly astonishing and impressive fantasist McKillip (*The Bards of Bone Plain*) travels the shadowy twilight realm between worlds and returns with the raw stuff of dreams."
—*Publishers Weekly,* starred review

"Mesmerizing. . . . Any collection of McKillip's short stories will be a valuable asset to any library and a joy to her many fans."
—*Library Journal,* starred review

"Anybody who loves fantasy—not just for what most fantasy does, but

for what the genre is really capable of—should definitely pick this book up. It's like a perfect encapsulation of fantasy writing at its most brave and beautiful."
—*io9.com*

"A casket full of wonders. I think each one is my favorite, until I read the next. McKillip has the true Mythopoeic imagination. Here lies the border between our world and that of Faerie."
—P. C. Hodgell, author of the Kencyrath series

"This brilliant new collection puts on display the audacity, the warmth, the intelligence, and depth of [McKillip's] huge and magnificent talent."
—Peter Straub, author of *Ghost Story* and *A Dark Matter*

"The lively and enchanting stories in *Wonders of the Invisible World* certainly deserve all the accolades I can summon."
—Paul Goat Allen, *Barnes and Noble.com*

"I loved all the stories in this collection, and if I still have to tell you to try this out, well, you haven't been reading my review. . . . Patricia McKillip is a master at what she does. Strongly recommended."
—*Locus*

"*Wonders of the Invisible World* is a wonderful collection of stories full of wit and insight wrapped in beautiful, effortless prose. McKillip's ability to convey so much in so few words is impressive, as is her ability with storytelling, characterization, and thematic elements."
—*Fantasy Cafe*

Praise for Patricia A. McKillip

"There are no better writers than Patricia A. McKillip."
—Stephen R. Donaldson, author of The Chronicles of Thomas Covenant

"Intricate, beautiful. . . ."
—*Chicago Sun-Times*

"A master storyteller."
—*Strange Horizons*

"Nothing less than masterly."
—*Booklist*

"Lush imagery and wry humor. . . . McKillip's rich language conveys real strangeness and power."
—*Starlog*

"World Fantasy Award–winner McKillip can take the most common fantasy elements—dragons and bards, sorcerers and shape-shifters—and reshape them in surprising and resonant ways."
—*Publishers Weekly*, starred review

"McKillip skillfully knits disparate threads into a rewardingly rich and satisfying story."
—*Amazon*

Other books by Patricia A. McKillip

The Riddle-Master trilogy

The Riddle-Master of Hed (1976)
Heir of Sea and Fire (1977)
Harpist in the Wind (1979)

Kyreol duology

Moon-Flash (1984)
The Moon and the Face (1985)

The Cygnet duology

The Sorceress and the Cygnet (1991)
The Cygnet and the Firebird (1993)

Other Works

The House on Parchment Street (1973)
The Throne of the Erill of Sherril (1973)
The Forgotten Beasts of Eld (1974)
The Night Gift (1976)
Stepping from the Shadows (1982)
Fool's Run (1987)
The Changeling Sea (1988)
Something Rich and Strange (A Tale of Brian Froud's Faerielands) (1994)
The Book of Atrix Wolfe (1995)
Winter Rose (1996)
Song of the Basilisk (1998)
The Tower at Stony Wood (2000)
Ombria in Shadow (2002)
In the Forests of Serre (2003)
Alphabet of Thorn (2004)
Od Magic (2005)
Harrowing the Dragon (2005)
Soltice Wood (2006)
The Bell at Sealey Head (2008)
The Bards of Bone Plain (2010)
Wonders of the Invisible World (2012)

Dreams of Distant Shores

PATRICIA A. McKILLIP

Tachyon | | San Francisco

For Dave, for so many reasons

With thanks to Susan Allison, Jonathan Strahan, and Terri Windling for inspiring, respectively, the Gorgon, the Crow, and the Sea Hare. . . . And very special thanks to Jacob Weisman for keeping track of my work and putting it in order.

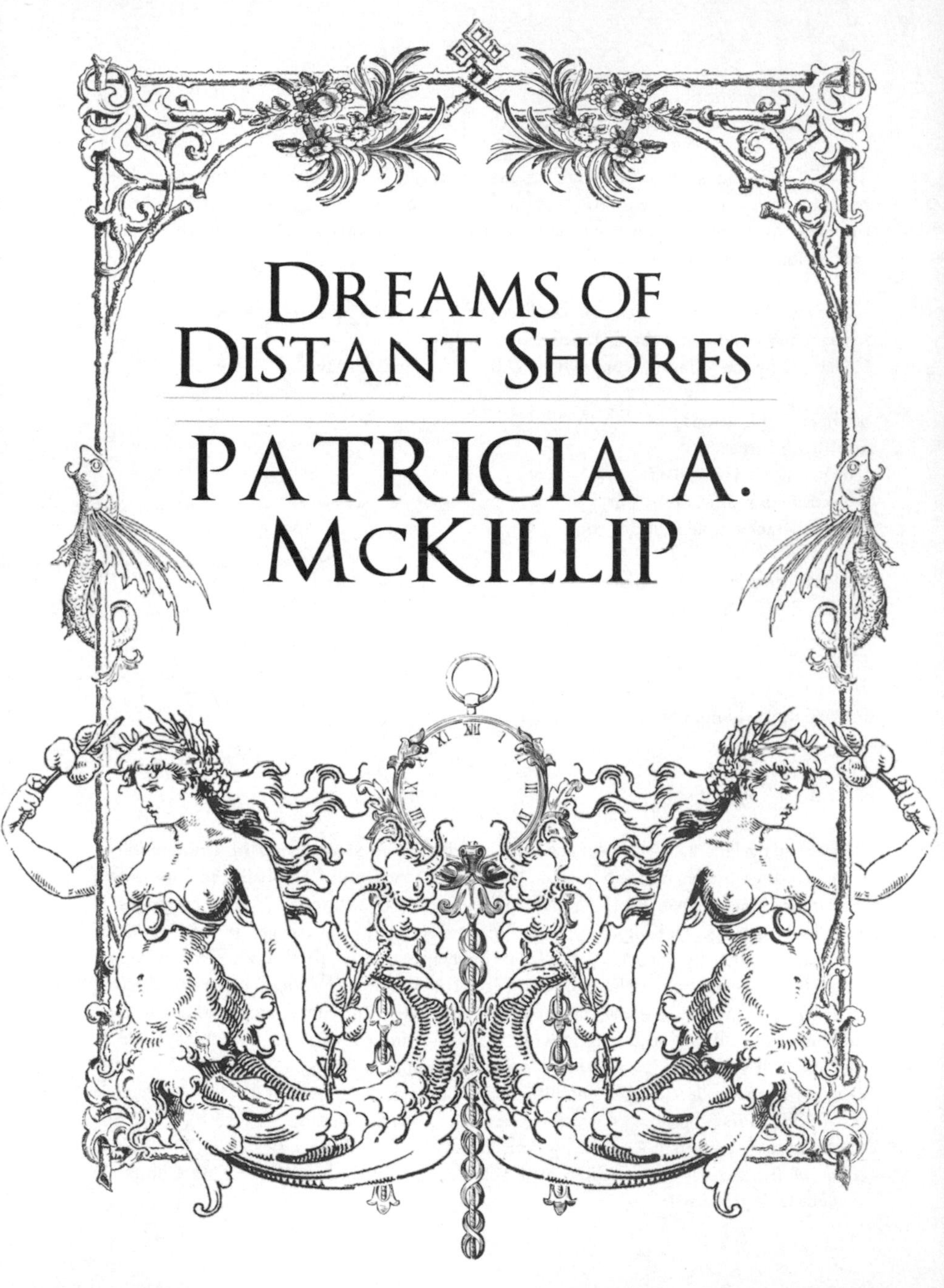

Dreams of Distant Shores

Patricia A. McKillip

Interior and cover design by Elizabeth Story

Tachyon Publications LLC
1459 18th Street #139
San Francisco, CA 94107
www.tachyonpublications.com
tachyon@tachyonpublications.com

Series Editor: Jacob Weisman
Project Editor: Jill Roberts

ISBN: 978-1-61696-218-0

Printed in the United States by Worzalla

First Edition: 2016
9 8 7 6 5 4 3 2 1

Table of Contents

WEIRD

"WHAT'S THE WEIRDEST thing that ever happened to you?" he asked.

"Weird," she repeated. "You mean like weird funny? Weird spooky?"

"Just weird." He brushed the crook of her elbow, the little hollow there, with one finger, lightly. "As in: for which there is no other word."

She thought. "You mean like the time I got swept up into an alien spaceship and examined by doctors who looked like talking iguanas wearing surgery gowns?"

He shook his head. "No. That's just silly. True weird."

"Well." She paused, lips parted, eyes dazzled by light, feeling his warm lips burrow into the hollow, leave a kiss that lingered there, an echo, a memory. "That would have to be what happened at my cousin Delaney's wedding when the shoe landed in the wedding cake."

He lay back, one hand under his head, the other touching, just barely with the tips of his fingers, the underside of her wrist. "Did it happen to you?"

"Not really. Except it being my shoe that landed in the cake. But it wasn't personal."

"That doesn't count."

She thought again. They were lying on every bath towel they could find. The bathroom floor was white and green tile, hard and cold but generously wide. They had piled hand towels under their heads, and used the bath sheets for blankets. The pretty gold wire wastebasket was filled with fruit, both fresh and dried, some Italian salami, packets of water crackers and digestive biscuits, a little jar of Kalamata olives, another of gourmet mustard, individually wrapped wedges of mushroom Brie, a bar of hazelnut chocolate, and a small vacuum pack of smoked, peppered salmon, along with the considerable length of purple ribbon that had been wrapped around the gift tray. The tray itself, a very nice bamboo hors d'oeuvres board, had gone out the window just before she slammed it shut and locked it.

They had water; they had plumbing; they were a little short on utensils, but, as he pointed out, they could use toothbrush handles, and the little files that slid in and out of nail clippers.

She remembered something suddenly. "Oh. My grandfather Pippin's funeral."

"Pippin?"

"Yeah. Like the apple. He was ninety-two. He wore leather bedroom slippers for twenty years because he kept his money in his shoes."

"Again," he said patiently, "is this about you?"

"No," she said. "But it is weird. The slippers seemed to have melted into his feet. In later years, they guessed, he showered in them. I won't even mention what state his toenails were in. They were sort of woven together—"

"You're making this up!"

She gave a little, liquid chuckle, like a pipe's gurgle. "Just the toenail part. Sorry. I got carried away. But the weird thing was, after they got him safely underground and came back to his house to clean it out, they found those slippers, a little worse for the wear, you know, bits of dirt and grass on them, right beside his bed, as if they had walked there after the funeral."

"You are so inventing this," he groaned. "And it's not even very good. Concentrate. The weirdest thing that happened to you. Not your cousin or heaven help us your demented grandfather or your pet tortoise—" The howling started; he had to raise his voice a little, close as they were, to be heard over it. "You do know what weird means."

"Fate."

"What?"

She turned her head, shouted into his ear. "Fate. It's one of the earliest meanings. I learned that when—" The menacing, furious, strangely desperate racket ceased as abruptly as it had begun; her own yelling softened into laughter. "Sorry. Anyway. Speaking of which—"

"Of what?"

"*Macbeth*. The three weird sisters. I did meet a witch once—a real one."

He sat up indignantly, sending hand towels rolling. Leaning on one arm, looking down at her, he demanded, "Are you making this up, too?"

"No. This is true." She paused, admiring the honey-amber glow of his skin; she held the back of her wrist against his breast, her ivory on his rich warmth. "Come back down. I'll tell you. And, yes, it happened to me."

She waited while he piled the hand towels again for his head, sank back down beside her. Then they both had to wait during the thundering clatter, like some gigantic backhoe scooping up a hundred old-fashioned metal garbage cans into its vast maw and dropping them from a great height onto a street jammed with empty cars, trucks, buses. She could feel the floor vibrate slightly under the appalling din. Her own voice sounded small, diminished, in the silence that followed.

"Her name was Jehane. She had long, wild, curly red hair and the most lovely, wicked smile, even though she had lost one eyetooth, maybe during an initiation ceremony or something." She felt him shift, but he didn't question the tale, not yet. "She told me she lived in an RV with a cat, a raven, and a snake, all with bizarre names. I mean, who would name a cat Tisiphone?"

"You," he said. "Where are you in this?"

"I met her in a bar where my crazy boyfriend at the time played bass in a band. Concert bass, not electric. She was drinking a mojito and writing a spell on a napkin when I came up and accidently knocked her glass over onto the napkin. Well, I thought it was an accident. But when I apologized, she said, 'There are no accidents.' She had an odd accent. Portuguese, maybe, or something Balkan. Ancient Irish? Anyway, I bought her another drink and she invited me to sit beside her. No. It was more like a command than an invitation. She told me that my boyfriend played the bass very well, and that he would dump me before the year ended for a singer-songwriter who wore only black."

"Did you still pay for her drink?"

"The witch offered to sell me a spell to keep him from leaving. She smiled her charming smile, which was itself a spell, and we both laughed. I didn't think about it again until he did leave me, a few weeks later, for a little whey-faced musician with a skinny voice who wrote morose songs on her acoustic guitar. I remembered then that there was no way for the witch to have known the bass player was my boyfriend, when she said what she said. No explicable way, I mean. Except that she was a witch."

"Is that as weird as it gets?"

She shook her head. "Not even close."

Someone or something pounded ferociously on the bathroom door. The door rattled and shook; the glass holding the toothbrushes clattered into the sink; her bathrobe fell off the hook on the door. The banging, fierce and energetic, was accompanied by deep, barking shouts in an unfamiliar language. Their hands shifted under the towels, seeking each other; their eyes locked. One final, exasperated pound was accompanied by a more familiar word, "Shit!"

They waited; the silence held.

He said finally, "Go on."

She drew a breath. "Well. The real weirdness started that first night. The bartender mopped up the puddle I made and threw the mojito-soaked spell away. I was about to stop him, but the witch said before I could speak, 'Don't bother. The spell hasn't gone anywhere.' Like she read my mind."

"Then why was she writing it down?"

"I asked her that. Someone at the bar had requested it, then left after paying for it and hadn't returned. I asked her what the spell had been for. She only told me, 'Spells are alive. Spoken about, they find carriers and travel like rumor until they reach the one who craves that particular spell and will pay for it. The spell will be turned into words, and therein lies its terrible and wonderful power.' Really. That's what she said. 'Therein.' Then the band took a break and my boyfriend came to the bar. I introduced them."

She paused. He said, "Go on."

"I still wonder why she bothered to wait through his affair with the singer-songwriter. I mean, she knew it would happen, so why didn't she cast a spell over the girl and make her lose interest in him?"

She heard him take a breath, hesitate. "You mean—"

"Yes. I mean. Far as I know, they're still together. The witch and my bass player."

He laughed a little, softly. "I didn't expect that. But the unexpected isn't necessarily weird. Complications and ironies in relationships happen to everyone."

She raised her head to look into his eyes. "Do they happen to you?"

His eyes flickered. But it could have been the lights going out, not in a normal blink into darkness, but vanishing more slowly, accompanied by a long, deep, growling, indrawn breath that seemed to suck the light into itself, swallow it whole.

She stared back at the absolute black. She couldn't even see the faint glow of city lights behind the window curtain; the entire planet had disappeared. Then the light came back in a stunning sheet, as though a gigantic eyelid had lifted to reveal the white of a monster's eye.

She blinked until she could see his face again behind the prickling dazzle of aftershocks across her vision.

"Parts of your witch story were weird," he admitted. A star gleamed in his nostril, went out; another flared and faded under his eye. "But as a whole, commonplace. Not truly weird."

She heaved a sigh. "True weird." She was silent, digging deep into memory. He got up after a time, rummaged through the wastebasket and pulled out the mushroom Brie. He rinsed the soap dish, a pretentious little rectangle with curved edges. He dried it, unwrapped the Brie and laid it on the dish. Then he found the fingernail clippers in his bathroom bag, rinsed and dried the little nail file tucked under the upper blade. She watched while he cut the pale, oozing cheese into chunks, wiping the file with a tissue when it got too sticky. He sat beside her on the towels, set the dish between them.

"True weird," he said inflexibly. "Try again."

She chose a piece from the soap dish, ate it dreamily, licked her fingers when it was gone. She settled back again. "This was when I was very young," she said slowly.

"How young?"

"I knew how to read a few words; I might have started school. Maybe not. Young enough that everything was new. I had no concept of history, and of course my past was very short. I used to sit and try very hard to remember where I had been before I became myself. I thought there must be some kind of before, before—you know. I didn't understand why I couldn't remember very far back. It was before I learned that there was nothing of me before I began. It was very strange."

"But not weird," he said, swallowing Brie.

"No," she said softly. "Not. Anyway, I was living overseas then. I had no idea what weird meant. Everything was, or nothing was. I had no context."

He nodded, hooked a bite of cheese on the tiny curved tip of the file and fed it to her. He watched the movements of her full lips, her throat as she swallowed. "Go on," he said.

"We lived in a small town, in a house so old that parts of the floor were slabs of stone. Milk was delivered in glass bottles, with the cream floating on top, so you had to shake it before you used it. A man drove a horse-drawn wagon down our street once a week. He had a strange, piercing cry, more like a bird than a person. He was called the Rag-and-Bone man. That's what he shouted, I was told. People gave him their garbage. His horse was slow and placid. I didn't know then, but now I know that I was seeing something out of a distant past that would one day ride out of the world and only exist in memory." She paused, reminiscing. "But that's not the weirdness, because nobody back then would have called it that."

"No," he said, though he sounded, she thought, not entirely certain. She smiled, a quick, private smile of satisfaction while he speared another piece of Brie.

"One day I decided I wanted to ride with him on his wagon, see where he went. I filled a paper bag with odd things I found around the house that I thought nobody would miss: a chipped coffee mug, a doll missing one arm and most of her hair, a mangy teddy bear with the stuffing coming out of its seams, an old pipe of my father's that had been lying on a windowsill for months, a pair of bedroom slippers my mother never wore—things like that. And since I thought he wouldn't accept the bag without them, I put a rag and a bone on top of the bag. The rag was a skirt with a torn pocket that didn't fit me anymore. The bone was something I'd found in the garden, a little hollow thing that had belonged to some bird or animal. I kept it because I liked the sound it made when I blew into it. I waited with my bag on the sidewalk until I saw the wagon coming. Then I walked into the middle of the street in front of the horse.

"It didn't stop until it was almost on top of me. The Rag-and-Bone man was making his bird cries, high and harsh and eerie, in the quiet street. He might have been telling me to move, but I never understood anything he said. The horse—"

There was an immense thump over their heads, as though a gigantic fist had punched the roof of the building. They both jumped. The walls shuddered around them; the floor seemed to undulate. They clung to it, as to a raft on a violent sea. In the room beyond the door something hit the floor and shattered.

They waited, silent, motionless. Nothing more happened. She cleared her throat finally; he eased upright again, reaching for the Brie.

"The horse loomed over me. It seemed nothing like the slow, placid animal I expected. It was massive; it exuded darkness. Its nostrils were huge, its eyes unrelentingly black. I stood transfixed under it, holding the paper bag in my arms, unable to speak or look away from its shadowy gaze. From very far away, from another world, I heard the Rag-and-Bone man's voice. The horse moved its head finally. I felt its nostrils whuff at my hair. Then it lowered its great head to the bag in my arms and whuffed at that.

"It opened its great, blocky teeth, picked the bone out of the bag and ate it. I heard it crunch. The Rag-and-Bone man gave a sharp cry. My legs refused to hold me; I toppled down in the middle of the street under the horse's nose. It shouted, then, a great, fierce blare that I swear blew the hair back from my face.

"Then it somehow slipped its traces and leaped over me. I smelled it, felt its bulk, its enormous hooves clearing my head. The Rag-and-Bone man jumped into the street. For a moment I heard hooves galloping down the cobblestones. The Rag-and-Bone man ran after them. I turned, scared and astonished, just as I realized that the sound of the hooves had stopped. I saw a barefoot boy with wild black hair turn a corner with the Rag-and-Bone man running after him, and bending now and then, as he ran, to try to catch the boy's shadow.

"They both disappeared around the corner. I scrambled to my feet, hurled the bag onto the hillock of trash in the wagon, then I ran as fast as I could back into the house and hid in the coat closet for the rest of the afternoon. When I finally peeked outside at twilight, the wagon was gone. I never saw the Rag-and-Bone man again." She looked at the soap dish, then at him, as he sat propped on one hand, motionless, gazing at her. She said reproachfully, "You finished the Brie."

He swallowed. "Did I?"

"Was that weird or what?"

He shook his head slowly, still holding her eyes. She felt the floor lurch again, or maybe it was her thoughts skittering over something that had suddenly loomed out of nowhere.

"Do you know," he began. His voice had gone somewhere; it was thin, hollow, like the note blown out of a bone. "What's even weirder?"

She tried to speak, could only shake her head in a no that turned by imperceptible degrees into a nod.

"You left your skirt with him. Your doll. Your bear. You left him things of yours to recognize you."

"It was you," she whispered, recognizing his dark hair, his black, black eyes.

"It was you. In trouble and hiding in a closet then. Now you're in—"

Their heads turned toward the bathroom door, as though they could see through it to the raging menace beyond. She began to laugh softly, weakly, until her laughter brought tears; she brushed at them as they fell, and then he did, his hand warm, very gentle. When she finally stopped, he moved the soap dish aside and lay back, shoulder touching hers, his hand finding hers.

"Is that," she said shakily, "what on earth all this fuss is about? It's your turn, now, you know. Was that the weirdest thing that ever happened to you?"

"Not even close," he said, and waited until the ancient cry filling the room, wanting, seeking the least scrap, the smallest bone of their lives, reverberated through the plumbing pipes, rattled the screws and hinges, and finally ebbed back into silence.

Mer

The witch had hitched a ride in some gorse plants that Lord Beale of County Cork, homesick for them, had shipped to himself in far Port Dido around the turn of the century, after he founded the town. The witch, napping amid the thorny prickles through the months of the sea journey to the Pacific Northwest, had lost track of her name when the vessel finally docked and she woke. Something to do with battles? Graculus or suchlike? Something about ravens? Never mind, it wouldn't be the first name she had mislaid. Leaving the gorse, she caught sight of letters on the door sign of a small, sturdy building overlooking the dock. Harbormaster, they said. Port Dido.

Dido, she thought. That might do.

A cormorant nesting in a tree greeted her with a gentle, woeful croak. She grunted back at it, then climbed gratefully into the heart of its nesting tree, a sturdy spruce, and, still feeling the slightest bit seasick, she went back to sleep for a time.

When she finally emerged, the birds had gone, the tree had died of their guano, and there was considerably more of Port Dido than there had been before.

She half-saw, half-sensed that. She could see in the dark; she could understand the gist of the language of leaves. She could hear laughter within the tavern on an island up the estuary a mile away, and she understood the gist of that as well. Most around her were asleep, lulled by the distant roar of tide at the mouth of the bay. But not everyone.

Spring, she thought, smelling it. And then she saw the face of the moon.

It was full and luminous, a great wide eye above the high forests and the silent waters of the estuary. It was staring straight at her. So, she realized suddenly, was someone—something?—else.

A goddess, she thought, startled, and she heard herself bleat like one of the dark, snake-necked birds she had last spoken to. She was still invisible to humans, but beyond that boundaries got nebulous. This goddess she recognized as one that took her power from the moon, but she had no idea what name that power claimed in this ancient place.

Nor, she remembered, did she know her own.

"I need a body," the goddess said inside the witch's head. "It's that time of the century. The one I have now is tired and needs a break." Her sacred voice sounded taut, restless, barely constrained; the witch felt her own bones smolder and shine, becoming illuminated with the intense, radiant scrutiny. "You recognized me. You know me—"

"I did once," the witch agreed, "but in a place very far away, and by a different name. Which," she sighed, "I have completely forgotten, along with my own."

"Perfect," the goddess said briskly. "Listen. Do you hear me?"

The witch did indeed: the roaring, growling turmoil along the edges of the earth, the rear and smack, the long, long roll, the break and thunder, the slow hiss, the whisper and pop of clams dancing in the tidal foam.

"Yes, Mistress," she said. She was fearless, adventurous—why else was she there?—and she had, as yet, no other place in the vast new world. Why not this?

"It's only for a hundred years," the goddess assured her. "And then you'll find someone to take your place. You will be feared, loved, cursed, praised, studied; you will be the flow of life; you will be bitter death; you will serve the moon, the sea, and all those your foamy fingertips can reach. Oh, and you will be worshipped. They're an odd lot, the worshippers, but very dedicated. You will be visible to them only once, near morning: the new face of my power." The goddess's voice was getting fainter, or the tide was getting louder, roiling into the witch's heart, into her blood. Her foamy fingers seemed everywhere, all around and very far away, following the path of the moonlight down the long pull of water. "Look this borrowed body up," she heard, "when you're yourself again. It'll be around."

She had no time to answer, learning names, shapes for everything she touched: every scale, worm, new thin shell, tiny unblinking eye, every floating strand of grass, transparent thread of jelly, everything new, just being born, all at once it seemed and already as moonstruck as she.

In the darkest hours she had reached the far edges of her realm, exploring every winding channel, every narrowing stream, every churning edge where the tide sculpted the world to its shape.

That's when she saw their fires and heard her name.

She appeared to them in the goddess's shape: a being made of spindrift, eyes of iridescent purple-black nacre, hair white and wild as spume, a voice like the most tender lilt and break of foam. She greeted them. The figures around the fires, all human, all women, all went as still as the great trees above them, boughs lifted as though to receive the descending moon.

Then they leaped to their bare feet, laughing, clapping, calling to the goddess, the same word again and again, which, the witch/goddess realized sometime later, as she busily withdrew herself across the mudflats and back into the sea, must have been her name. Her final coherent thought for a century was that, once again, she had forgotten it.

A hundred years later, give or take the time the moon took returning to the full, the witch, exhausted and desperate for a change of shape, poured all the powers of the tidal goddess into the first likely body that gave permission. The body, half-human and half-local spirits, seemed surprised at the forces, but on the whole quite curious, and responded with alacrity to her changed state.

The witch, herself again, crept with great relief into the heart of a wooden female shape nearby and went back to sleep.

Jake Harrow and Scott Cowell were trying to load the seven-foot wooden mermaid with her scallop-shell bra and her long blue tail with the cormorant perched in its curve off one end of the Port Dido bridge into the back of Markham Cowell's pickup truck when all hell broke loose.

It was after midnight and the town was asleep. Then it was dawn, or some lurid, colorless version of light, by which the two young men could suddenly see one another's pallid, surprised faces beneath the mermaid's cheery red smile. In the samc nanosecond the bell in the tower at Our Lady of the Cormorants pealed like someone had whacked it with a tire iron, and a cannon blew off next to them. They leaped. The mermaid slid out of their hands and toppled toward the back of the pickup, which is what they had wanted her to do in the first place. But the pickup was no longer there, Markham having stomped the accelerator at the sound of the blast, sending the truck careening halfway across the bridge.

The mermaid fell on her back and slid down the embankment into the bay.

For one stark moment, by the light of the streetlamp in the middle of the bridge, they saw her smile under the shallow wash of the tide. Then she sank a little deeper into darker water. Markham and Jake stared at where she had been, and then at each other. Lights were flicking on all around them in houses on the cliffs and along the water, in the Marine Institute's dorms, in the harbor where those who lived on their boats were scrambling onto the docks. There was a squeal of tires, a rattle of muffler as Markham backed wildly; Jake and Scott leaped to meet the truck, flung themselves inside.

"What the hell—" Markham breathed, shifting gears.

"Go," Jake said tersely.

"Where's the mer—"

"Go!"

They ventured back near dawn, on the off chance that the mermaid herself hadn't gone anywhere, and they might winch her out of the water before anyone else noticed her. But the slowly awakening sky revealed nothing, except that, where mermaid had been, there was now none. Most, Jake guessed, were so used to seeing her they didn't much notice her anyway, there or not. They would notice, maybe even remember, the three standing where she usually stood, looking down the bank for something in the water.

"Must have sunk like a stone," Markham murmured bemusedly.

"Most logs don't," Scott argued. "They float."

"Then she floated away."

"Let's take a walk on the docks," Jake suggested. "Look for her there. The bridge is going up, and people idling here are going to notice our faces instead of hers."

Fishing boats on the landward side of the harbor were heading out to sea. Two slabs of tarmac rose to sandwich air so they could get by, and traffic had begun to line up along the road. The three crossed between idling cars to where they had left the truck behind Sylvia's Bait and Tackle. When the bridge folded itself down again, they drove across, and turned onto Port Dido's single busiest street, where you could rent crab rings, buy groceries, find a beer and a barstool, or, at the far end of it, an education in marine biology. From there they took a side street, passed the fish-processing plant, several ancient restaurants, and the Landlubber, Port Dido's only motel. The street ended in the parking lot beside the harbor.

The three walked down a ramp and separated on the docks to search between trawlers, sailboats, cruisers, motorboats, and scows for the mermaid that might have gotten washed between them and wedged there by the tide. Everyone Jake passed, crabbers with their rings in the water, boat people gathered for coffee on one another's decks, talked about the same thing: the ferocious flash of light, the wild jangle of church bell like a call to judgment, the instantaneous detonation of thunder. Hell, he thought, even the harbor seals clustered on their favorite dock were probably barking it over.

Nobody mentioned the missing mermaid.

Yet.

She finally surfaced in the Foghorn Café where the three slid wearily into a booth for breakfast. The Foghorn cook, driving early to work, had marked the mermaid among the missing after that tumultuous night. Word spread quickly among the staff and passed to the diners along with every breakfast order. From what Jake could catch of the excited gabble, nobody was certain of anything, though nobody could get enough of it. The lightning, as sudden and vivid as a dead eye opening, the horrendous blast, the scarred, blackened bell tower, the vanished mermaid were puzzled over separately and together; nothing seemed to fit.

"That tall ship that comes to visit every year—the Lady Ysabelle—did she sail in last night? Maybe somebody shot off her cannon and hit the Cormorants' bell? Maybe it took out the mermaid along the way?" Jake, who had his back to her, recognized the lilting ebb and wash of Carey O'Farrell, who owned Sea Treasures, in which tourists could buy wind chimes made of jingle shells, local art and jewelry, and Port Dido tea towels.

"The Lady Ysabelle's not due until late summer," Parker Yeong, one of the Institute's professors, reminded her. "Besides, they only fire off gunpowder in their fake battles, not real cannonballs. I like your theory, though," he added cheerfully. "It's better than the single-bolt-of-lightning theory. That might explain the bell tower, but not the missing mermaid; she wouldn't have been in its trajectory."

"Yes, and what have those Cormorants been up to?" Emma Cadogan demanded darkly from the table on the other side of Carey. Her portentous, fluting voice caused Shirley Watson, of Watson Fishing and Whale Watching Excursions, to stiffen on her stool at the counter. "I always knew they are an evil bird. Blasphemous to think that the Mother of God would consort with cormorants."

Shirley spun on the stool, her whacked-out, sideways grin flashing her gold eyetooth. "So the Lord flung a lightning bolt, missed the birds, but got the church tower instead?"

Markham loosed a snort of laughter over his coffee. Scott, red-eyed, rattled, punched his brother's arm, but it was too late. Emma, loftily ignoring Shirley, trained her sights at the three young men in the booth. She was a massive, formidable woman who spent her hours at the Port Dido Visitors' Center, telling tourists where to go and showing them the quickest way to get there.

"What do you boys know about all this?" she asked, riveting them in an instant, like that snake-haired Greek with the snarky eyes who lingered in Jake's memory long after her name. "You must have been out late last night after graduation."

Jake heard Markham's breath again, freed from the stone he had almost become. "Graduated three years ago, ma'am," he said with a genuine edge of indignation. "Last thing on my mind back then would have been a woman made of wood with a fish tail instead of legs."

Emma's eyes didn't flicker, Jake saw; she might have pursued the matter for no other reason than to listen to her own voice. But

Sally Goshen edged between table and booth wielding a tray full of breakfasts.

"Did you all hear what happened last night?" she asked them breathlessly. "I just heard—I started my shift late. I was home all the way over in Greengage when that bolt woke me and my son Jeremy and the dogs. Louise in the kitchen said her boyfriend was out with the Coast Guard late last night in a cutter, and they saw the entire bay bright as day when the lightning flashed. He knew it got the Cormorants because they're the only church in the county with a real bell in the tower."

Dr. Yeong swiveled from his breakfast burrito to look at her. "Did he know anything about the mermaid?"

"What? No." She stared at him, giving Jake Markham's mile-high stack with bacon and extra butter. "He didn't say. Somebody found a mermaid?"

"No," Carey explained. "The mermaid on the bridge? She went missing last night."

"You're kidding!"

"Vanished," Markham said, gazing raptly at Sally's face, with its skin like a ripe, golden, finely freckled apricot. Scott joggled his elbow; he looked vaguely around, then focused on his plate. "Heck's this?"

"My Greek omelet," Jake said. "Spinach and feta and capers."

"Capers." Markham speared one on a fork prong. "Looks like bait to me."

"Oop—sorry," Sally said, putting Scott's salmon scramble in front of Markham instead. "Oh, yeah, that mermaid. Well? What happened to her?"

Jake shook his head, drawing in a deep breath of syrup and melting butter as he passed the pancakes to Markham, who handed his brother the scramble. "We have absolutely no idea."

They parted company after breakfast, Markham to work catching and baiting fish with huge hooks to catch the cormorants who swallowed the fish, Scott to the community college over in Myrtlewood to study Spanish and welding, and Jake to the South Coast Culinary Institute to learn the difference between hollandaise, béarnaise, and mayonnaise, and which belonged on what.

The witch opened her eyes and found herself floating on her back with a cormorant sitting on her front holding its wings out to dry.

Her whole being, whatever it was at the moment, protested the wakening. It was far too soon after a hundred restless years; she needed most of a year to sleep, not half a night—and why was she back in the tide?

The bird opened its long beak soundlessly, seeming to sense the witch's ire at the world through its great, flat feet. Then it levitated with a powerful, graceful thrust of its wings. The witch caught its eyes, its vision; for a dizzying moment, she looked down at herself, the wooden mermaid in the water, with her scallop shells and her bright yellow hair curved along her cheek and one side of her smile, her long tail curved upward, fin spread like a fan, the arc broad enough to hold something, the cormorant maybe, that might have perched there.

Oh, why not, the witch thought with exasperation. At least human, I could have a bed.

She guided the wood figure carefully away from fishing boats in the bay, from boat ramps and docks crowded with crabbers. Passing gulls took note of the mermaid's glowering eyes and changed their minds about landing there. After a century, the witch knew the waters—estuary, harbor and bay, every stone, barnacle, and bit of wrack—like she knew her own mind. She brought the stiff, heavy statue easily and unobtrusively to the sandy shore inside a half-hidden cove. There she let her powers flow everywhere into the wood, just as she had for the last century. Eyes blinked, hair shifted in the wash of water, the tree heart thumped, sap moved along its secret ways. The witch swallowed, spoke, making a hollow blat at first. When she tried to stand, she remembered what she had forgotten. Fin morphed into feet bigger than any she had ever had. She stumbled over them at first, and nearly bumped her head on the rocky ceiling. She touched her hair, examined her toenails, gazed with bemusement at the two scallop shells on her chest, no longer wood but real, and at the short, wetly gleaming, scale-patterned blue skirt that barely reached halfway down her thighs. She possessed nothing else: no shoes, no money, not even, she realized irritably, a name.

"Maybe," she said aloud, then, remembering, and her smile appeared, a living thing as responsive to her thoughts as language. "Maybe in this body I'm Dido."

She vanished for a while to climb up the cliff above the cave, a simple matter for her great, splayed feet and her long, hard arms; then she walked a back road down into Port Dido.

She let her oddly tall, ungainly but comely shape appear gradually on the sidewalks: a barefoot, very tired, very hungry young woman wearing only seashells and fish scales. People had changed, she noted with interest, during the hundred years she'd been in the water. Like the mermaid, they exposed anything at all of themselves, and much of what they exposed had colorful artwork on it, as though they kept their histories in living canvases on their skin. They let their hair do whatever it wanted; they put extraordinary things on their feet. Even so, some still gave her startled glances. Others grinned at her, or extended a thumb, which meant something, she guessed: maybe it warded away witches.

She was dawdling outside a cluster of shop windows in a little square, intrigued equally by the clothes in one, the bottles of wine in another, the little tarts and buns in a third. Her mouth watered; her chilly fingers and feet tried to warm each other. Money, she remembered distantly, was the difference between having nothing and having something. At least it was for mortals, but not necessarily for witches inhabiting the shape of a wooden mermaid turned temporarily human. She was debating in the mermaid's head the merits of pickpocketing, begging, scaring the change out of the next passerby, or enchanting a few dried leaves into coins, when a shop door flew open.

"There you are! I've been keeping an eye out." The witch, surprised by the young, brown, dark-browed face peering out, recognized under the thick curly hair and the flawless skin of someone not long in the world the force that had been the tidal goddess's previous body. She was part cormorant, the witch sensed, and part human, with some very old regional powers tossed into the mix. Like the witch herself, she'd been around a long time, and had many connections, not all of them innocent or unambiguous. "Come out of the cold. Port Dido blows in a fog bank every afternoon and calls it spring. I'm Portia. Did you remember your name?"

"Not yet," the witch answered, crossing the threshold. "But I've decided the mermaid is Dido. It's easy to remember." She smelled all good things then: meat, fruit, chocolate, fungi, grains, spices, and her knees shook. She sat suddenly; a chair caught her midway down.

"You poor thing."

"Something woke me before I had even begun to dream. I'm not sure what it was, but I found myself in this—this—"

"Yes." A dimple deepened in one firm cheek; in her smile a bit of ancient mischief sparked. "You did. I can give you a place to sleep for a hundred nights. Or I can give you dinner, a bed for the night, and a job in the morning. Not too early," she added quickly. "Pub hours. Your choice. Here. Eat this."

The witch, biting into strawberries, thick, heavy cream, dark chocolate, and golden pastry that crumbled and floated in air, decided in that moment, that mouthful, to stay awake and human for a while. There were benefits.

"But what do you get out of it?" she wondered. Even the most noble of witches had her own best interests at heart.

Portia dropped the lid over an eye dark as the backside of the moon.

"You'll see."

By the week's end, opinion seemed pretty evenly divided between blaming the mermaid's disappearance on the congregation of Our Lady of the Cormorants, whose passion for the demonic bird must have led them into unimaginable wickedness, or the Port Dido High School's graduating class, which was known for its pranks, or any of the rich tourists who might have driven off with the mermaid as a souvenir of the quaint little town where they had hired a boat for a day to haul salmon and tuna out of the sea. A reward donated by the Chamber of Commerce was posted for information leading to her whereabouts. Merchants set out donation jars to add to the reward. The local paper published a photo of the missing mermaid, the history of her life on the bridge welcoming visitors, and a plea from the chainsaw artist who had created her to return his master work, no questions asked.

Jake's girlfriend, Blaine, pretty much said the same thing, wailing into his cellphone as he sat with Markham and Scott in a shadowy corner of the Trickle Down Brewery and Pub, "Jake, how could you lose a seven-foot mermaid? You have to find her. I promised Haley! I promised her! That's the focal point of the whole color scheme of her wedding. My best friend is getting married and I want her day to be perfect. I don't care where she went, you have to get her back by Saturday."

"I know, baby," Jake said softly. "I will. Ah—where are you?"

"Here at Haley's with the girls, making the wedding favors. Oh, don't worry, nobody's here who doesn't know you're involved. Everything—the favors, the cake, our heels and dresses, the bouquets, the corsages and decorations—they're all her colors! Red and that dark, gleaming blue with yellow trim for her hair. Nothing will make any sense without her. You were just supposed to borrow her for a few days then put her back, not drop her into the bay."

"It just happened," he answered helplessly.

"I know, I know: the lightning whacking the church bell, the thunderclap—I understand that. But why did it have to happen to Haley?"

"We still have until Saturday. We'll find her."

"What can I get you guys?" the waitress asked.

Blaine's voice grew small and far away as Jake stared. She wasn't covered in blue scales; she had two legs under a short black skirt and black tights. But that red mouth, that generous smile, the curve of golden hair along one side of the smile, all that and the fact that she was taller than anyone in the room made his thoughts tangle to an abrupt halt, like an engine seizing up. He ended the call absently, forgetting Blaine. Beside him, Markham and Scott were absolutely still.

"Guys?" She twiddled the pencil between her fingers against the order pad. "Drinks?"

"You—" Jake breathed. "You."

"Oh, for—" She gazed at them with pity, one hand on her hip, and shook her head. "No. I am not the Port Dido mermaid come to life. What is it with everyone? I was the chainsaw sculptor's model. That's all."

"Lived here all my life," Markham managed. "Never saw you before."

"I've never lived here before." She raised the pencil. "Let's try again. What can I get you?"

She took their orders. They watched her return to the bar; then their heads swiveled slowly; their eyes met.

"No," Jake said flatly, to his own and everyone else's unspoken suggestions.

"But the timing—it's got to be more than coincidence," Markham said weakly.

"So? What?" Scott demanded. "So she really was a wooden mermaid a couple of days ago and the fall into the water turned her human?" He batted the back of his brother's head lightly. "Get real."

They were silent, watching her again. Markham mused, "She could come to the wedding anyway. Couldn't she? Don't suppose Haley would—"

"No. I don't suppose Haley would accept a human substitute dressed up as the Port Dido mermaid. Especially not one who looks like that." Jake drew a sudden breath. "Did I really hang up on Blaine? I'd better call her back."

The mermaid returned with their drinks. Their expressions transformed her enchanting smile into a broad grin. "Don't worry," she said briskly. "You'll get used to me."

On Sunday, the witch went to church.

Our Lady of the Cormorants was a modest chapel framed by a stand of old fir trees, its altar windows overlooking the blue-green estuary. Though its bell tower, tall and rounded like a tree trunk, had been scorched by the lightning, the bell still called the congregation to gather with a sweet, mellow toll. The congregation, the witch who called herself Dido noted, seemed to be all women. In fact, they were all witches with some level of power, though not all of them knew it. They simply felt comfortable, the witch guessed, among the eccentrically skewed worshippers dedicated to the smiling statue generically clothed in a long white robe and a blue mantle, her open hands outstretched over the dark pair of wiry-necked, long-billed, waddle-footed birds gazing up at her.

Seated on a pew smelling of cedar and candlewax, the witch napped through most of the service, waking only when the pastor, Reverend Becky, unsheathed an edge in her gentle, soothing voice.

"It's that time again, Ladies. Those of you with cormorant heritage will need to find and waken those powers to protect the nestlings from predators. Especially from Niall Parker at Davy Jones' Liquor Locker, who harpoons nests at night when he's drunk, and Markham Cowell, who gets paid to stuff freshly dead fish with hooks and run them fast underwater to attract the parent birds. Those who can will circle the nestling trees and grounds with your darkest powers so that humans can't pass among them. Those with other powers: get creative. Invent noises to scare the predators, swamp their boats if you catch them shooting the birds from the water, put whatever charms and distractions you dream up in places where they'll do the most good. Keep eyes and ears open for trouble, and stop it if you can before it starts. We are the faithful of our Lady of the Cormorants. It is our belief that we are all—even idiots like Niall and Markham—part of Holy Mother Nature, that we all belong to this earth, that cormorants are of an ancient and wild power that should be protected, and that the sea will provide for us all, human and bird, if we take care of one another and the sea. Amen, Ladies."

"Amen."

"Please stand for the closing hymn."

The witch yawned a great yawn, sent her body sprawling along the suddenly empty pew and went back to sleep.

She woke up in a tree.

It was night. She was surrounded by dreams of a fishy, feathery, egg-nesty kind, fraught with swift flights over water, sudden, deep dives, the struggles to stretch and shape a long throat and neck around the body struggling equally to wriggle out of them. She had to shield her human nose from the acrid smell of guano on the tree limbs, which seemed to cover them like perpetual moonlight. Parents, half-waking in their twiggy nests, made little blats and moans around her, disturbed without knowing why. The witch woke up a bit more, spread her rangy self more comfortably along the boughs, and got around finally to wondering why she was up a tree.

She heard voices.

The patch of forest, between the shops at one end of the street and the Institute at the other, overlooked the bay and a small beach over which the low tide gently sighed and slid, sounding like a contented dreamer. The only lights were distant: from the dorms, from vessels in the marina, from the occasional streetlamp. The half-dozen men gathering under the nesting tree had no reason to be quiet; the wakening parents above, some nervously croaking, weren't going anywhere. The men, the witch observed dourly, weren't much more articulate.

"Whaugh, this place stinks. Who's got the bottle?"

"Here."

"That one there, Niall. That big nest, higher up. Harpoon that one and it'll pull the others down along the way."

The witch heard a gulp, a spit, a sudden, sharp laugh. "Last time you'll snarf our fish, you up there. Look at them. All they do is eat and breed, make more mouths to take the fish out of ours. Do it, Niall."

A light went on; it searched the tree, falling short of where the witch sat. She could see a reddened, raspy face or two, the hands of the harpooner adjusting his line, raising the long weapon with its sharp, glinting dart, taking aim.

Get out, Portia's voice in the witch's brain said very clearly. *Fast. Now.*

There was a grunt, a whip of line, and a strangely solid thud. The witch, balanced precariously on the very tip of the tree, once again invisible, heard branches cracking, something heavy careening through them, men shouting in warning, the bottle breaking.

The thing finished its fall with a massive thud in the middle of the road.

There was utter silence. The witch, all her senses galvanized, powers she had forgotten she possessed, crouched, alert, waiting to attack, finally heard a dry swallow below.

"Damn, Niall. You harpooned the Port Dido mermaid."

Jake, driving back from his culinary classes at the end of the day, thinking of nothing more complex than a cold one at the brewpub, saw the mermaid at her post on the bridge giving him her familiar, welcoming smile. He was so used to seeing her, he barely noticed her, for as long as a couple of seconds. Then he swore, slammed on the brakes, and backed up without thinking once, let alone twice, and causing the car behind him to swerve onto the embankment.

Jake ignored the furious horn while he stared. The mermaid seemed her usual cheerful self, except for the large, oddly metallic fish scale in her tail near where human knees might have been. Jake squinted. The oversized fish scale looked weirdly like the bottom of a beer can, sliced off and nailed or glued into place to hide some—what?

Something fishy.

A face loomed into his open window, grey-browed, time-furrowed, and as annoyed with him as she had been all during second grade.

"Jake Harrow, you nearly ran me into the harbor!"

"Sorry, Ms. Priestly."

"Well, are you planning to move anytime soon? People are piling up behind us."

"Yes, Ms. Priestly. Sorry."

Something else he realized as he parked at the Trickle Down: something else was wrong with the mermaid. But what? The short, slender, dark-haired waitress who greeted him as he joined the Cowell brothers looked absolutely nothing like the mermaid they had seen there before. That fact he thought about briefly, then decided never, ever, to think about it again.

The expression on Markham's face, usually stolid and already set in its ways until now, told Jake exactly what he wanted to know.

"You put her back," he breathed, after the waitress had delivered his beer.

"We did. Late last night. I was with Niall and some of the fishers—they were nest-rustling—" He paused, drank, then stared, wide-eyed and stunned, into his glass. Jake wondered if he had forgotten how to blink.

"Well, where did you find her?"

Markham drank again. "Up a tree." Jake stared at him, then at Scott, who shook his head slightly.

"No, I wasn't there to see it, but I wish I'd been."

"Me, too,' Jake said fervently. "How'd she get up—"

"Ask him how she got down," Scott said, and answered for his brother. "Niall brought her down with a harpoon."

"He—what—what the hell, Markham?"

"We didn't know she was up there! Who would have guessed a mermaid up a tree? We were aiming for the cormorants' nests. But down she came instead, nearly fell on our heads." He paused to gulp beer. "But that's not the weirdest thing. The weirdest thing was that he shot up, she came down—all seven feet of her, and you know how heavy—but nothing else did. Not a bird, not an egg, not a feather, not a twig. Nothing. Birds all sat there and watched while Niall pulled out his harpoon, which should have just bounced off her—unless of course she'd been a real mermaid, and then—" He blinked finally, and shook his head, looking rattled. "And anyway, Adam Paring found some cutters in his tackle box and made a patch out of a beer can to hide the damage on her scales."

"But how did—who—? What, she climbed into the tree herself? A sneaker wave floated her up and left her there without drowning the nests?"

"You know what I know, and that's all I know," Markham said heavily. "Except that I need another beer."

"Well, that explains the beer can in her tail."

"You noticed that?"

"Well, yeah. It's not exactly subtle. Other than that, though, she seems. . . ." His voice trailed. He examined his first glimpse of her, felt the lack again, nothing where there should be . . . what?

"Her cormorant is gone," Scott said, and Jake nodded, relieved.

"Yes. That's it. That's what I was missing."

"Way things are happening, maybe it flew away when she slid into the water," Markham said, and reached for Jake's beer. "And maybe it picked her up later and dropped her in the tree. I don't know. You can't think about it too much. Things start happening in your head. Weird thing is—"

"What's weirder? What could be?"

"You know how the cormorant stood in the curve of her tail? And now it's gone. But there's no sign it had ever been there. No paint missing where its big, flat feet should have been. No bare patches in the tail. Just blue scales. So." He paused to drain Jake's glass. "Maybe it really did fly away." He looked around the pub. "And now we've got the mermaid back, but where's the waitress we thought was her?"

"I am so not thinking about that," Jake groaned. "I'd better call Blaine—"

"No," the brothers said together.

"Don't worry. I'm not going anywhere near that mermaid again. If the bride wants something blue and yellow and red I'll dye my hair and paint myself." He was silent then, musing over maybes, and what-ifs, and teasing the improbable out of the impossible. What did a lightning bolt, a church bell, a mermaid have in common? A cormorant, of course. A beer appeared in front of him like a lifeline, pulling him back out of his thoughts. "Promise me," he pleaded.

"What?" the brothers asked.

"If you ever figure all this out, don't tell me. I will never want to know."

"You might have warned me," the witch said grumpily.

"You were sleeping so soundly I didn't want to wake you," Portia said sweetly. They were back in her shop, inhaling tea and laying waste to a tray of sweet and savory tarts. The witch, who had forgotten what she looked like, even if she could remember where she had left her original self, had cobbled a body out of forgotten reflections she had coaxed from a mirror in a thrift shop.

"That harpoon might have killed me."

"Nope. I was guiding it all the way up, and the mermaid all the way down. I had everything under control, even the birds; it helps to speak their language. Reverend Becky told us to be creative against the predators." There was a look in her dark eyes, where antiquities lurked, that made the witch instantly suspicious.

"Now what?"

"Just a thought." Portia straightened a nicely painted index finger, licked chocolate off of it.

The witch felt a yawn ballooning in her, tried to hide it, then gave up and let it happen.

She said, tiredly, "I don't want to hear it."

"Well, I won't say anything if you don't want me to. But it would be a place to sleep for as long as you want. After all, they've got that mermaid attached to an antique ship's anchor now, and she's not going anywhere. They can't seem to find her missing cormorant."

"I suppose you haven't a clue."

Portia gave her a smile, lovely, carefree, inviting, not unlike the mermaid's. The witch stifled another yawn, felt herself drifting again on a slow ebb toward dreams.

"Well," she said. "Maybe. But promise me: no more surprises. I just want a long and very peaceful nap."

"You got it."

The wooden cormorant was back on its roost in the curve of the mermaid's tail sometime before dawn, where it remained undisturbed for months until it finally woke again and flew away.

The Gorgon in the Cupboard

Harry could not get the goat to stay still. His model, who was an aspiring actress, offered numerous impractical suggestions as she crouched beside the animal. In fact, she rarely stopped talking. Harry didn't like the look in the goat's eye. It wasn't very big, but it seemed to him arrogant beyond its age, and contemplating mischief.

"Give it something to eat," Moira suggested. "Goats eat anything, don't they? That old leather sack, there."

"That's my lunch," Harry said patiently. "And the less we put into the goat, the less will come out of it. If you get my meaning."

She giggled. She was quite charming, with her triangular elfin face, her large green eyes with lashes so long they seemed to catch air like butterfly wings as they rose and fell. She dealt handily with the goat, who was eyeing Harry's lunch now. It strained against the rope around its neck, occasionally tightening it so that its yellow eyes verged on the protuberant. A bit like hers, Harry thought.

"Try to remain serious," he pleaded. "You're a scapegoat; you've been falsely accused and spurned by the world. Your only friend in the world is that goat."

"I thought you said you were just sketching the outlines today. Putting us in our places. So why do I have to be serious?" The goat, in whose rope her wrists were supposedly entangled, gave an obstinate tug; she loosed one hand and smacked it. "You should have gotten a female. They're sweet-natured. Not like this ruffian." She wrinkled her nose. "Stinks, too, he does. Like—"

"This one was all I could borrow. Please."

They were still for a miraculous moment, both gazing at him. He picked up charcoal, held his breath and drew a line of the goat's flank onto the canvas, then continued the line with her flank and bent knee. She swatted at a fly; the goat bucked; they both seemed to *baa* at once. Harry sighed, wiped sweat out of his eyes. They had been there half the morning, and little enough to show for it. The sun was high and dagger-bright; the tavern yard where he had set his poignant scene was full of sniggering critics. Idlers, he reminded himself, resuming doggedly when the pair settled again. They wouldn't know a brush from a broom straw. Still. He paused to study his efforts. He sighed again. There was something definitely wrong with her foot.

"It's hot," she said plaintively, shaking her heavy hair away from her neck, disturbing the perfect, nunlike veil across her face.

"Ah, don't—"

"And I'm starving. Why can't you paint like Alex McAlister? He lets me sit inside; he dresses me in silks; he lets me talk as much as I want unless he's doing my face. And I get hung every time, too, a good place on the wall where people can see me, not down in a corner where nobody looks."

The goat was hunkered on the ground now, trying to break its neck pulling at the rope peg. Harry glanced despairingly at the merciless source of light, looked again at his mutinous scapegoats, then flung his charcoal down.

"All right. All right."

"You owe me for Thursday, too."

"All right."

"When do you want me to come again?"

He closed his eyes briefly, then fished coins out of his pocket. "I'll send word."

One of the critics leaning against the wall called, "Best pay the goat, too; it might not come back otherwise."

"I might have work," Moira reminded him loftily. Mostly she worked early mornings selling bread in a bakery and took elocution lessons in afternoons when she wasn't prowling the theaters or, Harry suspected, the streets for work.

"That goat won't get any younger neither," another idler commented. Harry gritted his teeth, then snapped his fingers for the boy pitching a knife in a corner of the yard. The boy loosened the goat from the peg, got a good grip on its neck-loop to return it to its owner. He held out his other hand for pay.

"Tomorrow then, sir?" he asked indifferently.

"I'll send word," Harry repeated.

"Don't forget your dinner there, sir."

"You have it. I'm not hungry."

He dropped the charcoal into his pocket, tucked the canvas under one arm and the folded easel under the other, and walked home dejectedly, scarcely seeing the city around him. He was a fair-haired, sweet-faced young man, nicely built despite his awkward ways, with a habitually patient expression and a heart full of ravaging longings and ambitions. He was not talented enough for them, this morning's work told him. He would never be good enough. The girl was right. His paintings, if chosen at all to be hung for important exhibits, always ended up too high, or too close to the floor, or in obscure, badly lit corners. He thought of McAlister's magnificent *Diana*, with the dogs and the deer in it looking so well-behaved they might have been stuffed. And Haversham's *Watchful Shepherd*: the sheep as fat as dandelions and as docile as—as, well, sheep. Why not scapesheep, he wondered despondently, rather than scapegoats? No goat would stand still long enough for mankind to heap their crimes on its head.

Then he saw that which drove every other thought out of his head.

Her.

She was walking with her husband on the other side of the street. He was speaking fervidly, gesturing, as was his wont, probably about something that had seized his imagination. It might have been anything, Harry knew: a poem, the style of an arch, a pattern of embroidery on a woman's sleeve. She listened, her quiet face angled slightly toward him, her eyes downturned, intent, it seemed, on the man's brilliance. He swept fingers through his dark, shaggy hair, his thick mustaches dancing, spit flying now and then in his exuberance. Neither of them saw Harry, who had stopped midstream in the busy street, willing her to look, terrified that she might raise her dark, brooding eyes and see what was in his face. She only raised her long white fingers, gently clasped her husband's flying arm, and tucked it down between them.

Thus they passed, the great Alex McAlister and his wife, Aurora, oblivious to the man turned to stone by the sight of her.

He moved at last, jostled by a pair of boys pursued through the crowd, and then by the irate man at their heels. Harry barely noticed them. Her face hung in his mind, gazing out of canvas at him: McAlister's *Diana,* McAlister's *Cleopatra,* McAlister's *Venus.* That hair, rippling like black fire from skin as white as alabaster, those deep, heavy-lidded eyes that seemed to perceive invisible worlds. That strong, slender column of neck. Those long fingers, impossibly mobile and expressive. That mouth like a bite of sweet fruit. Those full, sultry lips. . . .

I would give my soul to paint you, he told her silently. But even if in some marvelous synchronicity of events that were possible, it would still be impossible. With her gazing at him, he could not have painted a stroke. Again and again she turned him into stone.

Not Aurora, he thought with hopeless longing, but Medusa.

He had tried to speak to her any number of times when he had visited Alex's studio or their enchanting cottage in the country. All he managed, under that still, inhuman gaze, were insipid commonplaces. The weather. The wildflowers blooming in the garden. The stunning success of McAlister's latest painting. He coughed on crumbs, spilled tea on his cuff. Her voice was very low; he bent to hear it and stepped on her hem with his muddy boot sole, so that whatever she had begun to say was overwhelmed by his apologies. Invariably, routed by his own gracelessness, he would turn abruptly away to study a vase that McAlister had glazed himself, or a frame he was making. McAlister never seemed to notice his hopeless passion, the longing of the most insignificant moth for fire. He would clap Harry's shoulder vigorously, spilling his tea again, and then fix him in an enthusiastic torrent of words, trying to elicit Harry's opinion of some project or profundity, while the only thought in Harry's head was of the woman sitting so silently beyond them she might have been in another world entirely.

He walked down a quiet side street shaded by stately elms and opened the gate in front of the comfortable house he had inherited from his parents. Looking despondently upon his nicely blooming hollyhocks, he wondered what to do next.

If only I could create a masterwork, he thought. An idea no one has thought of yet, that would attract the attention of the city, bring me acclaim. Make me one of the circle of the great. . . . Now I'm only a novice, a squire, something more than apprentice yet less than master. Harry Waterman, dabbler at the mystery of art. If only I could pass through the closed doors to the inner sanctum. Surely She would notice me then. . . .

He went across the garden, up the steps to his door, and stopped again, hand on the latch, as he mused over an appropriate subject for a masterpiece. The goat, while original and artistically challenging, held no dignity; it would not rivet crowds with its power and mystery. At most, viewers might pity it and its ambiguous female counterpart, and then pass on. More likely they would pity the artist, who had stood in a sweltering tavern yard painting a goat.

Aurora's face passed again through his thoughts; his hand opened and closed convulsively on the door latch. Something worthy of those eyes he must paint. Something that would bring expression into them: wonder, admiration, curiosity. . . .

What?

Whatever it was, he would dedicate his masterpiece to Her.

The door pulled abruptly out of his hold. Mrs. Grommet, his placid housekeeper, held a hand to her ample bosom as she stared at him. "Oh, it's you, Mr. Waterman. I couldn't imagine who was making that racket with the door latch." She shifted aside, opened the door wide for him to enter.

"Sorry, Mrs. Grommet," he murmured. "Throes of creation."

"Of course, Mr. Waterman. I didn't expect you back so soon. Have you had your lunch, sir?"

"No. Just bring me tea in my studio, please. I expect to be in the throes for the rest of the afternoon."

"Yes, sir."

In the highest floor of the house, he had knocked down walls, enlarged windows to give him space and light, views from a city park on one side, the broad, busy river on the other. Mrs. Grommet came panting up with a great silver tray. He slumped in an easy chair, sipped tea as he flipped through his sketchbooks for inspiration. Faces, dogs, flowers, birds, hills, rocks, pieces of armor, horses, folds of heavy tapestry, drifting silk, hands, feet, eyes . . . nothing coherent, nothing whole, nothing containing the lightning bolt of inspiration he craved.

He read some poetry; words did not compel an image. He paced for a while, his mind a blank canvas. He beseeched his Muse. Anybody's Muse. Inspiration failed to turn her lovely face, her kindly attention, toward him. He wandered to his cupboards, pulled out old, unfinished canvases, studied the stilted figures, the fuzzy landscapes for something that he might redeem to greatness.

One caught at memory: a head without a mouth. He placed it on the easel, stood studying it. The head, when completed, would have belonged to Persephone at the moment she realized that, having eaten of the fruits of the Underworld, she was doomed to spend half her life in that gloomy place. The young model he had chosen for it had vanished before he could finish it. Harry gazed at her, struck by her beauty, which had inspired his normally clumsy brushwork. The almond-shaped eyes of such pale gray they seemed the color of sun-kissed ice, the white-gold hair, the apricot skin. A true mingling of spring and winter, his model, who had disappeared so completely she might have been carried away into the netherworld herself.

He tried to remember her name. May? Jenny? She had gotten herself into trouble, he suspected. Harry had noticed a certain heaviness in her walk, the frigidity of terror in her expression. Moved, he had offered, in his nebulous, hesitant way, to help. But she had fled. Or died, perhaps, he was forced to consider. In childbirth, or trying to get rid of the child, who could know? He had tried to find her so that he could finish the painting. But no one seemed to know anything at all about her.

He wondered if it might be worth finishing. Her eyes, gazing straight out at the viewer, compelled attention. Idly, he traced a mouth with his forefinger, rifling through all the likely mouths he might borrow to finish it. There was Beresford's cousin Jane . . . But no, even at her young age, her lips were too thin to suggest the hunger that had caused Persephone to eat forbidden fruit. . . . Or was that a different tale?

He recognized the invisible mouth his finger had outlined, and swallowed.

Some passing Muse, a mischievous sprite, tempted him to reach for crimson paint. The lips that haunted him burned like fire in memory . . . but darker than fire, darker than rose, darker than blood. He toyed guiltily with all those colors on his palette. Only paint, he told himself. Only memory. The color of wine, they were, deep, shadowy burgundy, with all the silken moistness of the rose petal.

Vaguely he heard Mrs. Grommet knock, inquire about his supper. Vaguely he made some noise. She went away. The room darkened; he lit lamps, candles. Mrs. Grommet did not return; the streets grew even quieter; the river faded into night.

He blinked, coming out of his obsessive trance. That full, provocative splendor of a mouth was startling beneath the gentle, frightened eyes of his Persephone. But the likeness transfixed him. Aurora's mouth it was; he had succeeded beyond all dreams in shifting it from memory into paint. He could not use it. Of course he could not. Everyone would recognize it, even on some other woman's face. Which he would need to go out and find, if he wanted to finish this Persephone. Maybe not his masterwork, but far easier to manage than the goat; she would do until inspiration struck.

He lingered, contemplating that silent, untouchable mouth. He could not bring himself to wipe it away yet. He would go down and eat his cold supper, deal more ruthlessly with the mouth after he had found a replacement for it. It did not, after all, belong to him; it belonged to the wife of his dear friend and mentor. . . . He tore his eyes from it, lifted the canvas from the easel, and positioned it carefully back in the cupboard, where it could dry and be forgotten at the same time.

He closed the door and the lips spoke.

"Harry!" Its voice was sweet and raucous and completely unfamiliar.

"You're not going to leave me here in the dark, are you? After calling me all afternoon? Harry?"

He flung himself against the door, hearing his heart pound like something frantic trying to get out of him, or trying to get in. He tried to speak; his voice wouldn't come, only silent bleats of air, like an astonished sheep.

"Harry?"

"Who—" he finally managed to gasp. "Who—"

"Open the door."

"N."

"You know I'm in here. You can't just keep me shut up in here."

"N."

"Oh Harry, don't be so unfriendly. I won't bite. And even if I did—" The voice trilled an uncouth snigger, "you'd like it, from this mouth."

Harry, galvanized with sudden fury, clutched at the cupboard latch, barely refraining from wrenching it open. "How dare you!" he demanded, feeling as though the contents of his inmost heart had been rifled by vulgar, soiled hands. "Who are you?"

"That's it," the voice cooed. "Now lift the latch, open the door. You can do it."

"If you force me to come in, I'll—I'll wipe away your mouth with turpentine."

"Tut, Harry. How crude. Just when I'm ready to give you what you want most."

"What I want—"

"Inspiration, Harry. You've been wishing for me ever since you gave up on the goat and gave me a chance to get a word in edgewise."

"You're a mouth—" He was breathing strangely again, taking in too much air. "How can you possibly know about the goat?"

"You called me."

"I did not."

"You invoked me," the voice insisted. "I am the voice of your despair. Your desire. Why do you think I'm coming out of these lips?"

Harry was silent, suddenly breathless. A flash went through him, not unlike the uncomfortable premonition of inspiration. He was going to open the door. Pushed against it with all his strength, his hands locked around the latch, he was going to open. . . . "Who are you?" he pleaded hoarsely. "Are you some sort of insane Muse?"

"Guess again," the voice said coolly. "You looked upon your Beloved and thought of me. I want you to paint me. I am your masterwork."

"My masterwork."

"Paint me, Harry. And all you wish for will be yours."

"All I wish. . . ."

"Open the door," the voice repeated patiently. "Don't be afraid. You have already seen my face."

His mouth opened; nothing came out. The vision stunned him, turned him into stone: the painting that would rivet the entire art world, reveal at last the depths and heights of his genius. The snake-haired daughter of the gods whose beauty threatened, commanded, whose eyes reflected inexpressible, inhuman visions.

He whispered, "Medusa."

"Me," she said. "Open the door."

He opened it.

Down by the river, Jo huddled with the rest of the refuse, all squeezed under a butcher's awning trying to get out of the sudden squall. In the country, where she had walked from, the roads turned liquid in the rain; carriages, wagons, horses, herds of sheep and cows churned them into thick, oozing welts and hillocks of mud deep enough to swallow your boots if you weren't careful. Here the cobbles, though hard enough, offered some protection. At least she was off her aching feet.

At least until the butcher saw what took up space from customers looking in his windows and drove them off. Jo had been walking that day since dawn to finish her journey to the city. It was noon now, she guessed, though hard to tell. The gray sky hadn't changed its morose expression by so much as a shift of light since sunrise.

Someone new pushed into the little group cowering under the awning. Another drenched body, nearly faceless under the rags wrapped around its head, sat leaning against Jo's shoulder, worn shoes out in the rain. It wore skirts; other than that it seemed scarcely human, just one more sodden, miserable, breathing thing trying to find some protection from life.

They all sat silently for a bit, listening to the rain pounding on the awning, watching the little figures along the tide's edge, gray and shapeless as mud in their rags, darting like birds from one poor crumb of treasure the river left behind to the next. Bits of coal they stuffed into their rags to sell, splinters of wood, the odd nail or frayed piece of rope.

The bundle beside Jo murmured, "At least they're used to being wet, aren't they? River or rain, it's all one to them."

Her voice was unexpectedly young. Jo turned, maneuvering one shoulder out from beneath a sodden back. She saw a freckled girl's face between wet cloth wrapped down to her eyebrows, up to her lower lip. One eye, as blue as violets, looked resigned, calm. The other eye was swollen shut and ringed by all the colors of the rainbow.

Jo, her own face frozen for so long it hardly remembered how to move, felt something odd stirring in her. Vaguely she remembered it. Pity or some such, for all the good it did.

She said, "Whoever gave you that must love you something fierce."

"Oh, yes," the girl said. "He'll love me to death one of these days. If he finds me again."

There was a snort from the figure on the other side of Jo. This one sounded older, hoarse and wheezy with illness. Still she cackled, "I'd one like that. I used to collect my teeth in a bag after he knocked them out. I was so sorry to lose them, I couldn't bear to give them up. I was that young, then. Never smart enough to run away, even when I was young enough to think there might be a place to run to."

"There's not," Jo said shortly. "I ran back home to the country. And now I'm here again."

"What will you do?" the girl asked.

Jo shrugged. "Whatever I can."

"What have you done?"

"Mill work in the country. I had to stop doing that when my mother died and there was no one else to—to—"

"Care for the baby?" the old woman guessed shrewdly.

Jo felt her face grow cold again, less expression on it than on a brick. "Yes. Well, it's dead now, so it doesn't matter."

The girl sucked in her breath. "Cruel," she whispered.

"After that I got work at one of the big houses. Laundry and fires and such. But that didn't last."

"Did you get your references, though?"

"No. Turned out without."

"For what? Stealing?"

"No." Jo leaned her head back against the wall, watched rain running like a fountain over the edge of the swollen awning. "I wasn't that smart."

The old woman gave her crow-cackle again. "Out of the frying pan—"

Jo nodded. "Into the fire. It would have been, if I hadn't run away. If I'd stayed, I'd have had another mouth to feed when they turned me out. So I came back here."

Another voice came to life, a man's this time. "To what?" he asked heavily. "Nothing ever changes. City, country, it's all the same. You're in the mill or on the streets from dark to dark, just to get your pittance to survive one more day. And some days you can't even get that." He paused; Jo felt his racking cough shudder through them all, piled on top of one another as they were. The old woman patted his arm, whispered something. Then she turned to Jo, when he had quieted.

"He lost his wife, not long ago. Twenty-two years together and not a voice raised. Some have that."

"Twenty-two years," the man echoed. "She had her corner at the foot of the Barrow Bridge. She sang like she didn't know any better. She made you believe it, too—that you didn't know anything better than her singing, you'd never know anything better. She stopped boats with her voice; fish jumped out of the water to hear. But then she left me alone with my old fiddle and my old bones, both of us creaking and groaning without her." He patted the lump under his threadbare cloak as though it were a child. "Especially in this rain."

"Well, I know what I'm going to do when it quits," the girl said briskly. "I'm going to get myself arrested. He'll never get his hands on me in there. And it's dry and they feed you, at least for a few days before they let you out again."

"I got in for three months once," a young voice interposed from the far edge of the awning.

"Three months!" the girl exclaimed, her bruised eye trying to flutter open. "What do you have to do for that?"

"I couldn't get myself arrested for walking the streets, no matter how I tried, and I was losing my teeth and my looks to a great lout who drank all my money away by day and flung me around at night. I was so sick and tired of my life that one morning when I saw the Lord Mayor of the city in a parade of fine horses and soldiers and dressed-up lords and ladies, I took off my shoe and threw it at his head." The old woman crowed richly at the thought. "I let them catch me, and for three months I had a bed every night, clean clothes, and food every day. By the time I got out, my lout had moved on to some other girl and I was free."

"They don't make jails nowadays the way they used to," the fiddler said. "They never used to spoil you with food or a bed."

Jo felt the girl sigh noiselessly. "I'd do three months," she murmured, "if I knew where to find a Lord Mayor."

Jo's eyes slid to her vivid, wistful face. "What will you do," she asked slowly, "for your few days?"

"I've heard they take you off the streets if you break something. A window, or a streetlamp. I thought I'd try that."

Jo was silent, pulling a tattered shawl around her. Jo had made it for her mother, years earlier, when her father had been alive to tend to his sheep and his cows, make cheese, shear wool for them to spin into thread. When she'd gone back, her mother had given the shawl to her to wrap the baby in. The sheep and cows were long gone to pay debts after her father died. Her mother's hands had grown huge and red from taking in laundry. Alf, they called the baby, after her father. Alfred Fletcher Byrd. Poor poppet, she thought dispassionately. Not strong enough for any one of those names, let alone three.

The man who was its father showed his face in her thoughts. She shoved him out again, ruthlessly, barred that entry. She'd lost a good place in the city because of him, in a rich, quiet, well-run house. A guest, a friend of the family, who had a family of his own somewhere. He'd found her early one morning making up a fire in the empty library. . . . The only time she'd ever seen him, and it was enough to change her life. So she'd run out of the city, all the way back home to her mother. And all she had left of any of that time was an old purple shawl.

That was then, she thought coldly. This is now.

Now, the rain was letting up a little. The young girl shifted, leaning out to test it with her hand. Jo moved, too, felt the coin or two she had left sliding around in her shoe. Enough for a loaf and a bed in some crowded, noisy, dangerous lodging house run by thieves. Might as well spend it there, before they found a way to steal it.

Or she could break a window, if she got desperate enough.

A door banged. There was the butcher, a great florid man with blood on his hands and a voice like a bulldog, growling at them to take their carcasses elsewhere or he'd grind them into sausages.

The girl wrapped her face close again, hiding her telltale eye. The fiddler coughed himself back into the rain, his instrument carefully cradled beneath his cloak. The old woman, wheezing dreadfully, pulled herself up with Jo's help. Jo picked up her covered basket for her. Flowers, she thought at first, then caught a pungent whiff of it. Whatever it was she sold, it wasn't violets. The woman winked at her and slid the basket over her arm. She trailed off after the rest of the bedraggled flock scattering into the rain.

Jo saw a lump of masonry, or maybe a broken cobblestone, half the size of her fist near the wall where the old woman had been sitting. She picked it up, slipped it into her pocket in case she needed it later.

You never knew.

Harry stood in the enchanted garden of the McAlisters' cottage in the country. Only a few miles from the city, it might have existed in a different time and world: the realm of poetry, where the fall of light and a rosebud heavy with rain from a passing storm symbolized something else entirely. The rain had stopped in the early afternoon. Bright sun had warmed the garden quickly, filled its humid, sparkling air with the smells of grass and wild thyme, the crushed-strawberry scent of the rambling roses climbing up either side of the cottage door. The cottage, an oddly shaped affair with no symmetry whatsoever, had all its scattered, mismatched windows open to the air. There was no garden fence, only a distant, rambling stone wall marking the property. The cottage stood on a grassy knoll; in nearby fields the long grass was lush with wildflowers. Farther away, brindled cows and fluffy clouds of sheep pastured within rambling field walls. Farther yet, in a fold of green, the ancient village, a bucolic garden of stone, grew along the river. On the next knoll over, John Grainger was battling the winds, trying to paint the scene. Occasionally, as a puff of exuberant air tried to make off with Grainger's canvas, Harry could hear his energetic swearing.

Harry had come up for the day to look for a face for his Medusa among the McAlisters' visitors. Painters, their wives and families, models, friends who encouraged and bought, and who brought friends who bought, wandered around the gardens, chatting, drinking wine and tea, sketching, painting, or watching McAlister paint.

McAlister was painting his wife. Or rather, he was painting her windblown sleeve. She stood patiently against the backdrop of climbing red roses, all of which, Harry noticed, were the exact shade of her mouth. He tried not to think of that. Thinking of her mouth made him think of the monstrous creation in his cupboard. In the sweet light of day, there in the country, he was willing to attribute his Gorgon to the morbid churning of his frustrated romantic urges. But she had inspired him, no doubt about that. Here he was in McAlister's garden, looking at every passing female, even the young girl from the kitchen who kept the teapot filled for his Medusa.

McAlister was unusually reticent about his own subject matter. Whatever figure from myth or romance he was portraying, he needed her windblown. He had captured the graceful curves of his wife's wristbone, her long, pliant fingers. The flow of her silky sleeve in the contrary wind proved challenging, but he persevered, carrying on three discussions at once with his onlookers as he painted. Aurora, her brooding eyes fixed on some distant horizon, scarcely seemed to breathe; she might have been a piece of garden statuary.

Harry drifted, trying not to watch.

He sat down finally next to John Grainger's mistress, Nan Stewart. She had modeled many times for John's drawings and paintings, as well as for other artists who needed her frail, ethereal beauty for their visions. Grainger had discovered her sitting in the cheaper seats of a theater one evening. A well-brought-up young girl despite her class, she refused to speak to an artist. Undaunted, he found out who she was and implored her mother's permission to let her model for him. Her mother, a fussy lump of a bed mattress, as Grainger described her, accompanied Nan a few times, until she realized that the girl could make as much in an hour modeling for artists as she could sewing for a week in a dressmaker's shop. Eventually Nan came to live with the brilliant, volatile Grainger, which explained, Harry thought, her pallor and her melancholy eyes.

She had fine red-gold hair and arresting green eyes. With marriage in view at one point in their relationship, Grainger had hired someone to teach her to move and speak properly. She smiled at Harry dutifully as he filled the empty chair beside her.

"More tea?" he asked.

A vigorous, incoherent shouting from the knoll beyond made them both glance up. Grainger, hands on his easel, seemed to be wrestling with the wind.

Nan shook her head. She had a bound sketchbook on her lap, as well as a pencil or two. Grainger encouraged her to draw. She had talent, he declared to the world, and he was right, from what Harry had seen. But that day her sketchbook was shut.

"Not inspired?" he ventured.

"Not today." She turned her attention from the painter on the knoll finally. "How are you, Harry?"

"Flourishing."

"Are you painting?"

"I have a subject in mind. I'm prowling about for a face."

"What subject?"

"It's a secret," he said lightly. "I'm not sure I can pull it off. I don't want to embarrass myself among you artists."

Her smile touched her eyes finally. "You're a sweet man, Harry. I'm still such a novice myself."

"John praises your work to the skies. He thinks very highly—"

"I know." Her face was suddenly angled away. "I know. I only wish he still thought so highly of me."

"He does!" Harry said, shocked. "He's loved you for years. You live together, you work together, you are twin souls—"

"Yes." She looked at him again, her expression a polite mask. "Yes."

He was silent, wondering what was troubling her. His eyes strayed to the group beside the rose vines. Children ran out of the cottage door; he recognized Andrew Peel's gray-eyed little beauty, and her baby brother trundling unsteadily after. Nan sighed absently, her eyes on the children. Harry's own eyes strayed. Across the garden, the statue came to life; the dark, unfathomable eyes seemed to gaze straight at him.

He started, his cup clattering, feeling that regard like a bolt from the blue, striking silently, deeply. He became aware of Nan's eyes on him, too, in wide, unblinking scrutiny. Then she set her cup down on a table; it, too, rattled sharply in its saucer.

"She's pregnant, you know," Nan said. Harry felt as though he had missed a step, plunged into sudden space. He started again, this time not so noisily. Nan added, "So am I."

He stared at her. "That's wonderful," he exclaimed finally, leaning to put his cup on the grass. He caught her hands. That's all it was then: her inner turmoil, her natural uncertainties. "Wonderful," he repeated.

"Is it?"

"Of course! You'll marry now, won't you?"

She gave him an incredulous stare. Then she loosed her hands, answered tonelessly, "Yes, quite soon. Next week, perhaps, and then we'll go away for a bit to the southern coasts to paint."

"I couldn't be happier," Harry told her earnestly. "We've all been expecting this for—"

"For years," she finished. "Yes." She hesitated; he waited, puzzled without knowing why. Something about the event, he supposed, made women anxious, prone to fear disasters or imagine things that were not true.

Grainger's voice, sonorous and vibrant, spilled over the group. He appeared tramping up the knoll, his hat gone, his canvas in one hand, easel in the other, paints in the pockets of his voluminous, stained jacket. He blew a kiss to Nan, leaving a daub of blue on his bushy, autumn-gold mustaches. Then he turned to see how McAlister's sleeve was coming. Above his broad back, Harry saw the statue's eyes come alive again; her cheeks had flushed, in the wayward wind, a delicate shade of rose. Ever the consummate professional, she did not move, while Grainger, lingering in the group, expounded with witty astonishment how like a wing that sleeve seemed, straining for its freedom on the wind.

Harry turned back to Nan, breath indrawn for some pleasantry.

Her chair was empty. He looked around bewilderedly. She had flown herself, it seemed, but why and on what wayward wind, he could not imagine.

Jo walked the darkening streets, fingering the broken cobble in her pocket. The day had been dryer than the previous one; that was as much as she could say for it. Sun seemed to linger forever as she trudged through the noisy, stinking streets. She asked everyone for work, even the butcher who had driven her out from under his awning, a shapeless, faceless, unrecognizable bundle he didn't remember in the light. But he only laughed and offered the usual, smacking with the flat of his hand the quivering haunch of meat he was slicing into steaks.

"Come back when you get desperate," he called after her, to the amusement of his customers. "Show me how fine you can grind it."

She got much the same at inns and alehouses. When she stopped at crossings to rest her feet and beg for a coin or two, she got threats from sweepers' brooms, screeches from ancient heaps of rags whose territory she had invaded, shoves from lean, hollow-cheeked, cat-eyed girls with missing teeth who told her they'd cut off her hair with a rusty knife if they saw her twice on their street.

Toward late afternoon she was too exhausted to feel hungry. She had money for one more night's lodging, or money for food. Not both. After that—she didn't think about it. That would be tomorrow, this was not. Now she had her two coppers, her two choices. And she had the stone in her pocket. She drifted, waiting for night.

When the streetlamps were lit, she made up her mind. Just in that moment. She was sitting in the dark, finally safe because nobody could see her nursing her blistered, aching soles. Nobody threatened, yelled, or made lewd suggestions; for a few precious moments she might have been invisible.

And then the gas lamps went on, showing the world where she was again. Caught in the light, she didn't even think. She was on her feet in a breath, hand in her pocket; in the next she had hurled the broken stone furiously at the light. She was startled to hear the satisfying shatter of glass. Someone shouted; the flare, still burning, illumined a couple of uniformed figures to which, she decided with relief, she would yield herself for her transgression.

There was a sudden confusion around her: ragged people rushing into the light, all calling out as they surrounded the uniforms. Jo, pushing against them, couldn't get past to reveal herself to the law.

"I did it," a woman shrieked.

"No, it was me broke the lamp," somebody else shouted. The crowd lurched; voices rose higher. "Give over, you great cow—it was me!"

"I did it!" Jo shouted indignantly. "It wasn't them at all!"

The crowd heaved against her, picked her off her feet. Then it dropped her a moment later, as it broke apart. She lost her balance, sat on the curb staring as the uniforms escorted the wrong woman entirely out of the light. She went along eagerly enough, Jo noted sourly. She pulled herself up finally, still smarting over the injustice of it all.

Then she realized that her purple shawl was gone.

She felt her throat swell and burn, for the first time in forever. Even when her mother had died she hadn't cried. Not even when the baby had died. She had taken the shawl off her mother, and then off the baby. It was all she had left to remember them by. Now that was gone. And she was blinded, tears swelling behind her eyes, because the tattered shawl had borne the burden, within its braided threads, of her memories.

Now she was left holding them all herself.

She limped to find some private shred of shadow, refusing to let tears fall. All the shadows seemed occupied; snores and mutterings warned her before she could sit. She wandered on and on through the quieting streets, unable to stop the memories swirling in her head. Her innocent young self, cleaning the ashes out of the fireplace in the fine, peaceful library. The handsome stranger with the light, easy voice, asking her name. Asking about her. Listening to her, while he touched her cuff button with his finger. Shifted a loose strand of her hair off her face. Touched her as no one had, ever before. Then gone, nowhere, not to be seen, he might have been a dream. And she, beginning to wake at nights, feeling the panic gnawing at her until she could bear it no longer, and upped and ran.

But there was something else. A street name dredged it up as she walked. Or the night smell of a great tree in a line of them along the street. She had run from someone else. Oh, she remembered. Him. The young painter. He had a gentle voice, too, but he only touched her to turn her head, or put her loose hair where he wanted it. He paid well, too, for the random hour or two she could spare him. It was his money she saved to run with, when she knew she could no longer stay. When her skirts grew tight. When the other girls began to whisper, and the housekeeper's eyes drew up tight in her head like a snail's eyes at the sight of Jo.

What was his name?

She walked under the great, dark boughs that shielded her from the streetlights. She could sleep under them she thought. Curl up in their roots like an animal; no one would see her until dawn. The street was very quiet; a sedate carriage or a cab went by now and then, but she heard no voices. He lived on a street like this; she remembered the trees. She'd walk there from the great house, his housekeeper would let her in, and she would climb the stairs to his—his what was it? His studio. He painted her with that strange fruit in her hand, with all the rows of little seeds in it like baby teeth.

He told her stories.

You are in the Underworld, he said. You have been stolen from your loving mother's house by the King of Hades. You must not eat or drink anything he offers you; if you refuse, he will have no power over you, and he must set you free. But, you grow hungry, so hungry, as you wait. . . .

"So hungry," she whispered.

You eat only a few tiny seeds from this fruit thinking such small things would do no harm. But harm you have done, for now he can claim you as his wife and keep you, during the darkest months of the year, in his desolate and lonely realm. . . .

What was her name?

Her eyes were closing. Her bones ached; her feet seemed no longer recognizable. Not feet any longer, just pain. Pain she walked on, and dark her only friend. . . . She didn't choose; she simply fell, driven to her knees in the damp ground beneath a tree. She crawled close to it, settled herself among its roots, her head reeling, it felt like, about to bounce off her shoulders and roll away without her.

What was its name?

She closed her eyes and saw it: that bright, glowing fruit, those sweet, innocent seeds. . . .

Pomegranate.

Would he want to finish his painting? she wondered.

But there was someone guarding her passage out of the Underworld. Someone stood at the gates she must pass through, protecting the serene upper realms from the likes of her. Someone whose word was law on the border between two worlds. . . .

What was her name?

Her eyes. Jo could not remember her eyes, only felt them watching as she fled into the ancient, timeless dark. Only her bun, the light, glossy brown of a well-baked dinner roll, and her chins and the watch pinned to her bosom, at one corner of her apron.

What would her eyes say when she saw Jo?

She remembered as she felt the strong arms seize her, pull her off the earth into the nether realms of sleep.

Mrs. Grommet.

Harry, having returned from the country without his Medusa, avoided his studio. He did not want to open the cupboard door again. He couldn't decide which might be worse: his painting talking to him or his painting not talking to him. Was expecting a painting to speak to him worse than having it speak to him? Suppose he opened the cupboard door with expectations, and nothing happened? He would be forced to conclusions that, in the cheery light of day, he did not want to think about.

So he left the house at midmorning and dropped in at a gallery where a new painting by Thomas Buck was hung. The gallery, recently opened, had acquired pieces indiscriminately in its desire to become fashionable. It aimed, it declared affably, to encourage the novice as well as to celebrate the artist. Tommy Buck's work showed promise. It had been showing promise for years. Harry, studying the new painting called *Knight Errant*, was gratified to see that Buck still could not draw to save his life. The horse was absurdly proportioned; its wide, oblong back could have been set for a dinner party of six. And the knight's hands, conveniently hidden within bulky gauntlets, gripped the reins awkwardly, as though he were playing tug-of-war. The young woman tied to a tree, toward whom the knight rode, seemed to be chatting amiably with the dragon who menaced her.

I could do better than that, Harry thought.

He felt the urge, remembered the anomaly in the cupboard, and was relieved when some friends hailed him. They carried him away eventually to dine, and from there to another friend's studio where they drank wine and watched the painter struggle with his Venus, a comely enough young woman with something oddly bland about her beauty. She bantered well, though, and stayed to entertain them over a cold supper of beef and salad. Harry got home late, pleasantly tipsy, and, inspired, went immediately up to his studio to view his work within the context of his friend's

The Gorgon spoke when he opened the cupboard, causing him to reel back with a startled cry: he had actually forgotten her.

"Hello, Harry."

"Hlmph," he choked.

"Have you found me yet?"

He tugged at his collar, tempted to slam the cupboard shut and go to bed. But he answered, venturing closer, "No. Not yet."

"Did you even look for me?"

"Of course I did! I looked for you in every female face I passed. I didn't see you anywhere." Except, he thought, in McAlister's garden, where Her eyes had immobilized him once again. "You aren't easy to find," he added, speaking now into the shadows. "You're a very complex matter."

"Yes, I am, aren't I?" she murmured complacently. "Harry, why don't you let me out?"

"I can't. What if someone sees?"

"Well, I don't intend to pass the time of day with Mrs. Grommet, if that's what worries you."

"No, but—"

"Hang a cloth over my face or something. Pretend I'm a parrot."

"I don't think so," he sighed, sitting down on the floor because he had been standing much of the day. A lamp on the wall above his head spilled some light into the open cupboard; he could see the edge of the canvas, but not the moving mouth. Less afraid now, lulled by wine and company, he asked her curiously, "Where do you think I should look for you?"

"Oh, anywhere. You'll know me when you see me."

"But to see you is to be—"

"Yes," she said, laughing a little. "You'll recognize your model when she turns you, for just a tiny human moment, into stone."

"Only One can do that," he said softly.

"Maybe. You just keep looking."

"But for what? Are you—were you, I mean, really that terrible? Or that beautiful? Which should I be searching for?"

"Oh, we were hideous," she answered cheerfully, "me and my two Gorgon sisters. Stheno and Euryale, they were called. Even in the Underworld, our looks could kill."

"Stheno?"

"Nobody remembers them, because nothing much ever happened to them. They didn't even die, being immortal. Do you think anyone would remember me if that obnoxious boy hadn't figured out a way to chop my head off without looking at me?"

Harry dredged a name out of the mists of youthful education. "Perseus, was it?"

"He had help, you know. He couldn't have been that clever without divine intervention. Long on brawn, short on brains, you know that type of hero."

"That's not what I was taught."

"He forced our guardian sisters, the gray-haired Graie, to help him, you must have heard. He stole their only eye and their tooth."

"They had one eye?" Harry said fuzzily.

"They passed it back and forth. And the tooth. Among the three of them." She gave an unlovely cackle. "What a sight that was, watching them eat. Or squabble over that eyeball. That's what they were doing when they didn't see that brat of a boy coming. He grabbed their goods and forced them to give him magic armor and a mirror to see me in, so he wouldn't have to meet my eyes. Then he lopped my head off and used me to kill his enemies. Even dead, I had an effect on people."

"He doesn't sound so very stupid."

"He had help," she repeated with a touch of asperity. "Anyway, it was loathsome, gray-haired old biddies who armed him to fight me. Not lissome, rosy-fingered maidens. You remember that when you paint me."

"I will." He added, brooding over the matter, "If I can find you."

"Oh, you will," she said more cheerfully. "Never fret. I do wish you would take me out of here and let me watch, though."

"No."

"I could advise you."

"You'd scare my model."

"I wouldn't talk, I promise you! And if I forget, just cover me up. Please, Harry? After all, I have inspired you. You could do me a favor. It's awfully dark in here."

"Well."

"Please? Harry?"

"Well." He got to his feet again, dusted off his trousers, yawning now and forgetting why he had come up. "I'll think about it. Good night."

"Good night, Harry."

He closed the cupboard door and went to bed.

The next morning, his ambition inflamed by what the gallery seemed to think worth hanging, he ate his breakfast hastily and early. He would not come home without his Medusa, he was determined, even if he had to search the ravaged streets and slums for her. No, he told Mrs. Grommet, she should not expect him home before evening, if then. He would go as far as he must to find his inspiration, even as far, he admitted in his inmost heart, as the country, to see if he might find that unexpected face in Aurora's shadow.

He got as far as the street. He paused to latch the garden gate behind him and was turned to stone.

A woman appeared out of nowhere, it seemed. She murmured something to him; he hardly knew what. He looked at her and time stopped. The normal street noises of passing carriages, birds, doors opening, voices calling simply vanished. He heard the faint hum of his own blood in his ears and recognized it as a constant, unchanging sound out of antiquity. The sound heard when all else is silent; nothing moves.

Her face was all bone and shadow, full of stark paradoxes: young yet ancient with experience, beautiful yet terrifying with knowledge, living yet somehow alive no longer. Whatever those great, wide-set eyes had seen had left a haunting starkness in them that riveted him where he stood. She spoke again. She might have been speaking Etruscan, for all the words made sense to Harry. Her mouth held the same contradictions: it was lovely, its grim line warned of horror, it hungered, it would never eat again.

Sound washed over him again: a delivery wagon, a yowling cat, a young housemaid chasing after it down the street. He heard his stammering voice. "Where—where did you come from?"

She gestured. Out of a tree, out of the sky, her hand said. She was very poorly dressed, he realized: her thin, tight jacket torn at both elbows, the hem of her skirt awash with dried mud, her shoes worn down and beginning to split. She spoke again, very slowly, as if to a young child, or a man whose wits had badly strayed.

"I wondered if you had some work for me, sir. If maybe you could use me for your paintings. Anything will do. Any amount of time—"

One of his hands closed convulsively above her elbow; his other hand pulled the gate open.

"Oh, yes," he said unsteadily. "Oh, yes. Miss. Whoever you—"

"Jo, sir."

"Jo. Come in." He swept her down the walk, threw the door wide, and shouted, "Mrs. Grommet! Mrs. Grommet! We need you!"

"You have lice," Mrs. Grommet said.

Jo, hearing her within a cascade of lukewarm water, thought her voice sounded simply matter-of-fact. The kitchen maid stopped pouring water, began to pass a hard, lumpy bar of soap over Jo's wet hair. It took time to work up a lather.

"I'm not surprised," Jo murmured. She knelt in her tattered chemise beside a huge tub, allowing Mrs. Grommet the sight of her cracked, filthy feet. She could only hope that whatever vision had possessed Mr. Waterman to let her in the house would not be washed down the drain. But, she told herself coldly, if that happens then I will be no worse than I was before, and at least I will be clean.

"Go on, girl," the housekeeper said. "Give it a good scrub. Pretend you're doing the front steps."

"There's such a lot of it," the maid ventured. Jo closed her eyes, felt the blunt, vigorous fingers work away at her until she imagined herself underwater, floating in some river god's grip, being flailed back and forth like water weed.

"Rinse now," Mrs. Grommet ordered, and the water flowed again, copious and mercilessly cold. "There," the housekeeper said at last with satisfaction. "That should do it."

Freed, Jo straightened. The maid tossed a towel over her head and began to pummel her again.

"Go and boil some water," Mrs. Grommet told her. She added to Jo when the girl had gone, "Sometimes they work and sometimes they don't, these new hot water pipes. He didn't recognize you, did he?"

Jo swallowed. Mrs. Grommet's eyes, green as unripe tomatoes, said very little beyond her words. She knows, Jo thought. She knows why I ran away. But what Mrs. Grommet felt about that, Jo could only guess. Anyone else in the housekeeper's position would have made her sentiments about this immoral, unwashed bit of dredge crossing her employer's threshold very plain, very soon.

"No," Jo said simply. "He doesn't. He saw my face and wants to paint it. That's all. I don't know if he'll feel the same when he sees it again. If not, I'll go."

Mrs. Grommet did not comment on that. "I'll see what I can find for you to wear while you wash."

"Mrs. Grommet—" Her voice faltered; the housekeeper, hand on the doorknob, waited expressionlessly. "I know my clothes are a disgrace, but they're all I've got, if I go. Please—"

"Don't worry, girl," Mrs. Grommet said briskly, "I won't turn you out naked into the street, whatever becomes of you."

An hour later, Jo sat at the kitchen fireplace, letting her hair dry while she ate some cold beef and bread. She was dressed in a dark, shapeless gown that had made its way, some time in the distant past, to Harry's costume closet. Made to fit tight at wrists and neck and beneath the bosom, it hung on Jo like a sack. The kitchen maid, chopping onions for a pie, could not stop staring at her. Jo, too weary to eat much, didn't wonder at her staring, until the cook, a great mound of a woman with cheeks the color of raw beef, who was rolling out pastry, made as though to swat the maid with a floury hand.

"Leave her be, then," she grunted.

"I'm sorry, miss," the girl murmured to Jo. "I can't help it. It's your hair."

Jo glanced sideways at it, as it fell around her face. It did look unfamiliar clean, but other than that it was just her hair.

"What's the matter with it? Have I got the mange, too?"

"No," the maid whispered, flicking her eyes to it again. "It's so beautiful, all long and gold and curly."

Jo blinked, at a loss. Her eyes rose helplessly, sought Mrs. Grommet's.

The housekeeper, sipping tea at the table and still inscrutable, gave a brief nod. "Oh, yes. He'll like that."

Jo, suddenly terrified, stood abruptly, her meal scattering out of her fingers into the fire. "I have to go, then," she heard herself babble. "I have to go. Where are my shoes? I had a couple of coppers in my shoes—"

Mrs. Grommet gazed at her wordlessly. Her eyes came alive suddenly, as she pushed herself to her feet. "There now, Jo," she said faintly, rounding the table to Jo's side. "Mr. Waterman's not like that. You know that. There's no need to run away from him again." She put her hand on Jo's arm and pointed to a grubby little pile near the hearth. "There's your shoes and clothes. The coins are in there, just as I found them. If you need them, you'll have them."

"Why," Jo asked her wildly, "are you treating me this way?"

"What way?" Mrs. Grommet asked, astonished.

It took Jo a moment to remember the word. "Kind." Spoken, it seemed to surprise them both. "Why are you being kind to me? You know—you—"

Mrs. Grommet's eyes went distant again. But she kept her hand on Jo's arm, patted it a little. "Stay a bit," she said finally, eluding the question. "Mr. Waterman will think we drove you away if you leave now. He'll only go looking for you."

"But I don't understand—"

"Well, you might ask him what he has in mind. You might stay long enough to listen to him. Whatever it is, I'm sure it's nothing more than a painting."

Jo, still trembling, sat down at the hearth again. She heard whispering; after a moment, the little maid brought her a cup of tea. She sipped it wordlessly, the kitchen silent behind her but for the thump of the rolling pin. When she knew she could stand again, she knew it was time. She rose, set the cup on the table. Mrs. Grommet looked at her.

"I'll take you up," she said briefly. Jo nodded gratefully, too lightheaded to speak.

She passed familiar hallways, paintings, patterns of wallpaper, carpets that seemed more real in memory. It was, she thought dazedly, like being in two places at once; she was uncertain, from one step to the next, if she were moving backward or forward in time. They went up the second flight of steeper stairs into the top of the house. There, as Mrs. Grommet opened the door, Jo saw another memory that was real: the long rows of windows overlooking the street, the park across from them, and on the other side of the house, the river. She could see the tree under which she had wakened in the other world at dawn. She smelled oils and pungent turpentine, saw the untidy shelves of books and sketches, the oddments everywhere—peacock feathers, beads, baskets, seashells, tapestries, rich shawls of taffeta, goblets, moth-eaten furs.

She saw Harry. He stood across the room, watching her silently as she entered. She had never seen anyone look at her like that before, as though she were something not quite human, a piece of dream, maybe, that he had to step into to see her properly.

He said absently, "Thank you, Mrs. Grommet."

"Yes, sir." She lingered. "Will you need—"

"Nothing. Thank you."

She closed the door behind her. Harry crossed the room, came close to Jo. Still in his dream, she saw, he reached out, touched her hair with one finger. She felt herself stiffen. He drew back hastily. She saw his eyes again, anxious now, tentative, fascinated. Like some mooncalf boy in love for the first time, she realized, and not even sure with what.

"Will you let me paint you?" he asked huskily.

"Of course," she answered, so amazed she forgot her terrors.

"I see you—I see you as a very ancient power, a goddess, almost, who is herself mortal, but who can kill with a look. To see her is to die. But not to see her is to live without living. I see you, in all her terrible, devastating beauty, as Medusa."

"Yes, Mr. Waterman," she said, completely mystified, and thought with wonder: he doesn't recognize me at all.

Much later that day, almost into the next, Harry sat on the floor beside the open cupboard door, babbling to the Gorgon.

"The lines of her face are stunning. They transfixed me the moment I saw them. They seem shaped—sculpted—by primal forces, like stone, yet very much alive. They are beauty, they are death, they are youth, they are ancient beyond belief. And her eyes. Medusa's eyes. They gaze at you from another world, the Underworld perhaps; they are portals to that grim world. Of the palest gray, nearly colorless, like the mist between life and death—" He heard a vague noise from within the cupboard, almost as if the Gorgon had sneezed. "I beg your pardon. Did you speak?"

"No," she said faintly.

"And her hair. I've never seen anything like it. White gold, rippling down from her face to her knees. Again that suggestion of youth and antiquity, knowledge gained too early from unearthly places—"

"Harry."

"Her mouth—there again—"

"Harry."

"Yes, what is it?"

"I think you should let me see her."

"Her mouth is like—"

"I promise, by Perseus's shield that bore my reflection and killed me, that I won't speak a word in her presence."

"Again, it contradicts itself—it should be mobile, plump, alluring, the delicate pink of freshwater pearls—"

"You can put me in a dark corner where she won't notice me."

"But it has long forgotten how to smile; its line is inflexible and determined—"

"Harry. It's me you're painting. I haven't seen myself in thousands of years. Have a heart. Let me see what humans think of me these days. I'm not used to being associated with beauty."

Harry was silent. He thought he perceived the faintest undertone in the Gorgon's plea, as though she were laughing at him. But her words argued otherwise. And it did seem an appropriate request. She had, after all, inspired him; how could he deny her his vision of herself?

"You'll forget," he said guardedly, "and say something impulsive and frighten her away."

"I won't. I have sworn."

"I'll think about—"

"Harry. Stop thinking about it. Just do it. Or I'll yell my head off here in the cupboard like one of Bluebeard's wives."

Harry blinked. "You could have done that—"

"Today, while she was here. Yes. But I didn't, did I? I am capable of controlling myself. I won't say a word in her presence, no matter how—"

"How?"

"No matter what."

"Do I amuse you?" Harry demanded indignantly.

"No, no," the Gorgon said soothingly. "No. I'm just incredibly old, Harry, and my sense of humor is warped. I'm very ignorant of the modern world, and it would do me good to see even a tiny corner of it."

Harry sighed, mollified. "All right. Tomorrow morning, before she comes."

"Thank you, Harry."

He got up early to hang the Gorgon above some high bookshelves, among other old sketches and watercolors scattered along the wall. The contradictions in the face startled him anew: the frightened eyes, the pale, anxious brows, the lush, voluptuous, wine-red mouth. His eyes lingered on that mouth as he descended the ladder. He would make a trip to the country soon, he decided. She was down there with Alex nearly every weekend. The mouth seemed to crook in a faint smile; his foot froze on the bottom rung.

"No," he said sharply. "You must be absolutely still."

The mouth composed itself. The eyes gazed unseeingly across the room. He had placed the painting where most often his model would have her back to it. She would only glimpse it as she faced the door to leave. And few people looked that high without reason, Harry had learned to his chagrin when his work had been hung near the ceiling in exhibits. She would never notice the peculiar face with its mismatched features unless she looked for it.

He spent a few days sketching Jo, learning every nuance of her face, experimenting with various positions, draperies. He decided, in the end, simply to paint her face at the instant she saw herself reflected in the young hero's shield. The Medusa turning her baleful gaze upon herself and realizing in that instant that she had slain herself. The shield would frame her within the canvas. The pale, rippling beauty of the model's hair would transform itself easily into gorgeous, dangerous snakes. Jo's stark-white skin, drained of life-force it seemed, hollowed and shadowed with weariness and strain, hinted of the Medusa's otherworldly origins. He positioned black silk in graceful folds about her neck to emphasize the shadows. That would be her only costume. That and the snakes in her hair, which might suggest, in their golden brilliance, the final light of the sun upon her dying and deadly face.

So lost he was in the excitement of inspiration that he scarcely remembered to speak to his model. She came in the mornings, murmured, "Good morning, Mr. Waterman," and sat in her chair beside his easel. He arranged the silk about her throat, giving her a greeting or a pleasantry. Then she became so still she hardly seemed to breathe. He worked, utterly absorbed, until the light began to fade. Then, her pallor deep by then, her humanity began to intrude upon him. She is tired, he would realize. She must be hungry. I am.

He would put his palette down and open the door. "Mrs. Grommet," he would call down the stairs. Then he would study the day's work until the housekeeper hove into view, bearing a tea tray and Jo's wages for the day. Jo would follow her down. Mrs. Grommet would feed her in the kitchen, for Harry was reluctant to glimpse, at this sensitive stage, his Medusa with her cheeks full of mutton.

The Gorgon above their heads watched all this silently, refraining from comment.

She hardly saw Jo, Harry knew, except when she rose to leave. Then the wan, beautiful face would be visible to the painting above her head. Jo never looked that high; she seemed oddly incurious about the studio. Other models had prowled around peering at his canvases, opening books, trying on bits of finery, fingering this and that. But Jo just came and left, as though, Harry thought, she truly vanished into another world and was not much interested in his.

The Gorgon finally asked one evening, after Jo had followed Mrs. Grommet downstairs, "Where does she go?"

"What?" Harry asked through a bite of sandwich.

"Your model. Where does she sleep at night?"

"How should I know?" He was sitting in a soft stuffed chair, weary from standing all day, and devouring sandwiches and cakes, he suspected, like a well-brought-up vulture. He could see the Gorgon's face from that position if he wanted. Her voice startled him; she hadn't said much for days.

"Aren't you pleased with me, Harry?"

"For being so quiet? Oh, yes, I'm very grateful." He swallowed another mouthful of hot, sweet tea, and looked up at her. "What do you think of her?"

"Oh, a great deal," the painting answered vaguely, and gave a sudden, crude snort of a laugh. "She's far too beautiful for the likes of me, of course. But I see your point in her."

"Do you?"

"Beauty that can kill. But Harry, she's bone-thin and she's not much use to you dead. She might sleep in an alley for all you know. Anything could happen to her, and you'd never know what."

Harry was silent, blinking. He took another scalding sip. "I hadn't thought of that."

"Well, think of it. What would you do if tomorrow she didn't appear?"

The thought brought him out of his chair to pace a little, suddenly edgy. "Surely I pay her enough for decent lodgings. Don't I?"

"How much is enough?"

"I don't—"

"And suppose she has others dependent on her? Who need every coin she brings to them?"

"Well, maybe—" He paused, still tramping across the room; then he dropped into his chair again. "I'll ask Mrs. Grommet."

"You could ask your model."

Harry rolled his head to gaze up at the painting. "How?" he pleaded. "She is my Medusa. She exists only in this little world, only to be painted. I dare not make her real. She might lose all her power, become just another woman in my eyes."

The Medusa snorted again, this time without amusement. "She'd still be there for you to paint her. Your brush knows how to lie. If she vanishes into the streets out there, where will you go to look for her? You might at least ask her that."

Harry tried, at least three times, the next morning, before he got a question out. His model, whose name he kept forgetting, sat silently gazing as he had requested, at the back of his easel. What she saw, he could not begin to guess. Her wide, eerily pale eyes seemed to glimpse enormities in his peaceful studio. Until now, he had absently confused her expression with the Gorgon seeing herself for the first time and the last. Now he wondered, despite his better judgment, what those eyes had truly seen to make them so stricken.

He cleared his throat yet again. Her eyelids trembled, startled, at the sound of his voice. "Tell me, er—Jo?"

"Yes, sir?"

"Do you have a decent place to stay at night? I mean, I do pay you enough for that, don't I?"

She kept her face very still, answered simply, "Yes, Mr. Waterman. I go to a lodging house on Carvery Street."

"Alone?"

Her eyes flicked up, widening; he caught the full force of the Gorgon's stare. "Sir?"

"I mean—I only meant—do you have other people to care for? Others dependent on you?"

"Oh." The fierce gaze lowered once again to the middle distance. "No, sir. They're dead."

"Oh," he said inanely. He painted in silence a while, aware, though he told himself he imagined it, of eyes boring into his head from above the bookshelves. He glanced up finally, was appalled to see the full red lips moving wildly in a grotesque parody of speech.

He cleared his throat again hastily. "Do you get enough to eat? I mean, you're very thin."

"I'm eating better now," she answered.

The question sent a faint, unwelcome patina of color into her white face that at first alarmed him. Then he thought, Why not? Medusa, seeing her own beauty for the first time, may well flush with pleasure and astonishment before she turns herself into stone.

"Do you know," he asked aimlessly, trying to make conversation, "the story of Medusa?"

"Something of it," she said hesitantly. "Some sort of monster who turned people into stone?"

"Yes."

"Ugly, wasn't she?"

"Hideous," he answered, "by all accounts."

He heard her take a breath or two then, as if to speak. Then she grew still again, so still that he wondered if he had somehow turned her into stone.

He let his model rest a day or two later and spent a tranquil afternoon in the country, watching others work. Arthur Millidge was there, putting a honeysuckle background to what would be his *Nymph Dying for Love of a Shepherd.* He kept knocking his easel over swatting at bees. John Grainger was there as well, to Harry's surprise, back on his windy knoll painting the distant village. McAlister had finished his wife's windblown sleeve; now he was engrossed in her bare feet and ankles, around which green silk swirled and eddied. Harry, after his first glimpse of those long marble toes and exquisite anklebones, took the first chair he found and tried not to think about them.

Arthur Millidge's wife, Holly, handed him a cup of tea and sat down beside him. She was a pretty, good-natured, giddy-headed thing, who could pull out an arrow and hit an astute social bull's-eye just when she seemed at her most frivolous. She was watching her suffering husband with a great deal of amusement.

"Oh, poor Arthur," she cried, when he batted at a wasp with his brush and actually hit it; it stuck, struggling, to the yellow-daubed bristles. "At least it's the right color."

Her husband smiled at her wanly.

"I thought," Harry said blankly, "that Grainger and Nan would still be at the south coast."

"Oh, no," Holly answered briskly. "They only spent a few days there."

"But they are—they did get married?"

"So it seems. She's wearing a ring."

"Is she here?"

"No, poor thing, the traveling exhausted her in her condition, so she let John come alone."

Harry's eyes crept back to Aurora. Her condition, as well, he remembered; he could not, for a prolonged moment, stop studying her. The flowing, voluminous silk hid everything. Her face seemed a trifle plumper, but then he had been gazing at his emaciated model for days, he reminded himself. Aurora's face seemed exquisitely serene, he realized, ivory, full and tranquil, like a midsummer moon.

"The condition suits Aurora," Holly said, reading Harry's thoughts in her uncanny way. "I think poor Nan will have a great deal of difficulty with it. She's frail anyway and suffers from imagination."

Harry pulled his eyes away from McAlister's wife, dipped his hand into a bowl full of cherries. "Which of us doesn't?" he asked lightly.

"I'm sure I don't." Holly laughed and helped herself to a cherry or two from Harry's hand. "I heard you're painting something mysterious, Harry. Tommy Buck said that he and some friends came to visit you, and you refused to let them into your studio."

"They frightened my model," Harry said, remembering the shouts, Mrs. Grommet's flurried protest, the stampede up the stairs. "I thought she might faint, she was trembling so badly."

Holly maneuvered a cherry pit daintily from lips to palm and tipped it into the grass. "But who is she? Someone we know?"

"No. I found her in the street."

"How exciting! And what are you making of her?"

"Oh, I'm experimenting with this and that," he answered airily. "Nothing much, yet."

"She must be very pretty."

"In a wild kind of way. She's very shy. Not used to company."

"Everyone," Holly sighed, "is full of secrets. Alex won't tell what he's working on, either. You should bring her here, Harry."

"I should?"

"It might calm her, knowing others like her who model. Besides, if you decide you can't make anything of her, someone else might, and then she wouldn't have to go back into the streets."

"True," he said absently, flinging a cherry pit at a bee buzzing in the honeysuckle. "Oh, sorry, Arthur. I was aiming for the bee."

"Don't try to be helpful, Waterman."

"I won't, then."

"Will you bring her, Harry?"

"I might," he answered vaguely and changed the subject. "What do you think McAlister is making out of his wife?"

"Oh, who knows?" Holly said, waving midges away from her face. "Blind Justice? Aphrodite? Maybe even he doesn't know. The point is to keep her here, don't you think?"

"Here?" Harry repeated, mystified. Holly turned her head, regarded him blithely a moment, chin on her fist. Abruptly she laughed and got to her feet.

"Oh, Harry. You are so unbearably sweet. Arthur, come into the shade with us and have something to drink before you melt in all that light. I'm trying to worm secrets out of Harry."

"Harry has secrets?" John Grainger's deep, vigorous voice intoned incredulously behind them. *"Mirabile dictu!"* He dropped into a chair, dipped into the cherries with cerulean blue fingertips, and demanded of the hapless Harry, "Tell all."

Jo sat in Harry's kitchen, eating her supper after he had returned from the country and began to paint her again. At his request, she had given Mrs. Grommet explicit instructions about where to find her if Harry needed her. Mrs. Grommet dutifully wrote the address down. Then, to Jo's surprise, she poured herself a cup of tea and pulled out a chair at the end of the table near Jo, where she sat close to the fire.

Mrs. Grommet said, "I know Mrs. Atkins, the woman who owns the lodging house on Carvery Street. She's a good, honest woman. Or at least she was when we worked together, in a great house over on Bellingham Road."

Jo's eyes slid uncertainly to her face. She managed an answer, after a moment. "She seems kind."

"She married unexpectedly. Lucky for her, her husband had saved a little money. And had a very loving heart. Married they were for thirty years before he died, and never a word passed his lips that their child wasn't his."

Jo coughed on a bit of pickled beet. The kitchen maid was on the far side of the kitchen, banging pots noisily in weltering dishwater. The cook was in the pantry counting spoons, which was her way of saying resting her feet and having a nip. Mrs. Grommet's green eyes opened meaningfully upon Jo, then lowered again. She sipped tea, half-turned at a splash from the sink.

"Go easy, girl! You're washing pots, not the flagstones."

Jo put two and two together, cleared her throat. Still, words came out with difficulty. "That's why—" She drew a breath, met the housekeeper's eyes. "That's why you're kind to me."

"Things happen," Mrs. Grommet said, the corners of her mouth puckering a moment. "They're not always our fault."

"No." She lifted her cup. It trembled badly; she put it down again quickly before she spilled. She folded her hands tightly, said to them, "It takes a special heart to see it that way, though."

Mrs. Grommet patted her hands. "I saw how you were with Mr. Waterman the first time you came here. So quiet and nicely behaved. Some of his models—well, the less said. Not that he was that way, at least not under his own roof. But I hear the young men talking about the girls they paint, about which would only pose and go, and which might stay around after for their bit of fun." She became aware of the maid handling the pots as gently as possible, and raised her voice again. "Finish up there, Lizzie, then go and see if Cook needs help in the pantry."

"Yes, Mrs. Grommet."

Jo said very softly, "You were friends, then, you and Mrs. Atkins, when you worked on Bellingham Road."

"Mary. Mary Plum she was, then. We started there very young, you see, and during the same summer. We were there together for five years. What happened to her seemed so unfair to me. It was one of the young friends of the family—"

"Yes," Jo whispered.

"Nothing to him, of course. He told her he loved her and would care for her. He couldn't even remember her name or her face, next time he came. He looked straight at her, she said, when she was serving dinner, and didn't even see her. She was at the point then when she had to leave. She had no choice. But then Martin—Mr. Atkins—found her weeping under the privet hedge when he went to trim it. He was a gardener there, then, and very well thought of. He'd saved all his money for years for an investment, he said. He asked Mary to be his investment." She paused, watching Jo's struggling face. "I've never seen you smile before."

"I've nearly forgotten how. Did he really put it like that?"

"She was a pretty thing," Mrs. Grommet said reminiscently. "He said he'd had his eye on her, but never thought he'd have a chance. Well, chance came, wearing an unexpected face, and he was brave enough to take it. She had a daughter who looked just like her. After some years, he'd worked so hard that—" She stopped abruptly. "Oh, dear."

The tears came out of nowhere Jo could name, hot, fierce, and seemingly unstoppable. She put her hands over her mouth, turned her back quickly to face the fire again. She heard Mrs. Grommet say something sharply to Lizzie; all sounds faded in the kitchen. Jo felt a tea towel pushed into her hand.

She buried her face in it, seeing, feeling, smelling all at once, as though memory, locked so carefully away, had crashed and blundered out of its door. His warm, slight weight in her arms, the smell of milk in his hair, his wide, round eyes catching at hers.

"Poor Alf," she whispered into the towel. "Oh, poor Alf. Poor little poppet. Oh, Mrs. Grommet, I did love him despite everything—"

"Now, then."

"He was just too frail to go on."

"There now." Mrs. Grommet patted her shoulder.

"I'm sorry."

"It's all right; Lizzie's gone. You have a good cry."

"I haven't—I forgot to cry, when—when—" Her voice wailed away from her, incoherent. She shook hair over her face and eyes like a shroud, trying to hide in it while tears came noisily, messily, barely restrained under the wad of tea towel. "Poor mite, he was all my heart. I think we must have gotten buried together, and I have been just a ghost ever since. No wonder Mr. Waterman sees me as that stone-eyed monster—"

"What?"

She drew a raw, ragged breath that was half sob. "Some—Medusa—who turns people into stone with her eyes. That's what he sees when he looks at me." Then she felt an odd bubble in her chest; loosed, it sounded strangely like a laugh. "I'd terrify anyone with these eyes now—"

"Let me see," Mrs. Grommet said faintly. Jo lifted her face from the towel, pulled wet strands of hair from her cheeks. Her throat ached again at the housekeeper's expression. But it was not grief so much as relief that she could still cry, she could still laugh. Which she found herself doing again amid her tears, in a damp, inelegant snort. "Look what I've done to you. You're stunned. . . ."

"You do look a bit fiery around the eyes," Mrs. Grommet admitted. "But no wonder Mr. Waterman doesn't remember you, with all that happened to you since."

"I was a maid when he began his first painting. Now, I'm Medusa." She sat again, drew a shuddering breath as she mopped her eyes.

"Maybe. But you look all the younger now for those tears." She refilled their cups. "Not that you're much more than a girl. But you just seemed . . . like you'd seen a Medusa, yourself. And lived to tell about it."

Jo wrapped her fingers around the cup, managed to raise it without spilling. "Mrs. Grommet, you've been so good to me," she said huskily. "I don't know how to thank you."

"Well. You reminded me so of Mary, when you disappeared like that. I couldn't see that you could have found any way to help yourself, except maybe into the river. Mr. Waterman looked for you when you left. He fretted about you. And not only for his painting. He wanted to help."

"I know." She got a sip past the sudden burn in her throat. "I was too frightened to think then. And now, I don't care if he never recognizes that terrified waif. I don't want him feeling sorry for me. I'm glad he doesn't know me."

"I did," Mrs. Grommet said, "the moment I saw you. I don't see how he can't. Being a painter as he is. Faces are his business."

"He doesn't see me. He sees the woman he wants to see. And I hope—" She touched her swollen eyes lightly. "I hope she's still there, in spite of my tears."

"Now he's got you thinking that way," Mrs. Grommet said roundly. "As if you're not yourself."

"But I never am, when he paints me. I am always the woman he has in mind. I think that's why he doesn't like to talk to me. He only wants to know the woman in his head. The dream he has of me. If I told him too much about"—she swallowed, continued steadily—"about Alf, about the streets, the mill, about my mother's hands all cracked from taking in laundry, about the purple shawl, the dream would be gone. All he'd have left is me."

Harry was gazing at his Medusa, a ham sandwich forgotten in one hand. With the other hand he was pointing out to the Medusa overhead various examples of his brilliance or his clumsiness, which seemed, judging by the Gorgon's expression, to be running about neck and neck that day.

"Look there. Putting that fleck of pure white just so, I've captured perfectly the suggestion of ice in her gray eyes. Do you see it? Of course the delicate line of the inner eye is a bit blurry, there; I'll have to rework it." Raptly, he took a bite of sandwich. "And there . . . ," he said with his mouth full, overcome. "You see what I did?"

"Harry. You still don't know anything about this woman."

"I told her to give Mrs. Grommet her address. You made a good point about that. Now, her hair. I shall have to go to the zoological gardens, observe some snakes." He paused, chewing, added regretfully, "I should have brought a few back with me from the country. I didn't think of it. Perhaps because I don't see the point of them. They just begin and go on and keep going on the same way they began, and then they end without any reason whatsoever." He paused again.

"Don't say it," the Gorgon pleaded.

Harry glanced at her, took another bite. "All right, I won't. But it is a bit like life, isn't it?"

"Harry!"

He smiled. "I'd give a lot to see your snakes, though. What color were they?"

"Ugly."

"No color is ugly."

"Maybe," the Medusa sighed, "but you must remember that I was hideous. I never looked at myself, of course, and my snakes were usually twined around my head. But now and then a loop or a head would lose its direction and slide near my eyes. They were fairly drab: brown, black, gray, without any interesting patterns. Big, they were, though. Thick as your wrists."

"Really? What did they eat?"

"Air, I suppose. Thoughts. They were my hair, Harry; they weren't meant to exist like ordinary creatures. Your hair feeds on you."

"I'll make hers like treasure," Harry said, studying the magnificent, haunting eyes again, the dangerous, irresistible mouth. "Gold, white gold, silver, buttercup, lemon. A shining, glittering swarm of colors. Tomorrow morning, I'll go—"

"She's coming tomorrow."

"I'll paint her in the morning then and visit the snakes in the afternoon."

"You could," the Gorgon suggested, "take her with you. You might get a better perspective on the snakes as hair if you see them both together."

Harry grunted, struck. "Possibly . . ." Then he blinked. "No. What am I saying? I can't possibly watch this devastatingly powerful creature wandering around looking at snakes in the zoological garden. Something would happen."

"Like what?"

"She'd step in a puddle, get a paper stuck to her shoe, some such. She'd mispronounce the names of things, she'd want tea and a bun, or peanuts for the bears—"

"I can't see that frozen-eyed woman tossing peanuts to the bears. But what you're saying, Harry, is that she would be in danger of turning human."

"Exactly," Harry said adamantly. "I don't want her human, I want her Gorgon—"

"I bet she'd be a charming human."

Harry opened his mouth. As though one of the Medusa's snakes had streaked down quick as thought and bit him, he glimpsed the potential charms in those eyes, warming in a smile, that hair, piled carelessly on her head, tendrils about her face playing in a breeze. He clenched his fists, pushed them in front of his eyes. "No," he said fiercely. "No, no, and no. This is my masterwork, and nothing—" He lowered his hands as suddenly. "What on earth is that hubbub downstairs?"

There seemed to be a good deal of shouting and thumping coming up the stairwell. Mrs. Grommet's voice joined it and it resolved itself easily then, into any number of friends in every stage of revelry pushing their way upstairs to join Harry.

He threw open the door, heard their chanting as they ascended. "Where is she, Harry? We must see her. We want to see your painting, foul as it may be. We have come to kneel at the feet of your Muse, Harry!"

Harry had just enough time to remove the painting from the easel and slide it carefully into the cupboard. Where, he hoped fervently, it would not also acquire a voice. He opened his study door, stepped into the landing. Half a dozen friends, a couple of them painters, one planning a gallery, others budding poets or philosophers, or whatever was fashionable this week, reeled into one another at the sight of him. Then, they rushed the second flight of stairs. Harry glimpsed Mrs. Grommet below, flinging her hands in the air, turning hastily back to the kitchen.

"Don't you dare lock your door this time," the honey-haired, sloe-eyed Tommy Buck called. "We'll sit on your stairs and hold them hostage until you reveal her. We'll—"

"She's not here," Harry said, with great relief. "She left an hour ago."

"Then let's see your painting."

"No. It's too dreadful." He turned adroitly as they reached the landing, and locked the door behind him. "You'll laugh, and I'll be forced to become a bricklayer."

"She's in there." Tommy Buck paused to hiccup loudly, then banged upon the door. "You've hidden her."

"I have not. She's a shy, sensitive woman and you lot would cause her to turn into a deer and flee."

"Prove it."

"Prove what?"

"Prove she's not there."

"All right, I will. But I don't want you all rummaging about my studio and tossing my bad paintings out the window. You can look in and see, Tommy. The rest of you go downstairs and wait."

"No," said one of the poets, a burly young man who looked like he might have flung bricks around in an earlier life. "Open up, Harry boy. Show us all."

"No. I shall defend all with my life."

"What's that in your hand?" Tommy asked, swaying as he squinted at it. Harry looked. "My ham sandwich."

"Ham. He has ham in there," someone said wistfully. "I'm hungry."

"Here," Harry said, tossing him the remains.

"I saw it first," Tommy said indignantly. "I'm hungrier." He paused, still swaying lithely, like a reed in a breeze. "I've got an idea."

"He has an idea."

"I'd rather have a sandwich."

"Silence! I will speak! My idea is this. We all leave—" He waved his arms, fending off protests. "Listen. If we all go out to dinner, and Harry goes out to dinner with us, and then goes wherever we happen to go after that, it will prove that he hasn't got a model locked up in his studio. Won't it?"

"He could get the Grommet to unlock her," someone muttered.

"I won't speak to her," Harry promised. "And—" he dangled it. "I have the only key."

Tommy made a snatch at it. Harry tucked it out of reach. "She really has gone home," he told them. "And I think Tommy has an excellent idea. Maybe, if we hurry out, we'll catch a glimpse of her on the street."

They were quiet, staring at him, faces motionless in the stair lights.

Then, as one, they turned, clattered furiously back down the stairs. Harry followed more slowly, brushing crumbs off his shirt and rolling down his sleeves. He heard the street door fly open, voices flow down the hall and out. Someone called his name, then the sounds faded. He didn't hear the door close. He wondered if Mrs. Grommet had taken refuge in a closet until the barbarian horde had gone.

He reached the hall and nearly bumped into his Medusa, coming quickly out of the kitchen with Mrs. Grommet at her heels.

"Jo—" he exclaimed, startled.

She pulled up sharply, staring at him, just as surprised.

"Mr. Waterman," she breathed. "I thought you had left with them."

He was silent, studying her. Something was awry with her face. It seemed streaked, flushed in odd places; her cold, magnificent eyes looked puffy and reddened, oddly vulnerable. He caught his breath, appalled.

"What have you done?"

"Sorry, Mr. Waterman," she said tremulously, brushing at her eyes. "It'll be gone by morning."

"But—" Something else was happening to her face as he stared. Lines shifted. Memory imposed itself, rearranging a curve here, a hollow there. He swallowed, feeling as though the world he knew had vanished for an eye blink, and then returned, subtly, irrevocably altered.

"Jo," he said, feeling his heart beat. "Jo Byrd."

She said simply, "Yes."

She returned the next morning as she promised, though not without misgivings. She looked for the same apprehension in the artist's eyes, searching for his Medusa in her face while he arranged the black silk around her neck, to draw out her pallor as he said. She wasn't certain about the pallor. The face in the tiny mirror above her washstand had been more colorful than usual. Nor was she at all certain what Mr. Waterman was thinking. He was very quiet, murmuring instructions now and then. She would have described his expression as peculiar, if he had asked. He looked like someone who had swallowed a butterfly, she thought: a mixed blessing, no matter how you turned it.

She said finally, hesitantly, "Mr. Waterman. If you can't see your Medusa now for seeing me, I'll understand."

He gave his head a quick little shake, met her eyes. "As the Gor—as someone pointed out, I tell lies with my brush. Let's see how well I can do it."

"But—"

"We'll give it a try," he insisted calmly. "Shall we?"

"If you say so, sir." She subsided, prepared herself to sit as silently as usual. But, strangely, now he seemed in a mood to talk. "I am," he said, touching white into the black around the Medusa's throat, "incredibly embarrassed that I didn't recognize you."

"I've gotten older."

"By how much? A year? I'm a painter! I've been staring at you daily. Not to mention—" His lips tightened; whatever it was, he didn't mention it.

"Yes, sir."

He looked at her again, instead of the silk. "I can't imagine what you've gone through. Or, rather, I can only try to imagine it. The child . . . it must have died?"

Her voice caught, but she had no tears left for that, it seemed. "Yes. He was never strong."

"Where did you go, when you vanished in the middle of my painting?"

"I went home to my mother's, in the country."

"I looked for you."

"I know. Mrs. Grommet told me."

His mouth crooked ruefully. "So she recognized you."

"The way I see it," Jo explained, "Mrs. Grommet was protecting your household. She has to know what she opens your door to. You remember what I looked like, then."

"Yes."

"She had to make decisions in her own mind about me. You were only seeing your painting. She was seeing a hungry, filthy wreck of a girl and trying to judge all in a moment whether I would steal the silver, eat with a fork or my fingers, go mad and break all the crockery. She was looking for reasons not to be afraid to let me through the door. You just saw your dream and let me walk right in."

He ran his hand through his hair, nearly tangling the brush in it. "Makes me sound like a fool."

She thought about that, shrugged. "I don't know. How do you like your painting?"

He looked at it, his eyes going depthless, still, like water reflecting an empty sky. They were, she realized suddenly, the exact blue of the dragonflies in the stream behind her parents' cottage. She'd lie and watch them dart and light, little dancing arrows as blue as larkspur.

Mr. Waterman blinked; so did she. They both drew back a little from what they'd been examining. She recognized that expression on his face; it was how he had been looking at her until now.

"I think—" he said, still gazing at his painting, and stammering a little, "I think—I wasn't a fool, after all. I think it's at least better than anything I've done so far. Jo. . . ." He turned to her abruptly. "I have such amazing visions of your hair. Are you afraid of snakes?"

"No more or less than anything else that might bite me. But, sir," she amended warily, "surely you're not going to put them in my hair? I don't think I want to wear them."

"No, no." His thoughts veered abruptly. "I have to fix that eye before I go on. Look at me. Don't blink." He added, after a moment or two, "You can talk."

"About what?"

"Anything that won't make you cry." She felt her eyes flush at the thought; he looked stricken. "I'm sorry, Jo."

"It's just—somehow I never got around to crying before."

"Tell me something, anything you remember, that once made you happy. If there was anything," he added carefully.

"Well." The tide retreated; she gazed, dry-eyed, at her past. "When my father was alive, he kept a small flock of sheep for wool. I liked to look at them, all plump and white in their green field, watch the lambs leap for no reason except that they were alive. He'd shear them and we'd spin the wool into yarn to sell. Sometimes we'd look for madder root to dye it purple."

"We?" he asked, busy at the corner of her eye, from what she could see. "Sister?"

"My mother. I didn't have sisters. I had a little brother for a couple of years once, but he died."

"Oh. But you chose not to stay with your mother? To come back here instead?"

"She died, too."

"Oh. I'm sorry."

"Yes," she said softly, but without tears. "So was I. So I came back here. And you rescued me."

He looked at her, oddly surprised. "I did?"

"You did," she said huskily. "I couldn't find work, I was exhausted, I had two coppers to my name. I found my way to your street just muddling around in the dark, and then I remembered you. I slept under a tree, that night before I came to your door. I didn't have any hope, but I didn't have anything left to do. I even—I even tried to get myself arrested for breaking a streetlamp, to have a place to sleep."

He was watching her, brush suspended. "When you do that—"

"What, sir?"

"Even when you only think about smiling, you change the shape of your eye. Medusa does not smile." He stopped abruptly, cast an odd glance above her head, and amended, "At least we have no recorded evidence that she smiled."

"You asked me to think about something happy."

"You didn't smile, then. It was irony, not happiness, that made you smile."

She mulled that over. "You mean trying to get into jail for a bed?"

"Yes. What happened? Did you miss the streetlamp?"

"No. I hit it dead on. But a dozen others stepped up on the spot and swore it was them that threw the stone. Someone else got my bed. So I wandered on—"

"And," he said softly, his brush moving again, "you found me."

"You found me," she whispered.

"No tears. Medusa does not cry."

She composed her face again, summoned the icy, gorgeous monster to look out of her eyes. "She does not cry."

"But," he said after a while, "she might perhaps like to come with me this afternoon to look at snakes. No blinking."

"No blinking."

"But snakes?"

"Looking at snakes," she said, suddenly aware of his own fair, tidy hair, on a nicely rounded head, his young face with its sweet, determined expression, "would make Medusa happy."

Harry stood on the ladder in his studio, detaching the Gorgon from her nail. He had gotten in late. After spending a few hours among the reptiles and other assorted creatures, he had walked Jo to her lodging house on Carvery Street. Then he had wandered aimlessly, oddly light-headed, dropping in at studios here and there to let his friends tease him about his imaginary model, his hopeless daub of a painting so dreadful he was forced to keep it hidden behind locked doors. He laughed with them; his thoughts kept straying back to his studio, sometimes to the reptiles, none of which had done justice to his Medusa's hair.

But my brush can lie, he told himself. He had insisted on buying Jo peanuts in the zoological garden. But instead of throwing them to the animals, she had simply given them to a wiry, dirty-faced boy who had somehow wriggled his way in and was begging near the lions' den.

His elbow hit a book on top of the shelves as he maneuvered the painting down and under his arm. The book dropped with a thud that probably woke the house. He breathed a curse, trying to be as quiet as possible. The ladder rungs creaked ominously.

The Gorgon, who had been blessedly silent until then, said sharply, her mouth somewhere under his armpit, "Harry, you're not putting me back into the cupboard."

"Shh—"

"Don't shush me. Just because you don't need me anymore."

"What do you mean I don't need you?"

"I saw the way you looked at her."

"I was not aware that I looked at her in any particular way."

"Ha!"

"Shhh," Harry pleaded. "Mrs. Grommet will think I'm up here entertaining lewd company."

"Thank you," the Gorgon said frostily. But once started, she could never be silent for long, Harry knew. He felt the floor beneath his foot at last, and her curiosity got the better. "Then what are you going to do with me?"

"I just want to look at you."

He positioned a wooden chair beside the easel, propped the painting on it. Then he drew the black silk off the new Medusa. Side by side, Jo past and Jo present, he studied them: the young, terrified girl; the haunted, desperate woman. A year in the life. . . . "What a life," he breathed, moved at the thought of it.

The Gorgon spoke, startling him again. "What are you looking for?"

"I wanted to see why it was I didn't recognize her. I understand a little better now. That hair—I should have known it anywhere. But the expressions are completely different. And the skin tone. . . . She was at least being fed when she came to me the first time." His voice trailed away as he studied them: Persephone who had innocently eaten a few seeds and transformed herself into the doomed Medusa. He asked, suddenly curious himself, "Where do you live? I mean, where were you before you took up residence in my painting?"

"Oh, here and there," she answered vaguely.

"No, really."

"Why? Are you thinking of ways to get rid of your noisy, uncouth Gorgon?"

He thought about that, touched the Medusa on the easel. "Who inspired this out of me? No. Stay as long as you like. Stay forever. I'll introduce you to my friends. None of them have paintings that speak. They'll all be jealous of me."

"You invited me," she reminded him.

"I did."

"I go where I'm invited. Where I am invoked. When I hear my name in someone's heart, or in a painting or a poem, I exist there. The young thug Perseus cut my head off. But he didn't rid the world of me. I've stayed alive these thousands of years because I haven't been forgotten. Every time my name is invoked and my power is remembered anew, then I live again, I am empowered."

"Yes," Harry said softly, watching those full, alluring lips move, take their varying shapes on canvas in ways that he could never seem to move them in life. "I understand."

"You understand what, Harry?" the Gorgon asked so gently that he knew, beneath her raucous ways, she understood a great deal more than he had realized.

"I understand that I must go to the country again soon."

"Good idea. Take Jo with you."

"Should I? Really? She might be uncomfortable. And Grainger will try to seduce her away from me. He tries to steal everyone's models."

"That will happen sooner or later in any case, unless you are planning to cast her back into the streets once you've finished with her."

"No. I don't want to do that. I hadn't really thought ahead. About sharing her. Or painting her as someone else. Until now she was just my inspiration." He paced a step or two, stopped again in front of the paintings. Jo then. Jo now. "She's changed again," he realized. "There's yet another face. I wonder if that one will inspire another painting."

"Something," the Medusa murmured.

"Something," Harry agreed absently. "But you're right. I certainly can't put her back on the streets just so that she stays my secret. If she can get other work, she should. If I decide I don't—"

"Harry," the Gorgon interrupted. "One thing at a time. Why don't you just ask her if she'd like to come to the country with you and be introduced to other painters? She'll either say yes or she'll say no. In either case, you can take it from there."

Harry smiled. "That seems too simple."

"And find her something nice to wear. She looks like a bedpost in that old dress. Went out of style forty years ago, at least. I may not have a clue about what to do with my hair, but I always did have an eye for fashion. Though of course, things were incredibly boring in my day, comparatively speaking. Especially the shoes! You wouldn't believe—"

"Good night," Harry said, yawning, and draped the black silk over her. "See you in the morning."

Jo sat in the McAlisters' garden, sipping tea. She felt very strange, as though she had wandered into a painting of a bright, sunny world strewn with windblown petals, where everyone laughed easily, plump children ran in and out of the ancient cottage, and a woman, still as a statue at the other side of the garden, was being painted into yet another painting. Some guests had gathered, Harry among them, to watch Alex McAlister work. Jo heard the harsh, eager voice of the painter, talking about mosaics in some foreign country, while he spun a dark, rippling thundercloud of his wife's hair with his brush. Aurora McAlister, a windblown Venus, it looked like, her head bowed slightly under long, heavy hair, seemed to be absorbed in her own thoughts; her husband and guests might have been speaking the language of another world.

Someone rustled into the wicker chair next to Jo. She looked up. People had wandered up to her and spoken and wandered off again all afternoon; she was struggling hopelessly with all the names.

"Holly," this one said helpfully, "Holly Millidge." She was a pretty, frothy young woman with very shrewd eyes. She waved a plate of little sandwiches under Jo's nose; Jo took one hesitantly. "They're all right. Just cucumber, nothing nasty." She set the plate back on the table. "So you're Harry's secret model. We've all been wondering."

"I didn't know I was a secret," Jo said, surprised.

"I can see why."

"Why what?"

"Why he tried to keep you secret. Tommy Buck said he'd been twice to Harry's studio trying to see you, and Harry locked the door on him."

Jo remembered the clamoring voices, the thunder up the stairs. "Why," she asked warily, "did he want to see me that badly?"

"To see if he should paint you, of course." Holly was silent a little, still smiling, studying Jo. "They're noisy, that lot. But they're good-hearted. You don't have to be afraid of them."

"I'm used to being afraid," Jo said helplessly. "I'm not used to this."

"It's not entirely what you think," Holly said obscurely, and laughed at herself. "What am I trying to say? You're not seeing what you think you see."

"Painters don't, do they?"

"Not always, no." She bit into a strawberry, watching the scene on the other side of the garden. "They'd see how pretty you are and how wonderful and mysterious the expression is in your eyes. But they wouldn't have any idea how that expression got there. Or the expression, for instance, in Aurora's eyes."

Jo looked at the still, dreaming face. "She's very beautiful."

"She is." Holly bit into another strawberry. "Her father worked in the stables at an inn on Crowdy Street. Aurora was cleaning rooms for the establishment when Alex met her. Barefoot, with her hair full of lice—"

A sudden bubble of laughter escaped Jo; she put her hands over her mouth. "Her, too?"

"And whatever her name was then, it was most certainly not Aurora. Most of us have a skewed past. As well as a skewed present." She gave a sigh, leaned back in her chair. "Except for me; I have no secrets. No interesting ones, at any rate. When they put me in their paintings, I'm the one carrying the heartless bride's train, or one of the shocked guests who finds the thwarted lover's body in the fishpond."

Jo, feeling less estranged from her surroundings, took another glance around the garden. Seen that way, if the goddess had been a chambermaid, then everyone might be anyone, and no telling what anybody knew or didn't know about life. Except for Harry, she thought. And then she glimpsed the expression on his face and had to amend even that notion.

Nothing, apparently, was plain as day, not even Harry. While the other guests were laughing and chatting, Alex's voice running cheerfully over them all, Harry was standing very quietly among them, his eyes on the tall, dark goddess. Jo drew a breath, feeling an odd little hollow where her certainty had been.

"Harry," she said, hardly realizing she'd spoken aloud.

Holly nodded. "Oh, yes, Harry. And John Grainger, and half the painters in the McAlister constellation, including one or two of the women. Dreamers, all of them, in love with what they think they see instead of what they see."

"John Grainger. The one with the wild hair and rumbly voice and the black, black eyes?"

"Yes, that's him."

"He talked to me earlier."

"Everyone talked to you earlier," Holly said lightly. "I was watching. They're making their plans for you, don't you fret."

"I didn't like him," Jo said. "He has a way of putting his hand on you as though it's supposed to mean something to you. It made me uncomfortable."

Holly laughed. "Then he'll have to watch his manners with you. He's a fine painter, though, and very generous; if you let him paint you, you'll be noticed. Others will find you, if you want." She lifted her bright face to greet a lovely, red-haired woman with somber green eyes. "Nan! Have you met Harry's painting yet? Jo Byrd. Nan Grainger."

"Jo Byrd. Why do I know that name?" Nan eased herself into a chair, gazing at Jo. "Harry must have talked about you. But that was some time ago. Oh!" She gave a little start, her pale skin flushing slightly. "I remember now."

"I ran away."

"Yes. In the middle of his Persephone. He was bereft."

"Yes, well," Jo said, her mouth quirked, for everyone seemed to know everything anyway. "So was I."

Nan was silent, gazing at her without smiling. What have I said? Jo wondered, and then saw what lay beneath Nan's hands clasped gently over her belly.

Holly interrupted Nan's silence adroitly, with some droll story about her husband. Jo sighed noiselessly, her eyes going back to the group around the goddess. John Grainger stood closest to Aurora, she saw. They did not look at one another. But now and then the trailing green silk around her bare feet, raised by a teasing wind, flowed toward him to touch his shoe. He would glance down at that flickering green touching him, and his laugh would ring across the garden.

Secrets, she thought. If you look at this one way, there's a group of cheerful people standing together on a sunny afternoon in a garden. That's one painting. If you look at them with a different eye, there's the story within the painting. . . . She looked at Harry again, wanting the uncomplicated friend she thought she knew, who got excited over the golden snakes in the reptile house, and who made her go shopping with Mrs. Grommet for a dress, he said, that didn't look as if his grandmother had slept in it.

Unexpectedly, as though he'd felt her thoughts flow in his direction, against the wind, he was looking back at her.

"What beautiful hair you have," Nan said, watching the white-gold ripple over Jo's shoulders. "I'd love to paint it." Her green eyes were gathering warmth, despite the silk fluttering over her husband's shoe, despite her fears and private sorrows; for a moment she was just a woman smiling in the light. "Jo, have you ever tried to draw? You might try it sometime. I forget myself when I do; it makes me very tranquil."

I might try it, Jo thought, after I lose this feeling that I've just fallen off the moon.

But she didn't say that, she said something else, and then there was another cup of tea in her hand, and a willowy young man with wayward locks the color of honeycomb kneeling in the grass at her feet, who introduced himself as Tommy Buck. . . .

Harry watched Tommy kneel beside Jo's chair. Their two faces seemed to reflect one another's wild beauty, and he thought dispassionately: I would like to paint them both together. Then, he felt a sharp flash of annoyance at Tommy, who could barely paint his feet, dreaming of capturing that barely human face of Jo's with his brush.

His attention drifted. He watched the green silk touch Grainger's shoe, withdraw, flutter toward him again. Seemingly oblivious,

Aurora watched the distant horizon; seemingly oblivious, her husband orated in his hoarse, exuberant crow's voice about the architectural history of the arch. Harry thought about Aurora's long, graceful hands, about her mouth. So silent, it looked now; he had gotten used to it speaking. He wondered if he could ever make this mouth speak.

And then she moved. The little group was breaking up around McAlister. "Too sober," he proclaimed them all. "Much too sober." Lightly he touched his wife, to draw her with him toward the cottage. As lightly, she slipped from his fingers, stayed behind to find her shoes under the rose vines. Grainger glanced at his wife across the garden, then at Aurora, then at his wife again. In that moment of his indecision, Aurora put her hand out to steady herself on Harry's arm as she put on her shoes.

"She's lovely, Harry," he heard her say through the blood drumming in his ears. "I like her. Where did you find her?"

"In the street," he stammered. "Both times. She—she has been through hard times."

"I know." She straightened, shod, but didn't drop her hand. Behind her, Grainger drifted away. Her voice, deep and slow and sweet, riveted Harry. "I know those times. I hear them in her speech, I see them in her eyes. I know those streets."

"Surely not—"

She smiled very faintly. "Harry, I grew up helping my father shovel out the stables until I was old enough to clean up after humans. Didn't you know that? I thought everybody did."

"But the way you speak," Harry said bewilderedly. "Your poise and manners—"

"A retired governess. Alex hired her to teach me. Beyond that I have my own good sense and some skills that Alex finds interesting. He likes my company."

"He adores you."

"He thinks he does. He adores the woman he paints. Not the Livvie that I am."

"Livvie?"

Her mouth crooked wryly; he saw her rare, brief smile. "Olive. That's my real name. Livvie, they called me until I was seventeen and Alex looked at me and saw painting after painting. . . . He said I was the dawn of his inspiration. So Olive became Aurora."

"Why," he asked her, his voice finally steady, "are you telling me this?"

"Because I've often thought I'd like to talk to you. That I might like having you as a friend, to tell things to. But for the longest time you could only see me the way Alex sees me. But then I saw how you looked at Jo today, knowing all you know about her. So I thought maybe, if I explained a thing or two to you, you might look at me as a friend."

She waited, the dark-eyed goddess who had pitched horseshit out of stables and whose name was Livvie. Mute with wonder, he could only stare at her. Then his face spoke, breaking into a rueful smile.

"I hope you can forgive my foolishness," he said softly. "It can't have been very helpful."

"I do get lonely," she confessed, "on my pedestal. Come, let's have some tea with Jo, and rescue her from Tommy Buck. He's not good enough for her."

"Will you come some day and see if I'm good enough to paint her? I would value your opinion very much."

"Yes, I will," she promised and tucked her long sylph's hand into the crook of his arm, making him reel dizzily for a step. He found his balance somewhere in Jo's eyes as she watched them come to her.

Much later, he reeled back into his studio, stupefied with impressions. Jo had promised, sometime before he left her at her door, to sit for the unfinished Persephone as well. So he would see her daily until—until he dreamed up something else. Or maybe, he thought, he would do what Odysseus's Penelope had done to get what she wanted: weave by day, unweave by night. He pulled the black silk off Persephone's head, saw the lovely, wine-red mouth and smiled, remembering the real one speaking, smiling its faint sphinx's smile, saying things he never dreamed would come out of it. But he no longer needed to dream, and he did not want Jo to see that mouth on her own face and wonder.

He was wiping it away carefully with cloth and turpentine when he remembered the Gorgon.

Horrified, he dropped the cloth. He had erased her entirely, without even thinking. What she must be trying to say, he could not imagine. And then he realized that the voluble Gorgon, who had talked her way out of his cupboard and into his life, had said not a word, nothing at all, to rescue herself.

Perhaps, he thought, she had nothing left to say. Perhaps she had already gone. . . .

He picked up the cloth, gazing at the clean, empty bit of canvas where Persephone's mouth would finally appear. He heard the Gorgon's voice in his head, having the last word as usual.

If you need me, Harry, you know how to find me.

He left them side by side, his unfinished faces, and went to bed, where he would have finished them, except that he could not keep Persephone from smiling in his dreams.

Which Witch

Liesl, that grinch, stole my G string. "Borrowed," she said. Ha! So I had to limp along on a Spinreel G so old it was liable to snap at any moment with a twang in pure Country, while she wailed along like she was summoning the devil to dance, with her long black hair tangling in her bow until it seemed she was pulling the song out of her hair instead of her fiddle.

Maybe she did. Summon up the devil, I mean, since that night was when Trouble joined the band.

I know Cawley warned me. I know that. But it had to have been while I was on the floor slithering like the snake in the Garden into my tightest black jeans, or trying to bend over after that to buckle the Mary Jane strap on one seven-inch lollipop red heel, and then zip a black ankle boot on the other foot, or surrounding myself with puddles of sequins, satin, leather, and lace, trying to find just the right top for my mood. Pirate Queen, or Good Fairy/Bad Fairy, or maybe I'd just wear my glasses and my crazy-quilt jacket and Cawley on my shoulder and be Scholar Gypsy.

Cawley hates being used as an accessory, unless I'm in Dire Need. Which I wasn't then. Or at least I didn't know it, then. Though I would have if I'd listened to him. But I was on the floor, etc., while he was fluttering on his wooden perch trying to take my attention off my clothes. Translating crow requires concentration. I thought he was asking me to open the window so that he could fly out, and I finally did give it a shove up, in the middle of putting on a shirt covered with roses and skulls.

"There," I said. "Bye. You know where I'll be."

But he didn't leave, just kept squawking. Since he had hopped from his perch to the sill, I thought he was talking to his clan, which had covered the tree outside like very dead leaves. They were all chattering, too. Where to go to dinner, or the sun about to go down, or somebody spilled a ginormous order of french fries in the middle of B Street. Something like that.

So you can't say I wasn't warned. I pulled off the shirt, which wasn't right, and limped in one-shoe-on, one-boot-on mode to the window, and pushed it shut behind Cawley. I nearly caught his tail feathers. He whirled in a black blur and could have cracked glass with the word that ripped out of his open beak.

I yelled back, "Sorry!"

But what I thought he squawked wasn't what he said at all.

I hadn't really had him that long. Some witches find their familiars; some familiars find their witches. Liesl's smoke-colored cat with golden eyes had been put in an animal shelter along with her seven siblings. Liesl had a dream about her, and went searching. They recognized each other instantly. Liesl smiled; the cat started a coffee grinder purr that rattled her tiny body. Of course Liesl named her Graymalkin. Why not? Who'd guess that names among familiars are remembered through vast webs of families and histories, way back into antiquity? Naming a cat Graymalkin is like adding yet another Josh or Elizabeth to the human list.

As for Cawley, yes, that too is pretty much obvious. At the time, I thought it was clever of me. To name a crow Cawley. Duh.

Cawley found me.

Liesl had it easy in the sense that she didn't have to learn to understand Cat. They just read each other's minds. If Graymalkin presents herself with her back arched and every hair standing up on end, that pretty much says it all. But Cawley doesn't have a stance for: be afraid, very afraid. When I first saw him, he was pacing on a rain gutter next door and imitating the endless barking of an obnoxious dog in a neighboring yard. The noise had crept into the background of a dream I was having, and finally woke me up way too soon after a long night. I stumbled to the window and pushed it open to find out what exactly was the dog's problem. Then I saw the crow waddling to and fro on the gutter and barking back at it. I laughed, and the crow flew over to me like he'd just been waiting for me to get up.

I didn't understand a word he said. But I felt as though somebody—something—had slipped a fine, gold chain onto my wrist and said, "Mine." I didn't argue. I liked that feeling of having been chosen, of belonging to a dark, mythical bird that had my best interests at heart. Also, Cawley gave me status. I was True Witch, now, not Apprentice, or Journeyperson Witch. Familiars don't stay with witches who are not yet True.

I had gotten into the habit of watching crows. I never guessed they were watching me back. Who does? City crows mingle so easily with people that people hardly notice them. Crows know the habits of cars. They don't even bother to stop pecking at roadkill or bugs or a spilled bag of chips in the middle of a street until a car is almost on top of them. They move aside grudgingly for the monster outweighing them by several tons, but with no real sense of urgency. They have the same hysterics teaching their fledglings to fly that human parents have teaching their kids how to drive. They imitate noises that catch their interest; that's what Cawley was doing when we met. They get bored; they play tricks. And, at sundown, they all fly the same direction to some mysterious place, a coven of crows gathering at dusk for reasons Cawley can't yet explain in ways I can understand.

A murder of crows. That's what they were called in medieval times. Maybe for their habit of chowing down on the dead. Maybe for something more sinister. But the city crows I see seem basically civilized. True, they might peck at people when they're nesting, or chase a pet across the yard for fun. But mostly they act like they're beneath our notice.

I notice. Maybe that's why Cawley came to me.

The others in Which Witch, except for Rune, have their familiars, of course. Madrona, the skinny, white-haired whippet on the percussions, has a parakeet named Hibiscus. Pyx, our lead singer, has a white rat named Archibald. Makes sense: Pyx is bald. They have squeak-fests together. Sometimes Pyx wears Archibald on her clothes along with a lot of ugly old brooches her mother left her, made of gold and diamonds and sapphires.

So that's us, Which Witch: Liesl and Madrona and Pyx and her boyfriend, Rune, on bass, and me, Hazel. I know. Just like the witch-hazel bush. Like Graymalkin and Cawley: with a name like that, what else could I be?

Where was I?

French fries, indeed. Granted, we crows like a snack now and then, and are not above a discarded bit of burger, preferably with pickle, or a salty, lightly tailpipe-smoked fry. But what I tried and failed so miserably to get my witch Hazel to understand was exactly why we had chosen the tree outside her window for our Twilight Coven. The monster creeping toward her as her attention flitted like a magpie to this red shoe, that purple sequin was ancient, powerful, and thoroughly nasty.

And we were not just any tree full of gabbling city crows. We were a gathering from all over the land, most of us experienced, some of us with powers, and a few of us scandalously older than we had any right to be. My great-grandmother on my father's side was still with us. She spotted the peril first. She had recently retired to live on warm southern beaches where plump briny critters and picnic leftovers were readily available. Having no human to guard, she watched everything else.

"It broke out of the sea on a wave, crawled up to dry sand on a roll of froth and foam in the moonlight," she said excitedly. She was looking pretty good for an old crow, though her tail feathers were a bit scraggly. "In the wee hours of the morning it gathered itself up and chose its human form. Cutest lifeguard you ever saw. Great abs. Spent the day sunning on its high chair, watching behind its dark glasses and flirting back at the girls who came up. I searched everywhere, couldn't find what it had done to the real lifeguard. It was gone after sunset. I lost track of it while I watched the sun go down.

"So I took to the air. I never spotted it again, but I followed rumors of it in the night roosts and covens between ocean and here.

"Here, it stopped."

"I saw it last night," I said, clutching the branch in my claws so tightly that the tree gave a little, irritated twitch. "Last night, where my witch Hazel plays music."

"Did you warn her?" my Uncle Rakl asked sharply. What did he think? That I'd recognized it and gone on preening my feathers and picking at fleas?

"I tried." Uncle Rakl was watching me out of one eye, a bleak, annoying gaze, as though he expected nothing more or less from me.

"You tried."

"We haven't been joined long. I forget what human words I've learned when I'm agitated, and she is still struggling with crow."

He made the noise like his name, causing a half-dozen youngsters on a bough beneath us to explode into raucous mimicry. They were screeched into silence by various parents; the fledglings subsided, perching sedately and pretending they didn't know each other.

"What shape was it?" my great-grandmother asked practically.

"I felt it long before I saw it. The club was shadowy and very crowded. My witch's band is extremely popular," I added proudly and unnecessarily, then got back down to business before Uncle Rakl could open his beak. "I found the source of the dark emanation in an aging biker's body, with stylishly frayed jeans, black leather boots, and a long, gray-brown braid down its back. Earrings, thumb rings, tattoo of a skull with roses in the eye-sockets. No other visible piercings. Wealthily scruffy."

There were mutterings and soft rattles throughout the tree: that dead body shouldn't be hard to spot if it was still in any recognizable form. A couple of messengers left immediately to spread the word to the night roost in the city park, a couple of miles away as we crows fly.

"I smelled the death and the power in it. And it smelled me, so I had to leave."

"You left your witch?" Uncle Rakl again, ever ready to believe the worst of me.

"Only," I rasped back, "to get it to follow me. Which it didn't. But when I flew back inside the club it was gone. I stayed with my witch, but she roosted with a friend that night; I had to sleep outside. They gave me no chance to try to warn her until this evening. She didn't understand. As you saw."

I glanced over to my witch's window. She had finally chosen her costume for the evening, a process I will never understand, and was giving herself a wide-eyed glare in a mirror, brushing the small hairs in her eyelids with a mixture of glitter and blue paint.

"Perhaps," Uncle Rakl said heavily, "it went its way already. Whatever it wants or seeks isn't in this city at all."

"Maybe," my great-grandmother said. "And maybe not. What kinds of powers does your witch have?"

"I wonder," my young cousin Ska mused, "how that glitter would look on my tail feathers."

There was another rackety outburst of hilarity from the fledglings, during which my great-grandmother forgot her question. Just as well, since I had no idea. All I really knew of my witch Hazel's powers is that she had drawn me to her side. And the ooze that had shaped itself into a semblance of the dead to watch her in the shadows of the bar, she might have drawn to herself as well. It was my fate and my duty to make such distasteful assumptions, and to go where few self-respecting crows should ever go.

"Anybody up for some music? I can get us in as stage props."

Uncle Rakl rackled. My cousin Ska preened. The fledgling chorus erupted, along with most of the coven, until my witch turned her stare to the window, and, across the way from her, somebody threw a beer bottle at the tree.

"Pipe down, birds!"

We all fluttered up, with a great deal of noise and confused energy. A window slammed. As was our habit, we came to our decision suddenly, reading each other's thoughts, including the image of where to go in mine, before we settled back down again in leisurely fashion, all of us talking at once.

"That's it, then," great-grandmother said briskly. "We'll all go. But you go with her. Cling to her, do what you must to make her understand. Peck her head if you have to, Whatever-it-is-she-calls-you. Cawley."

I had to listen to the derisive echo of that—*Cawley, Cawley, Cawley*—as the black cloud flowed out of the tree and swarmed away into the twilight sky over the city. I flew to my witch's window, stood on the sill, and pecked at the glass until she let me in.

Cawley was still trying to give me a language lesson when I left for the club. It was only a few blocks away and Quin would meet me there. Quin was Quinton Matthew Tarleton III. He had wandered with some friends into a place we were playing a couple of weeks before, looking earnest and geeky and too sweet for words. He had taken me out for ice cream on our first date. For breakfast. Later, after our first kiss, he had bought me a gecko pin for my hair. So it was a little hard for me to concentrate on what Cawley was saying, what with the slight weight of the gecko sparkling just above my ear and making me think of Quin.

Finally one word penetrated, making me stop dead in my tracks, or rather, wobble to a halt in my high-heeled lace-up boots.

"What? Wait. Did you say danger?"

I was so proud of myself for picking that out of all his noises that I forgot for a moment what it meant. He flew around my head three times, squawking so excitedly that people ducked away from us, alarmed.

"Cawley." My voice did something strange, then: it got sharp and slow and focused all at the same time. "Please. Stop. Sit. Start over."

He shut up abruptly and fluttered onto my shoulder. Luckily I was wearing a retro 1940s-style jacket with some major shoulder pads in it; even so, I could feel his claws, loosening and tightening nervously. "Danger," he said again, then another word I actually recognized. "You."

"Me? I'm a danger?" I looked at my outfit bewilderedly. "Why? Because I'm showing four inches of skin and a fake garnet in my navel between my shirt and my skirt, or I would be except I've got my jacket buttoned now and nobody can—Cawley, why are you suddenly sounding like my mother?"

He pecked my head. Not hard, just a fingernail thump, but I couldn't believe he had done that.

"Cawley!" I yelped, seriously irritated. I wanted to smack him with my fiddle case. I shrugged my shoulder hard instead, shaking him off. "Go," I told him in that voice again. "Just go. Leave me alone until you can talk to me like a normal familiar. You're pretty much useless to me like this."

He hovered a moment in midair in front of my face. Then he made a sound, a sort of crow-rattle of total frustration that I understood completely. He sailed off in the direction of the club. I stomped off after him, still smoldering, and wishing I had a familiar that was easier to talk to, like maybe an iguana.

When I walked into the club it was like walking into some weird power field. I could feel the hair lift on my head and I prickled everywhere, like a cat coming nose to nose with the Hound of the Baskervilles. I knew immediately: this is what Cawley meant, what he had been trying to say. I could feel it creeping under my skin, dragging at my bones, like a cold, bleak fog, or the nasty breath of some animal that's been eating roadkill. It weighed me down, fogged my brain, so that when I glanced around the club to see what caused it, the candles on the tables dimmed to a yellowy-brown, and the shadows looked like solid blocks of black.

I recognized Quin through the haze in my brain. He stood at the bar, sipping at his usual undrinkable mix of sparkling water, tomato juice, and lime he called a Toothless Vampire. He lightened the air a bit, inside me and out. I took a step toward him. Then I saw what stood beside him, holding a mug and gazing at the ceiling.

I glanced up, too, and saw every single fake axe-split rafter in the place crowded with crows, silent and motionless in the shadows, as though they were all waiting for someone to die.

I wanted to shrink down into something very small and skitter my way out between the incoming feet. The thing beside Quin poked him in the shoulder and made some comment, laughing. It looked like the dark-haired, blue-eyed fry cook from the club's kitchen, idling at the bar before her shift began. But she—it—forgot to change its shadow. What clung to her cowboy boots and slanted away underfoot across the floor didn't look like anything remotely human.

People were crowding into the place behind me, paying the cover and getting their hands stamped. I forced myself to move, wave at Quin until I caught his eye. I didn't dare glance at the shape beside him. It would have looked through my eyes and into my brain and seen everything I was thinking. When Quin saw me, I slapped a smile on my face and tapped my wrist: late for work. He waved a kiss at me, then tapped his head where, on my head, the little, glittery gecko was pinned. He made a circle with his thumb and forefinger. I grinned like a pumpkin and nodded so hard the gecko nearly fell off.

I felt its attention then, as though a new moon had looked at me, enormous, invisible, full of black light.

I turned away fast and headed for the stage.

Walking into the tension there was like trying to hurry underwater. Everyone seemed normal enough, dressed by a passing tornado and wearing the usual assortment of animals except for Rune, who was still Journeyperson status. He was tuning his bass, looking like a hairy Viking who had forgotten to do his laundry. He thumbed a note as I picked my way through cords and equipment, and said, without looking up, "Which witch are you, I wonder?"

It was our code for: man, have we got Trouble. Anybody know what that is?

Even the familiars looked spooked. Pyx was wearing every brooch she owned. Gold and diamonds, dirty silver and hunky jewels of every color flared on her orange silk vest. Usually she wore Archibald in the middle of them, the white rat with his garnet-red eyes splayed and clinging with his strong little paws to her threads among the treasures. But he was on her shoulder, snuggled as close to her ear as he could get and probably wishing she had left some hair on that side of her head for him to crawl under. Madrona's yellow parakeet was half-hidden in her wild white curls. Hibiscus's feathers were completely puffed out, as though she tried to convince Trouble she was two or three times her tiny size. Graymalkin was in her usual spot inside Liesl's open violin case. But she wasn't curled up and napping. She was crouched, motionless, staring into the crowd like she watched a ghost. I had a feeling that if I put a hand on her fur I'd get a shock that would untie my bootlaces.

"I'm the Wicked Witch," I answered, which meant: I know. I'm armed and dangerous.

Well, I could hope.

"You look more like the Good Witch," Liesl murmured, stroking her strings with her bow. I puzzled over that for a moment until I realized it wasn't code, it was a comment.

"Sorry," I said meekly. "I couldn't figure out who I am tonight."

Madrona, who lived, slept, and possibly showered in black, said sweetly, "You look nice," which of course is code for: your grandmother would love what you're wearing. She sat down and picked up her drumsticks, which usually caused Hibiscus to take cover in the violin case with Graymalkin. But the parakeet only deflated a bit and shifted farther back into Madrona's hair. She bopped a cymbal lightly and asked, "Do we have a set list?"

Of course we did; we always had a set list. That was code for: does anyone have the slightest idea what to do?

Liesl shrugged speechlessly. She was the gypsy that night, from the rings on her bare feet to the gold loops in her ears and the ribbons in her long black hair. I opened my case and took out the bow, tightened the strings, then picked up the violin, which, freed from years of lessons, turned promptly into a fiddle.

"Wing it?" I suggested, and above my head a crow—maybe Cawley—rustled feathers noisily. I hoped they might know what to do, not that any of them could tell me. I listened to Liesl's tunings, tightened my A, then my G, which promptly snapped and curled with a little mournful wail. I said something I hoped the mikes didn't pick up and scrabbled among the strings in the case. "Where is that—Liesl, did you take my G string?"

"Borrowed," she said unrepentantly. "In rehearsal yesterday—you were in the bathroom. You have another one."

"You took the good one. Do you know how expensive those are?"

"Sure, I do. Why do you think I grabbed it?"

Madrona gave us a drum roll and a bling on the cymbal. "Pick it up, ladies. We've got a heavy night ahead of us."

That was pretty much code for: if we get out of this alive, I'm calling my mom every week, I promise, and if I ever think of buying another pair of frivolous shoes, I'll donate the money to the food bank instead. I clamped my teeth, changed the string, and wished with all my heart that Cawley would fly out of the shadows and come and sit on my shoulder.

"Where is Cawley?" asked Liesl, who sometimes read my mind. I shrugged, and her eyes narrowed incredulously. "Did you guys have a quarrel?"

"How would I know?" I muttered. That thing at the bar had one hand on Quin's shoulder and he wasn't smiling anymore. "We can't understand a word we say."

Madrona raised her sticks, woke the Thunder Gods with them, and announced to us and the cheering crowd, the coven of crows above us, and whatever familiars and aliens were among us, "Which Witch Can Dance."

They all took off without me.

I was still tightening the new string. Worry makes Liesl edgy and feisty. She was all over the notes I needed to tune; I half-expected to see smoke rising off her strings, the way her bow danced. Pyx was blasting away at the song with her eerie voice that could slide deep, then shoot freakily high on the same word. She sparked as she moved, colors from all those cut jewels flinging out spangles of red, green, yellow, ice-white. Archibald must have decided that her bare neck was too slippery. He had crawled down among the pins, hanging onto a diamond with one hind claw, a chunk of topaz with another, his foremost claws on a coil of tarnished silver and garnets. I finally finished tuning and positioned my bow to jump in.

I saw Cawley, then, perched on the beam where the bar glasses hung, right above Quin's head.

He might have been carved out of wood himself, he was that motionless. The monster fry cook beneath him still had its hand on Quin's shoulder, and it was staring across the room at us. I forced myself to look away from the weird little group of Quin and crow and creepy thing. As I started playing, something flashed across my brain. Something glittery, green, catching light like Pyx's pins. It flew in and out of my thoughts a second time; I saw a golden eye. I hit a sour note, recognizing it. The gecko pin. It was on my hair; what was it doing in my head? Liesl caught my eye and grinned maniacally; she loves it when I screw up. The gecko skittered across my thoughts again. This time it made a sound. I had no idea geckos sound so much like crows.

My fingers froze. Gecko. Gecko pin. That was what Cawley said to me. The thing at the bar let go of Quin. He swayed a little, blinking confusedly. It was staring at me now, grabbing at me with its eyes. I felt my skin crawl; insects skittered all over me. My bow was still stuck in place. Liesl lost her smile and covered for me. What about the gecko? I cried silently at Cawley. What about the pin?

The monster took a step toward us, and Quin upended his Toothless Vampire onto its head.

Then he jumped all over the fry cook, which caused the startled bartender to shoot him with the tonic water hose. The fry cook melted away. A black shape, familiar but bigger than I'd ever seen, streaked over the crowed, aiming not at me and my worthless-but-of-sentimental-value gecko, I realized then, but at Pyx's pins.

Cawley came to life, went flying off the rafter after it.

A note came out of Pyx that I'd never heard before. But I recognized its power and so did one of the pins on her vest. The spiral of blackened silver and garnets started spinning, covering the open-mouthed crowd with gyrating red stars. Everybody applauded wildly. I felt the colorful force shoot past me and added something of my own: a shriek of bowed string and a word my mother taught me early on to yell in emergencies. Of course it was the Spinreel G string, and it promptly broke. Liesl added her version to mine, and Madrona walloped a cymbal so hard the reverberations scudded like fast flying golden ripples across the air at the incoming magic. Rune hit the lowest note on the bass while a deep demonic sound came out of his mouth, making the crowd go crazy again. Through it all, Archibald hung on to that pin with one claw, whirling around and refusing to budge, and Graymalkin yowled like the walking dead out for your brains.

All that didn't stop the thing flying at us, but it did slow a bit, bouncing over Madrona's waves and splashing into the wall of power we raised against it. I heard a strange, muffled squawk in my head, which was the only way I could have heard anything in all that uproar. It sounded like Cawley, only sort of squashed, like something was sitting on him.

Then I saw him, fluttering furiously against the grip of a claw bigger than my head.

Several things, all of them incoherent, flooded into my head at once. Cawley might be a disaster of a familiar, but he was my disaster, and nothing could break that bond without losing teeth. Or in this case, feathers. I felt myself fill like a balloon with outrage; in the same moment I glimpsed Hibiscus, who was puffed up like a yellow cloud on top of Madrona's head, facing off something nineteen hundred times her size. A good idea, it looked like, so I puffed, and I puffed, staring that looming monster smack in its moon-black eye, until it seemed that feathers were breaking out all over me. My fiddle wailed a couple of times; more strings broke. I dropped it. A black cloud came down out of the rafters all over the club, covered the gigantic crow-thing from beak to tail fathers, and, I discovered, as we started pulling and shredding, that I was one of them.

A murder of crows.

The crowd went totally bonkers, especially when Pyx hit the note she did and caused a sizzling short in the stage lights overhead. I hung upside down on the humongous claw, pecking and biting at it, while some gigantic feathers drifted into me from the rumpus on the monster's back. Cawley got his head free and grabbed a beak full of claw. I couldn't tell if we were winning or losing. But judging from the things flying around us—high heels, baseball caps, lit keychain flashlights, even a T-shirt or two—the crowd was loving our act.

Then a wave of garnet came at us like an exploding red star, and all the lights in the club went out.

I hit the floor and realized that my bones were back where I was used to them being. "Cawley!" I yelled in the dark. I felt claws tangle in my hair. I scrambled to get up, managed an undignified wobble onto my heels, and started off toward where I thought I had left the stage, worried about Pyx and her exploding pin. Cawley squawked in my ear. I said, "Oh," and turned the opposite direction. His claws left me abruptly. I stepped on someone's feet, and we grabbed each other for balance. Then a few of the lights went back on, and I found my hands full of Quin.

He stared at me. His mouth opened, worked noiselessly a couple of times in goldfish mode. Then he got words out. "That was—" he breathed. "That was. That was. Truly. Awesome."

I straightened the gecko pin and smiled, still feeling a bit wobbly. "You were great. The way you tackled the fry cook?"

Behind him the crowd, dead quiet now and standing in a litter of fallen flying objects, including various drink garnishes, lipsticks, and an order of fried onion rings, still faced the stage, waiting for more.

"She was evil," Quin said flatly, and I felt him shudder. "Bad wicked evil."

"I know." I glanced around. It was gone, whatever it was, and so were all the crows, including Cawley. I wondered if they had finished the brawl, or just taken it outside. I listened. But there was no Cawley in my head. I looked for him, saw the bartender, the waiters, the kitchen staff, all motionless, gazing speechlessly at each other, at the band.

I counted heads onstage, found four humans, to my relief, and four familiars. Four? I counted again. Rune had one, I realized suddenly. He was grinning crookedly at the garter snake wound around his wrist like a cuff. Archibald still clung to the garnet pin; it smoldered, flaring red now and then, like fire dying down. Graymalkin had quit her caterwauling and Hibiscus had dwindled to her usual size, but they still looked alert, tense.

Pyx cleared her throat but even she was speechless. Madrona brought her sticks very lightly down on the snare and said shakily, "We'll slow things down a bit for our next number, shall we? Hazel? Are you out there?"

Cawley! I called again, this time silently, wanting to know what happened to him, where he had gone, and was he coming back? Every other witch in the band, even Rune, now, had a familiar; where was mine? *Cawley!*

An eerie image formed in my head: a monster crow under a tree, surrounded by a wide ring of hundreds and hundreds of crows, all watching it while only one spoke. Now and then the huge bird twitched a wing or a tail feather, but it didn't seem able to fly.

". . . for the terrible deeds upon which all crows should look with abhorrence and which deeds no crow deserving of the name shall commit and still remain crow . . ."

Cawley! I cried again into that dark, still place in my head, and the crow-voice I heard interrupted itself petulantly.

"Your witch Hazel seems to be listening in to private coven matters."

"Uncle Rakl, she became crow and helped us fight." I realized, with surprise, that I recognized Cawley's voice. "My witch Hazel earned the right, by the powers that she possesses."

"I think he's right, Rakl," an unfamiliar voice, higher and more rattly than the first, said. "Private coven matters weren't so private in that place, and she fought well and fearlessly for my great-grandson. And for her friends, who seem to be in possession of ancient jewels of extraordinary power. Now can we get on with this? My tail feathers are a mess and my claws are killing me."

I went back to the stage. The crowd sent up a cheer when I reappeared, maybe just because I made it up the stage steps without toppling over. Madrona clanged the cymbal for me. Liesl handed me my fiddle; she had already replaced a couple of broken strings. I'd have to play around the missing G but that seemed a piffling matter by then. Rune's snake flicked its tongue in friendly fashion at me as I passed. It was a sleek, sturdy, pretty thing with a fine golden stripe down its back. Rune grinned proudly. He was True Witch now, and he had earned it with the subhuman growl that had come out of him.

Pyx still seemed a little stunned by the ugly old brooches she'd been wearing without a second thought.

"Sorry," she said softly to us. "My mother never had time to teach me about them before she died. I just wore them to remember her."

Liesl nodded, looking very curious. "Soon," she promised, "we'll help you find out if they can do more than summon evil monster crow god thingies."

Madrona hit the cymbal again, this time a thorough whap to bring the crowd back to life. People were still crowding the floor, wanting more, even while they picked up their stuff and dodged brooms sweeping up the squashed onions. The sweepers watched us mindlessly, running into people as they waited to see what we could follow that act with.

"Gentle people of every persuasion," Madrona said into the mike, "Which Witch Are You?"

Midway through that song, Cawley fluttered onto my shoulder where he belonged.

"Thank you, Witch Hazel. Very impressive work indeed."

I wasn't sure any more which language he spoke, human or crow, or if I heard it with my brain or my heart, but I understood exactly what he said.

Edith and Henry Go Motoring

The pile of oranges in the bowl was dwindling, the full, round, bright orbs shrinking, withering as Harry sucked, squeezed, palpated their liquid into his mouth. He seemed to exude it in sunny droplets; he plumped as the oranges shrank. But he looked no happier. His face bore an expression of patient resignation, like a martyr feeling the little eager flames springing up under his sandals.

He sighed, voluminously and unconsciously.

There was only one thing for it, Edie thought, glancing at her guest. They sat in white wicker on the terrace of Hill House, itself white on white marble overlooking the pond, drowsy with light, and beyond it, on down the gently sloping paths through the gardens she had designed, the shallows of the lake in the distance, framed by birch and maple, a splash of molten silver in the eye.

"There really is only one thing for it," she said briskly. "We must go for a drive."

He gazed at her in astonished disbelief, as though she were the cheerily smiling angel with the bucket descending to douse the fire. "My dear lady," he managed, overwhelmed. "My good woman—"

As though, she thought with amusement, they had not said these things, they had not done this a dozen times before on those stagnant, broiling late summer days.

"Of course, yes," she said, rising instantly to summon Thompson and the car, the housekeeper to find Ned, the cook, for a basket of chicken sandwiches, cold tea, more oranges, in case they rolled themselves into a ditch. Sunshades, she debated, for the Pope-Hartford had no roof. But Harry never seemed to mind the heat with the wind blowing around him. The faster the better, such was his opinion, and she let the idea of sunshades go, for that is what they would do at such speeds: turn inside out and fly away.

Thompson, their resourceful driver, was alerted; Edie heard the engine harrumph into life as she changed out of her thin lawn into more practical dark linen. There came a message from her husband: Ned had a headache and had taken to bed. She focused a moment's thought on him, gazing into the mirror as the maid pinned her hat. Ned's sick headaches, requiring dark rooms and absolute quiet, had been frequent that summer. They were followed by his moods, a couple of black days when he looked critically upon Edie, avoided their guests, and spoke mostly to the dogs.

Perhaps, she hoped, when the weather changed he would brighten. . . .

They were out at last, the shiny red tonneau idling, the basket stowed, dear Harry in his seat smiling once again and talking to Thompson behind the wheel.

"Going south, as it were, is what we seldom do. East and we are well acquainted; we are in complete accord; our views seldom surprise. North not so much so, but then north is vague and wanders off into endless forest without a view or a house for miles. West brings us to the river, for which we need a bridge. In short, what I have in mind is a foray west, and then south, and then again west. Can you, do you think, manage? Might there be, to put it plain, a bridge?"

"Harry, do you mean to take us into the wilderness?" Edie asked, settling herself beside him in the back. Ned usually rode up beside Thompson; she would have a peculiarly unencumbered view without his head. She felt a tiny pang: some future road without him, she envisioned for a breath.

"Only think of that cool air above the rushing river," Harry exclaimed. "Can anything be more agreeable?"

The efficient Thompson interjected himself here with delicacy, for Harry regarded himself as the intuitive authority on matters of direction. "I think, ma'am, there is a bridge across the river at Tattersclaw."

"There, you see?" Harry beamed. "How could we not be drawn irrevocably by the idea of Tattersclaw? The possibilities of it? The very existence of such a name demands our immediate awe and all our scrutiny."

"Very well." She settled herself in the soft leather, adjusted her veil against wildlife careening through the air. "The fabulous Tattersclaw it shall be."

"And do not consider our feelings," Harry instructed Thompson. "Drive every bit as fast as you like."

Which he did, to Harry's evident relief; he smiled even as the warm wind buffeted him, and the bees and grasshoppers from passing fields and hedgerows performed death-defying skids through his hair. With his usual adroitness, Thompson turned the tangle of dusty cart roads into something workable: he threaded his way through the fields and villages west of Hill House until he reached the mighty Humber. He turned south, then, down an ancient river road. That he'd known such a road along the water must exist impressed Edie. Harry, on the other hand, seemed to have expected it, though Edie suspected he had assumed it would be there because he wanted it. For a while they motored down the tooth-rattling road, dodging antique cartwheel ruts and the occasional terrified animal. They glimpsed water now and then, glittering, smooth, and deep, through shrubbery that Edie longed to take in hand.

Then there was a choice: they could continue south, or they could veer suddenly west down a branch of road that led, so a worn wooden post stated, to TATTERSCLAW AND BRIDGE. Thompson turned the wheel heroically, without a waver. Trees on both sides of them leaned close; leaves brushed them. Abruptly they straightened, thinned, and there, spread along the riverbank, was Tattersclaw. And Bridge.

The road plunged them down into the village first, as was proper, Edie thought, for such a hard, old, wizened rind of a wagon path that existed for who knew how many centuries to serve the crofters and fishers along the river. She peered curiously at the houses. They were wooden, tall, narrow and dark, set far too close to the road. Dusty panes glinted at them, flicking light, like the shy, sly glances of birds. The doors were all shut tight. And why not, she decided, at that busy hour of the day? But there were not even children about, nor maids on their errands. Just houses, the occasional slate-stooped shop with oddly opaque windows, and dirt lanes running now and then between them, empty and silent.

"Where is everybody?" she murmured. "You'd think somebody would be out gardening. Look at the weeds around that lovely clematis."

"Perhaps they keep European hours," Harry guessed. "They delve at dawn, and sleep like the dead through the hot, onerous afternoon, to come to life again with the cool breezes riffling over the water at dusk, becoming more and more visible, like fireflies, showing at their most brilliant, their most lively, in full night."

They passed beneath the shadow of the bridge, a modern contrivance with steel girders to uphold the road, and massive stone columns and arches rising across the water to allow the boats to pass under it. A thin layer of houses followed them along both sides of the road, then scattered away as the road, too, at last became modern, curving onto the bridge, wider, flatter, and suddenly tarred.

There was a tollhouse.

Edie caught her breath at the sight: a tiny, dark hut with a couple of filthy windows awaiting them in the exact center of the bridge. Behind a window, a face turned toward them, bristling and indistinct with hair.

She laughed, wondering what, in this outlandish place, they might possibly be expected to pay.

Harry, dear Harry, absently slapped a pocket at the suggestion of money. The gesture never came up with anything more material than good intentions. Thompson pulled up to the hut and stopped; he glanced back, questioningly, at Edie, who was working her fingers into her handbag. Ned usually kept the coins as they traveled, but she had remembered to bring a few for emergencies and tips.

The toll-taker pushed out of his flimsy turret by means of a door that scraped the tar; he stumped to the middle of the road in front of the car. Edie nearly laughed again, for he seemed a fantasy that only a village named Tattersclaw would come up with. He was quite short yet burly, with a great deal of black, hairy eyebrows, mustachios, muttonchops, and tangled, untidy waves falling across his shoulders. All that, she marveled, and a wooden leg, a plain honed stump like an old sailor's; the great black boot on his other leg was trimmed with a huge, rakishly turned cuff.

A belted coat and a cockaded hat completed the splendor.

He looked them over as even Harry sat stupefied by the vision, and then gave judgment: "A half."

"A half?" Edie echoed, her voice quivering giddily. "A half of what, pray?"

"A half," he said. His eyes, she saw, were as black as his boot, with a well-polished gleam in them. "A half of what you bring back from the other side."

"But—my good man—don't you think that's somewhat excessive? I mean, suppose we were a hay wagon. Would you take half our load?"

"Naw," he said shortly, turning his shoulder to them and stumping back to his hut. "You're not a hay wagon. You are what you are and that's your toll."

Harry loosed a delighted yelp. "Oh, Tattersclaw," he exclaimed. "I am in love with Tattersclaw. Of course we will pay with whatever we bring back. Half for us, half for you, is that not right? A hatful of gold, a wheel of cheese, a basket of mushrooms from that wilderness ahead. Is this not wonderful, Edie?"

"Wonderful," she agreed a trifle breathlessly, gazing at the green wall of mountains on the other end of the bridge. "Drive on, Thompson."

Indeed, the vast green seemed to loom as they crossed, become a frozen sea of massive waves rising, one after another, peak after peak stretching to a distant blue-gray upwell, to the end of the world, it looked like, and all about to come crashing exuberantly upon the heads of the innocent travelers. Even the road at the far end seemed swallowed by the waves, running a short way into shadow and vanishing.

But Thompson made nothing of that; he plunged fearlessly into the unknown, enjoying, Edie knew, his own proficiency as he spun them around one coil of road to the next, all wonderfully ornamented with great boulders and ferns and wild streams. Harry became very quiet, infinitely soothed by the cool air, the smells of wet moss and earth, the shadows of birch and hemlock.

"Lovely," he breathed finally, fixated upon a little rill splashing down stones beside the road. "Lovely. But," he added after a breath, "I wonder to what point?" Edie opened her mouth, perplexed; he enlightened her. "Where, in short, does the road go? There are no signs pointing onward to villages, no isolated houses, not even a farm readily visible, and yet this road."

"Patience, dear Harry, patience. We have only gone a little way. It will reveal its purpose."

Which it did, in the next curve, running abruptly upward on an oddly widened expanse of lane. Rough fieldstone walls appeared here and there, strengthening the steep hillside. The road continued up and up in a long, winding spiral through the forest. Edie's fascinated eye recognized, among the still green locals, outlandish trees and shrubberies from distant countries, unexpected continents. They had been ruthlessly transported from their native soils and dropped, willy-nilly, into this unkempt wilderness. Remnants, she wondered, of some overgrown, long-untended garden?

"The sign!" Harry suddenly exclaimed.

And there it was: a wooden slat, weathered and grey, hanging from a rusty chain on a pole. Upon it, looking very freshly painted, a word: RÊVE.

A black rose bloomed beneath the word. A black raven stood above it. Unlike the rose, the bird was alive, and emitted its own word, a remarkably accurate imitation of the Pope-Hartford backfiring into the trees.

"Dream," Harry translated. He sounded absolutely delighted. "Oh, this is beyond expectation. The bridge where we wanted it, the stump-legged toll-collector, and now—" He gestured, rendered uncharacteristically inarticulate. "This."

The raven flew off the sign, sailed up the road ahead of them. The car labored around a final curve and, to Edie's relief, achieved level ground.

Thompson stopped the engine.

For a moment, even the raven was silent.

They were parked on a precipice, a slab of solid rock that seemed, in its dizzying height, the pinnacle of the world. Farther below them than should be possible, Edie glimpsed a ribbon of the river, and in the distance beyond, a pale blur that might have been her own Hill House on a miniature mound of green.

In front of them stood row upon row of blank, dark, rectangular windows above a broad, regal swath of veranda interspersed with many lofty pillars overlooking the stunning view of the world, and, it seemed, entirely empty.

Or maybe not, Edie thought, as movement, like a thought, flickered across one of the high, hollow windows. But no: it was the raven, falling like a black tear down the face of the abandoned structure.

She consulted the strangely motionless Harry; he gazed, engrossed, at the vision, his own face as still, as thoughtless as that many-eyed dreamer now inhabited, from the look of it, only by ravens and ghosts.

Thompson glanced back at Edie, his brows raised, and she made a decision.

"Tea," she said. "On those steps, I think, leading up to the porch. Can you put us closer, Thompson? Perhaps there is a caretaker of some sort who can explain this marvel to us. Does that suit you, Harry? Harry?"

But he was already out and gone, as quickly as his patient bulk would permit, every step across stone and weedy drive in an unhesitating line for the broad, elegant stairway leading up to the pillared veranda and the entryway, whose doors were shut as tightly as the mouth of a housekeeper over the secrets of the house. His attention never swerved, even when Thompson passed him to park discreetly to one side of the steps, so as not to intrude upon their view.

Harry went up the steps, opened the doors, and vanished.

Edie felt a word, dark and harsh, try to fly from her lips; she put her hand over them quickly. The imperturbable Thompson spoke, sounding shaken.

"Should I unload the picnic basket, Mrs. W.? Or should I go after him?"

"I'll go," Edie answered quickly. "Why should dear Harry have all the adventures?" She rose to let herself out. "By all means unpack the basket. There's tea, there are sandwiches, and some blueberry tarts. If we get captured by desperate mountain folk living inside, find a way to let Ned know so that he can pay the ransom." And hope, she thought, that he's having one of his better days. She smiled cheerfully, for Thompson was looking dubious. "I'll be out shortly, I promise."

She gained the top of the rigorous ascension of treads, and crossed the veranda, empty now of the long lines of white wicker lounges and sturdily slatted rockers upon which guests must have once perched to admire the stunning view. Midway, time shifted, it seemed; the moment merged with memories, like layers of torn wallpaper, revealing earlier broad verandas, and piazzas in far-flung places across the sea: ancient lights slanting across them, hues of sky mirrored in rain puddles on cobblestones, great clouds of pigeons or doves startling upward, and then wheeling, adrift, behind spires, between towers, over palaces centuries older than this naïve place, barely past its callow youth before it had hollowed out.

The high double doors opened easily. She left them open to reassure Thompson, who still watched her from the bottom step, and entered.

"Harry?"

There he was, reflected in a great, gilt-edged mirror at the end of the passageway. He receded; she quickened her pace, and saw the raven again, swooping in and out of the mirror behind Harry. It cried once, but soundlessly, as though only its reflection had made a noise, and only Harry's might have heard it.

Someone else appeared in the mirror then, passing it noiselessly. The caretaker? Edie guessed, and hurried to catch up. She had the vague impression of a suit, black, hair, also black, and longer than now stylish, but this was country after all, remote, indeed aloof, and even time took a while to get there.

She reached the end of the passage and passed in and out of the mirror herself, as she pushed wider the door angled open beside the mirror.

The man in black, tall, with a long, youthful step, seemed preoccupied with matters as he strode the length of a large, airy, completely empty room. A dining room, it might have been, or a ballroom with windows on three sides overlooking the immensity of space and light around it, the river far below, the distant horizons, mountain slopes, a waterfall plunging endlessly over what looked like the edge of the world.

"Excuse me?" Edie called as the man opened doors in the inner wall at the far end of the room. He did not hear her; he disappeared again as he closed them quickly, competently behind him. Where could he be going? she wondered as she pursued him. What business could compel him so thoroughly in this deserted place? His dinner?

And where was Harry?

She flung open the doors to what must have been the reception room, with its high ceilings and pillars imitating those on the outer veranda. Neither the stranger nor Harry was anywhere in sight. Corridors and stairways to other rooms and floors branched away from this room. She called again through the accumulated silence of seasons, of years: "Harry?"

She heard faint, rhythmic footsteps above her, and she headed for the stairs.

At the top, a corridor of doors stretched the length of the entire building. Some were open, spilling afternoon light moted with golden dust onto the bare floorboards. Others were shut. She walked slowly, noiselessly down the hall, listening; light, shadow, again light filled her eyes. Ancient afternoons flickered past her from a time when every room was full, every window golden, and every door was closed.

She heard a murmuring, maybe doves, maybe at last a human voice, behind a door, and reached out to it quickly, opened it.

She had a confused, startling vision of color, of opulence, before she began to recognize what she saw: gold and blue velvet drapes, satin sheets edged with lace tumbling to the floor, a woman's face turned quickly away from the interloper, her youthful skin the color of cream, her chestnut hair unbound, loose across the satin. Her gown, ivory white and peach, tossed among the sheets, was sliding toward a dark, lovely carpet strewn with tiny red roses upon which her silver-buckled shoes lay where they had been tossed, and another shoe had just fallen.

The dark-haired man sitting among the bedclothes, gazed at Edie. He had not finished undressing. He was shirtless but had not yet taken off his trousers. His shoulders glowed in the gentle light behind the sheer inner curtains pulled loosely over the windows so that hawks and the heads of mountains could not peer in at them. The hair on his chest, a fine, soft dark, seemed as neat and carefully arranged as a garment. Half-naked, he still seemed clothed, exquisitely so, in his own body, his long, perfect bones, the muscles delineated with such precision under his gleaming skin that Edie's fingers longed to trace them, feel that hard warmth glide and shift under them.

The man, his young, comely face surprised, asked very politely in French, "Is there some way I can help you, Madame?"

Edie opened her mouth to answer.

Then she felt herself on fire, every inch, every pore of her, with horror and embarrassment. What had she almost said, what had she wanted to do? Ned had never inspired her fingertips; she had never felt his skin before she touched it. She had never seen, he had never, she had no idea, even naked, he or she, how such things could be, how wildly different, if. . . .

She answered, babbled, something back, and found herself in the hallway again, the door closed before she realized it, feeling as disheveled, mentally, as if she had been with them in that rumpled bed.

She drifted then, not seeing much, forgetting even Harry, until, eventually, she wandered back into the reception room and saw him there.

She looked at him across a distance, as though they had not seen, nor even thought of, one another in many years, and for a moment, she could not remember. . . .

Then she blinked and recognized the expression on his face: he seemed as bemused, as stunned, as she.

"Harry?"

"My dear Edie."

"You vanished so quickly—I was searching—"

"I thought I saw—" He hesitated. "I did see. In the end."

"What?" she breathed, astonished that he might tell her. She had no intention of revealing her own vision. Not, at least, to him.

"I thought I saw someone inside. A face, looking out at us as we drove up. At me. Someone I thought—I thought I recognized. So I followed."

"You left us," she reminded him, "without a word."

"No. Surely not. I distinctly remember saying—"

"No."

"Maybe it was something I heard," he said enigmatically. Even then, he scarcely saw her, she realized; his eyes were wide, haunted by his own vision. "So I went to find this man I thought I knew."

"And—" Her voice failed her again. "Did you?"

"He was always ahead of me, always just closing a door when I opened one, climbing stairs before I reached them, showing himself in mirrors when I thought I had lost him. I scarcely saw his face, just a quick profile, a half-turn, never anything so profound as an expression, and never his eyes."

Yes, she thought. Until the end.

"But every time I glimpsed him, he changed—"

"He—"

"In some small detail. In some strange emanation, as though in the air around him, or in his shadow. I could sense the changes, feel them. He never entirely disappeared, you understand, he stayed always within my glimpse, and yet—" He paused, drew a breath so full, so profound it might have been his last. "With every glimpse, I felt him grow farther and farther away from me. He made changes in himself that in the end I did not understand. As though we had ceased speaking the same language, and had never known each other at all."

"Who was he? Harry?"

He finally saw her again, his eyes clearing, yet strangely sad, mourning something he had never known.

"He finally let me see his face; he turned deliberately to look at me. He was myself. If I had taken a different path, made other choices, above all known that I had choices, and the strength to choose."

She stared at him wordlessly; he smiled, faintly, ruefully. "And you, my dear? What did you see?"

The choice, she thought. She answered simply, "Much the same."

The drive back to Hill House was very quiet. Somehow Thompson found his way out of the tangled forest and back to the bridge where Edie, out of habit, stirred from her trance and felt for her handbag. Absently, she proffered coins to the short, hairy figure who stumped out of his booth to stop them in the middle of the bridge. He seemed somehow less fantastical than he had been that morning. Or perhaps, she thought, her world had shifted, expanded, to let the fantastic in.

He huffed a snort at the coins in her hand, his mustachios fluttering in his breeze. "We agreed on half. Half of what you're bringing back."

"But that's all I've got—"

"Hah!" His eyes, dark as the water now and shrewd, almost seemed, in the last glow of light, to smile. "I want the other half of your stories."

Speechless, Edie dropped the coins back into her bag. She glanced at Harry, found his own eyes narrowed, half-dreaming, already beginning to calculate his half.

She felt the quickening in her own mind, the bloom of possibilities, the shift of image to word to structure, of dream awakening to true.

The toll-collector swept the great hat off his head and stepped aside with a flourish.

Thompson drove on down the suddenly unfamiliar road.

Alien

My grandmother Abby was sixty-nine when she got sucked up into the bowels of an alien spaceship and thoroughly examined. My grandfather had died a couple of years before, which we—her children and grandchildren—felt pretty much explained the incident of the alien, while at the same time illuminating what none of us had any desire to think about: the sex lives of our elders.

"Loneliness," my Aunt Sabrina decided.

"Dementia?" my husband, Gage, guessed tentatively, reluctant to let the word in the door in case it stuck around, refused to leave, became part of our family.

My sister Miranda's cute and icky boyfriend, Wallace, balancing precariously on the back legs of his chair, brought the front legs down with a thump. "Drugs," he declared officiously. "She taking anything new? My mom's on something that makes her see elephants in her bedroom. Sometimes an albino buffalo."

We looked at Beau and Sabrina, Abby's children, for that one. My parents hadn't arrived yet. My father, Abby's younger son, had laughed himself silly over the phone when he heard the news. So far that was the only opinion I'd heard from him. While my aunt and uncle sorted their thoughts, I heard the battle raging in the living room between Jedi Knights and the Evil Empire, punctuated with outraged accusations.

"You're dead!"

"Am not!"

"I shot you!"

"You missed!"

None of us sitting around the kitchen table with beer and seven kinds of roasted nuts wanted to deal with that. But when my one-year-old, Bertram, tottered like a drunken caveman into eyesight, his diaper drooping, his plump, milky body naked but for one sock, a look on his face of pure primal merciless focus as he stalked across the doorway, raising the plastic green baseball bat in his hands, I guessed I'd better take notice.

"Bertram!"

I joggled the table jumping up. Wallace's beer fell over and drained into his lap. He was up again on two chair legs; trying to go forward to right himself and get back away from the cold wet at the same time unbalanced him completely. He toppled back against the wall with a cry, echoed piercingly in the living room by the object of Bertram's attention. Miranda loosed an appalled "Shit!" The space war went suddenly silent; curious warriors slunk toward the doorway, avoiding the ruthless tangle on the floor of my two sons, both scrabbling for the bat and howling at the top of their lungs.

My husband sighed as he rose to the occasion. "So she got abducted by aliens. Does that mean she can't babysit anymore?"

We were supposed to be having our yearly family reunion. That meant RVs, tents for the kids, mountains and trees and lakes to absorb their relentless energy, while we watched in leisure from camp chairs, propping our feet on the beer coolers. My grandmother, materfamilias, was the still point of our gyrating lives, the one dot on the timeline from which the family radiated. We fretted over her after my grandfather died, wondering how, after forty-five years with him, she could survive without. She could and did, though to my youthful eyes she grew smaller, more vulnerable; even I had glimpsed the enormity that loomed over us all. She smiled and teared more easily, rarely criticized; she seemed genuinely grateful for the genial chaos we provided for her, as she sipped her single bottle of beer through the day and contemplated the distant peaks.

So it wasn't alcohol, and we didn't think it was depression, either, that made her quietly, stubbornly, refuse to leave her house for this summer's reunion.

"What if they come back?" she asked us, as, individually, we pleaded, cajoled, argued that it was not possible to have a family reunion without her.

So we all crowded in with Uncle Beau's family, who lived out of town on several acres, in a rambling old farmhouse. They had the biggest driveway for the RVs, the widest lawns for the children's tents, and were only a few miles from Beau's mother's place.

"What the heck does she mean by that?" Beau was the first to demand. "You'd think she wants them back. That's not how it happens in the movies."

His and his wife Greer's children were my age, twenty-something; so were Uncle Sam and Aunt Sabrina's two. Miranda and I had grown up running barefoot through hot, dusty forests in late August with our cousins, then leaping into lake water to clean ourselves off. In later years, we lay outside our tents at midnight, watching shifting stars and planets, roaming satellites and the occasional distant airplane, in a sky so vast and black, it could roll over us and pull us into itself like a tide. I could feel the earth moving under me on those nights, a little whirling ball working its way around the sun, which was busy finding its own path around the galaxy in great, slow, astonishing measures of time that gave no more thought to my tiny life than I gave to the ant I slapped off my ankle. On those nights I could imagine that flying saucer with blue lights like a scallop's fringe of eyes around its shell, or that humungous birthday cake lit like a Vegas casino descending out of the stars, drawing us all up into its lights, and just maybe, before it sent us all back to our mundane lives, giving us an altered point of view, a glimpse out of alien eyes, of what all this dark, this fire, this unimaginable infinity meant. I was a minute flicker of fire aware of its existence, aware that it could be blown out at any second. What was the meaning of everything?

Then I did those other things: fell in love, went to college, went to work, fell in love again, got married, had two boys. I learned to live without answers. After a while, I forgot the questions.

"Drugs," Uncle Beau repeated blankly, after Wallace had mopped himself off and Gage had put out the brush fires in the living room. Beau cocked an eyebrow at his sister. Women kept track of everyone's ailments and who was taking what for them. Aunt Sabrina only looked questioningly at me. I had bought Grandma Abby her first cell phone, taught her how to use it. She became an avid fan, calling and texting at whim. But she hadn't told me that.

I shrugged. "She hasn't mentioned anything new lately. My mother might know."

But my parents were still on the road, having stopped for a visit to the more sedate reunion of my father's family, which involved restaurants and hotels instead of burned hot dogs under a pine tree. Also among the missing were Sabrina's two children, my cousins Alys and Sydney. Sydney and her husband, Lyle, were still on the road with their two little girls, Meade and Dulcie, who loved my impossible toddlers and even had a soothing effect on Reed and Holly's turbulent boys, Luke, Han, and Indiana. What, we all wondered, had they expected, with those names? Choirboys? Reed and Holly had dropped them off at Uncle Beau's earlier and fled to a wedding a couple hundred miles away. They'd be back soon as possible, they'd assured us. Aunt Greer was running a betting pool on that promise. My cousin Alys had just started a new job and couldn't get away. Beau and Greer's son Marshall had gone off to do good in some impoverished country rather than face the wild horde of his own family, and was out of the loop re: alien spaceships.

I made a sudden decision then, and stood up, this time without spilling beers and boyfriends.

"I'll call her and ask."

I went outside onto the wide wraparound porch for a quiet place to talk. The moon was a spill of light and a silvery rim pushing up behind a dark peak. I looked for ships in the inky sky while my grandmother's cell sounded. I had a sudden vision of her phone calling an empty house, her favorite chair still rocking, something—the umbrella stand—knocked over, the front door wide open. I was actually startled when she said my name.

"Maggie! Where are you, sweetheart? And why are you there and not over here with me?"

"I'm at Uncle Beau's with everybody. Shall I come over and get you?"

She didn't answer immediately; I waited.

"Oh," she said slowly, "I don't think so."

"But the little ones—they'd love to see you."

"Maybe tomorrow. During the day. I'll drive over then."

"Promise?"

"I do, dear."

"If I don't see you, I'll come and get you."

"Oh," she said again, a definite sigh this time. "I do get tired of all the questions. Nobody really wants to hear my answers. Their eyes glaze over; they turn everything I say into some one-word explanation. Boredom. Or gin."

I swallowed a laugh, feeling guilty at the same time. "Well, nobody's suggested boredom yet. But they did wonder if Dr. Gresham prescribed any new drugs."

"Drugs? Not since Scott died. And I stopped taking those ages ago. Why?"

"Miranda's new boyfriend says his mother takes a prescription drug that makes her hallucinate elephants."

"No—really?"

"And a white buffalo."

"What's she on, dear? I might like some of that."

I let her hear my laugh this time. "I'll ask him."

"And how is this new boyfriend? Do we approve?"

I made a face only the moon saw. "He's okay. Lots of muscle, cute face, pretty pleased with himself. Maybe I'm just too protective. No one will ever be good enough for my sister."

"And how are you, Maggie? You and Gage."

I smiled again. We talked a while. I told her funny stories about the boys; she reminisced about my grandfather. Then she said, out of the blue, as we were drawing the conversation to a close, "Do you know that their mating rituals are entirely different?"

My fingers tightened on my cellphone; it beeped. I pushed it against my ear as though that would help me understand her. "Who? Buffalo, you mean?"

"No, they're nothing like the buffalo," she answered patiently. "Nothing at all. More like—well—salmon, if anything on earth. I have to go, sweets. I'm supposed to turn on my TV now. I'll come and see you all tomorrow."

"Gran. I'm coming over now."

But she had ended the call before she heard me. I went back inside and Bertram grabbed me, pushing his face against my knees and wailing. Fargo barreled into both of us, got an arm-lock on my thighs, trying to outwail Bertram. I could smell Bertram's diaper. Through the kitchen doorway I saw Gage pop an almond into his mouth, chase it with an upended beer.

In that moment, the spaceship flitted into my mind, layered like a wedding cake, ringed with lights, engines humming in lovely harmony, vast portals sliding slowly open to draw me up and away, far, far away, to the place where nobody knew where I was, and I would never know what was going to happen next.

Aunt Greer and I wrestled my two into bed; Aunt Sabrina came to read them a story while Greer and I got Holly's boys into their sleeping bags in the pup tent on the lawn. We left them with their ray guns for protection and enough cheesy snackie thingies to dye their teeth orange by morning.

By that time my grandmother's space alien had dwindled in memory; all I wanted was an ice-cold beer.

Uncle Beau glanced up vaguely as we came back into the kitchen; he had forgotten we had gone. Then he heard the quiet. His face brightened and he sighed expansively. "Ah. Peace." His wife and his sister glared at him; he didn't notice that either. He went back to frowning, cracking a peanut between his thumbs. "Thing is, if it is dementia, we've got decisions to make." He looked across the table at me as I slid into my chair next to Gage. "Did you get hold of her? Or was she off gallivanting in the stars?"

"I talked to her." I paused to drink, and bits of our conversation came back. "She said she wasn't taking any new meds. She seemed—well, like herself. Clearheaded and cheerful." Then I remembered more. "At least—"

"At least what?" Miranda prodded.

"Well." I rubbed my eyes with beer-cold fingers. "We talked about the kids and about Grandpa; she said she'll drive herself over here tomorrow. Then she made some weird comment about alien mating rituals. How they were sort of like salmon. Then she said she had to go turn on the TV and she hung up." In the sudden silence, I added reluctantly, "It sounded as though turning on the TV had something to do with the aliens."

"Wow," Miranda said softly.

Uncle Beau's jaw set; he consulted Aunt Sabrina with his eyes. Wallace remained tactfully silent, letting his expression tell us that he could have told us so.

Gage had a funny look on his face, as though he were chewing on something bizarre in his mind.

"Salmon," he said. "They find their way back to the place where they were born to spawn. Is that what she meant by alien mating rituals?"

"Wasn't that a *Star Quest* episode?" Uncle Beau muttered.

"They come back here?" Miranda said, straightening suddenly. "To earth?"

"Well, this is where she saw them."

"Then they'd be—"

"Our older smarter ancestors," I finished. "Yeah."

"Very much older," Gage said. "Like before dinosaurs."

"And so much smarter they figured out how to fly way back then."

"But wait," Wallace said, catching up. "What if the aliens were just passing through on their way to someplace else and—"

"And got stopped cold by mom's stunning beauty and obvious ability to procreate," Aunt Sabrina said wryly. "Sure."

"Well, maybe they're just scientists taking a look—"

Uncle Beau dropped his hand flat on the table, causing bottles to tremble. "You're all talking like it might have happened," he complained. "The point is she invented it. It's a dream. Her imagination. That's what we've got to deal with. Aliens in her brain, not in the sky. There's got to be a pill for that." He cracked another peanut, emptied the shell into his mouth. His eyes went to his sister again, questioning. "When she comes over tomorrow, we'll make an appointment for her with Dr. Gammon. Okay?"

Aunt Sabrina shrugged, picked up her beer. "Can't do any harm," she said wearily. "But let's not make her feel bad. Let's try to get her to stay here with us. She can turn on the TV for them here if she has to. They can land on your lawn."

"Sure," Uncle Beau said. "We'll feed them hot dogs."

A young face peered around the doorway behind him; not one of mine, I saw with relief.

"Mom?" It was Indiana, with his ray gun in one hand. "I mean, Grandma?"

"What do you need, Hon?" Aunt Greer asked.

"There was something funny in the sky. I think I shot it."

Nobody breathed. Then we all moved at once, scrambling over toys, books, each other for the screen door, left unlatched for the campers. We spilled out onto the porch, all of us assuming the same position: gripping the porch railing, heads tilted, staring up at the starry sky, hunting for whatever moved.

Then Gage spoke. "Wait."

"It's plastic," Uncle Beau said heavily. "It's a toy. We gave them to the boys for—" He turned his head toward Aunt Greer. "Last Christmas? Wasn't it?"

She nodded, her hands loosening on the railing. "Runs on double D batteries. Like a flashlight. And just about as dangerous."

Wallace gave a dry little chuckle. But I had seen his face, as stunned and thoughtless as any of us before we hit the porch.

"She's got us all going," Gage breathed.

Indiana gestured vaguely at the moon with his ray gun. "It was over there."

"What was, son?" Uncle Beau asked without a great deal of curiosity.

"Whatever it was. I shot it with my ray gun and it blinked out."

"Well. Good work." He took the plastic weapon, aimed it at a passing moth. Neither the eerie noise nor the whirling coils of colored light seemed to have any effect; the moth fluttered on by, ignoring the attack entirely. Uncle Beau gave the gun back. "You probably saved the universe. Now get into your sleeping bag and hold your fire until morning so you don't wake Maggie's boys."

He dropped a kiss on Indiana's head and sent him down the porch steps.

"What did we all come running out here to see?" I asked bewilderedly, as Indiana squirmed back into the pup tent.

"Pre–dinosaur age salmon flying back here in their spaceship to spawn with our grandmother, I guess," Miranda said.

"Well, that doesn't make sense on any level," Wallace declared earnestly. "Number one, fish don't spawn with humans. Number two, why would they want somebody as old—" We were all laughing by then; he gave up. "Oh, never mind. The whole thing's ridiculous."

Gage lingered with me as the others filed back in. He put his arms around me. We watched the stars, wanting and not wanting strangeness, change, danger. Wanting and not wanting aliens.

My grandmother drove herself over the next day, as promised. She sat on the porch with a beer in her hand, listening patiently but without a great deal of attention to our questions and suggestions. Maybe she'd be happier in a place where she could make friends? Maybe her house, where she and Grandpa Scott had lived for a quarter of a century, had gotten too empty for her?

"How would they find me if I moved?" she asked puzzledly, causing Uncle Beau, grilling burgers for lunch, to flip a patty onto the lawn.

"Why," he demanded, "do you want a bunch of mutant fish to find you?"

"Oh, hush, Beau," Greer said, though my grandmother seemed to be doing a fine job of ignoring everyone. She sat in the glider with Bertram on her lap and Fargo pushed close against her. Her shoes were off; she ran fingers through her hair, smiling gently into the summer breeze. She was there and not there, waiting for someone who hadn't yet arrived. She looked, I thought incredulously, exactly like a woman in love.

"Grandma Abby?" I said, my voice going small, childish.

She looked at me, still smiling, without seeing me. "Yes, dear?"

"Mom," Sabrina said gently, sitting on the other side of Fargo, rocking the glider with the tip of her shoe. "We're worried about you. This story about space aliens—it can't possibly be true. Why would you make something like that up?"

"Well, I wouldn't, would I?" she answered, taking a small, precise sip of beer. "That would be just silly."

"We'd like to make an appointment for you with Dr. Gammon. Okay, Mom?"

She shrugged. "I feel fine."

"I—we thought maybe you could have a little chat with him. About your aliens."

My grandmother's expression changed; she looked directly at her oldest child, her lips thinning. "My aliens. You don't believe anything I've said."

Sabrina drew a big breath, let it out. "Not a word."

"Well." Grandma Abby leaned back again, her gaze shifting back to the horizon that, last night, we had all stared at, mesmerized by intimations of aliens. "You weren't there, were you."

Sabrina rolled her eyes at the porch roof, shook her head mutely. She got up after a moment, went inside to make the phone call, I guessed. I left my perch on the porch railing, and went to lean on the glider frame. Bertram was asleep on my grandmother's lap; Fargo uncurled into the space Sabrina had vacated, propped his head on a cushion and hummed a faint little tune while he ran a tiny toy Ferrari up and down his bare leg. Aunt Greer was setting the picnic table; Miranda and Wallace had wandered off into the trees. I heard Gage inside the house, playing some kind of online game with Holly's boys.

I said very softly, "What are they like, Gran?"

She answered after a moment, still watching the empty sky above the trees. "Like nothing you could possibly imagine."

I tried anyway. The swamp monster? Something dark, mysterious, capable of passion? A silvery, scaly Cary Grant? A reptilian creature with three sets of teeth and a sense of humor? A being that could change its shape to match anything you wanted?

I studied my grandmother, with her short white hair, her skin drooping, melting away from her bones. I had inherited her blue-gray eyes, her oval face, her hair that once had been heavy, dark, and smooth. With a sudden prickle of premonition I saw myself in her, that alien in me, waiting patiently, appearing little by little, line by line, hair by turning hair, until one day I was taken over by nothing I could possibly have imagined.

She glanced behind her, listening for Sabrina, and began to stand up. I took Bertram from her before he woke. Uncle Beau and Aunt Greer had their backs to her, turning hot dogs and burgers on the grill. "I have to go," she whispered, and put her forefinger on her lips. She touched my lips with that finger, that kiss.

"I'll come with you, Gran. Let me come. Let me see."

She shook her head, picked up her sandals, walked quietly down the steps. "They only come if I'm alone."

"Gran—"

"I'll call you later, I promise."

"Don't go anywhere," I begged, and she smiled again, that look back in her eyes of anticipating wonders.

Years later, when I was middle-aged and she was very old, I went to visit her at the rest home and she broke her very long silence. I had wheeled her outside to the tiny, sunny rose garden; I sat on a bench beside her, amusing her with tales of Bertram's upcoming wedding, which at that point in the preparations involved surfboards.

Reminded, maybe by the fierce, underlying point of all the froth and bother, she said out of the blue, "Something must have disturbed them. Frightened them away. Or they saw something that they couldn't make sense of in their terms. You know. They interpreted it badly." Oddly enough, after all that time I knew exactly what she was talking about. "That night when you called me from Beau and Greer's house, that was the last night I saw them."

A child's plastic toy gun popped into my mind for no reason, I thought, until, examining the image idly, I remembered. I closed my eyes, saw Indiana's small, worried face, Uncle Beau shooting the ray gun, how it wailed and spat its colored rings of light while the moth fluttered through them. How we had all stood on the porch, gripping the railing, staring into the stars, seized, shaken, possessed by the possibility of aliens.

I opened my eyes again, saw my grandmother smiling faintly, reminiscently. I leaned over, kissed her cheek, and tried not to wonder if one day far into my future they might return to look for her, misinterpret my aged face for hers, and come for me instead.

Something Rich and Strange

Full fathom five thy father lies;
Of his bones are coral made: Those are pearls that were his eyes:
Nothing of him that doth fade, But doth suffer a sea-change
Into something rich and strange.
—The Tempest

ONE

MEGAN DIPPED HER HAND into the tide pool, drew the shining out of the sea.

It was the gold foil, wire, and cap from a champagne bottle someone had flicked into the water. She dropped it into the capacious pocket of her jacket, already jingling with beer caps, the plastic lid off a gallon of milk, a couple of sand dollars, blue and yellow sea glass, half of a Styrofoam float, a flattened Orange Crush can, and a three-quarter-ounce weight knotted to a foot of fishing line. She waited for the water to still, then studied the pool again. A dozen sea urchins, a starfish, chitons, anemones. . . . She pulled the sand dollars out of her pocket, poised them in the sand beneath the starfish, waited for the ripples to subside. Something she had disturbed on the bottom rose to the surface of the pool. She fished it out: foil from a cigarette pack. She rolled it into a ball between her fingers, dropped it into her pocket, her mind still absorbed by the pool, the line of rock that formed it, the bits of broken shell, sandstone, agate jumbled on the bottom. She eased into a smooth place among the barnacles beneath her, and began to draw rapidly, before the tide turned.

She was a tall, lean, taciturn young woman, with long straight pale hair that she let grow past her waist. Her blue-gray eyes could be found, not easily, under the drift of her hair, or beneath the reflections in her glasses. She drew seascapes in ink and pencil and hung them in Jonah's shop, among the jewelry and fossils and shells and other oddments he sold. Three years before, he had hired Megan to paint a shop sign. She had shown him her seascapes; he had hung a few; tourists had bought them. Somehow, despite his crotchety manner and her reticence, they had, in the sort of dart-and-dance courtship displayed by mute and easily startled fish, indicated an interest in one another. His eyes opened and glittered beneath his shaggy hair; she flashed her sudden, rare smile. So they lived together above Things Rich and Strange, the shop beside the sea, where changing tides of sound tumbled constantly about them as if they were creatures in some invisible tide pool.

Something waved at Megan from a cleft in the stone: a tiny crab, venturing out. She waited for it, drew it as it picked its way across the bottom. She studied the drawing, added some graceful fronds of sea moss. Lately she had started experimenting with pale, delicate washes of color over black ink. Jonah, who thought pastel colors were trendy, commercial, and sentimental, disapproved. "Next thing," he grumbled, "you'll be making kittens out of cowrie shells." But, as Megan pointed out, shoving massive oceanography books under his nose, the secret sea, beneath its bland surface, was garish with color.

Wind rippled the water. Megan, waiting for the starfish to come into focus again, debated color. The starfish was crimson; she could try a light red wash. Something popped suddenly to the surface and floated: the champagne cork. She stared at it, and then at her drawing, wondering if she had absently sketched a cork in among the sea anemones. She picked it out, put it in her pocket. Gulls cried overhead; pelicans flew low over the distant tide. She tasted salt on her lips. The water shivered again, wind-stroked; the wind was rising. She felt chilled suddenly, sitting on a cold gray rock under a gray sky. She leaned down to gather her sand dollars. The wind grabbed her hair out of her jacket, tossed it over her shoulder, into her mouth, into the water. She spat hair irritably, groping for the shells. An anemone sucked at her finger. A pen she had balanced among the barnacles rolled into the water. She groped for that, too, stirring sand into a roiling cloud. Her fingers hit something smooth, hard. She pulled it out: a beer bottle.

She checked her drawing incredulously: no sign of a beer bottle. It must, she decided, have been buried in the sand; her groping had uncovered it. She stuffed it into her pocket, retrieved the shells and, finally, the pen. She gazed into the pool, thinking: now what? The champagne bottle? The pool, suddenly limpid, gave her back her face: great, square eyes, a little hard mouth, like a parrotfish's mouth, fit for nibbling coral, long pale tentacles that searched the air for microscopic life. Entranced by the fishy vision, she no longer recognized herself.

She pulled back, remembered her own face. She slid the drawing pad into its waterproof case and stood up slowly, cramped and weighted with flotsam and jetsam. "You can't sweep the sea," Jonah would say as she pulled garbage and treasure from her pockets. "No," she would answer, "but I can tidy a tide pool." Then she would show him her drawings.

She had three that day: one a mound of sea urchins, one a carpet of anemones, and the last, which he lingered over longest, intent, musing, picking at his teeth with his thumb. He took his hand away from his mouth finally, pointed.

"I don't recognize this."

Megan looked over his shoulder; their heads touched. Sea lettuce, she was about to say, glancing at the shapeless, fluid lines. The word caught; her mouth stayed open. It wasn't algae; it had an eye; it crawled across the bottom, small, rippling, horned. She took a breath, perplexed.

"I don't either."

Jonah watched her as she pored through her books. She sat on a stool beside the counter dividing the kitchen and dining room, drinking tea out of a clay mug, her head bent, her smooth, pale hair spilling over the book, her hands, her knees. He loved her hands: slender, long-boned, beautifully proportioned. She could moor a boat with those hands, hammer a nail, pitch a tent. She could fold origami paper into a bird; she could draw a spider web strung with dew. Now her hands were flicking pages as she searched through photographs of underwater life for the odd little animal wandering through her drawing. The wind was rattling the windows; the full tide sounded as if it were heaving great driftwood logs and old sunken ships across the beach to their doorway.

He said, "What was that old tale about a ship? A flying ship?" He was sorting through rocks and fossils he had pulled from the cliffs that day: bits and pieces of sandstone, half a clam, a worm tube. They were scattered over the dining table; he was not particularly tidy. She tugged at her lip, studying something.

"The USS *Enterprise*?"

"No—you know. An old sailing ship. A ghost ship, wanders around scaring sailors on foggy nights."

"Oh. *Flying Dutchman.*"

"Yeah."

"Why?"

"I think it's at the door."

Her eyes lifted, regarded him vaguely behind her glasses. Had he, they wondered, said what he had said? They lost interest, dropped again, to what looked like a floating candy store. Tropical fish: he had a tank when he was a kid. The thermostat broke one day; the temperature plummeted and fish went belly up, floating like petals on top of the water.

"One of those?" he asked, bored. She got obsessed, sometimes, working. She disappeared on him, the way an anemone did, drawing in tighter and tighter the more you prodded. But she heard him; she shook her head.

"No. It's not a fish. But look at those colors—lemon, turquoise, indigo—"

"Pepto-Bismol."

"Orange sherbet."

"Pickled ginger."

"Puce."

"Lime," he shot back, but weakly; she had disarmed him with the puce. She had already submerged herself in the coral reef. He leaned over his collection: a tall, wiry man with long red-brown rippling hair, cobalt eyes, glasses in round black frames he aimed at customers like cannon muzzles if they annoyed him. He had hired Jenny Elwood to work the register for him, at Megan's suggestion; he looked, she said, too pained when someone wanted him to handle money. Megan herself looked incredulous behind the register. She picked at it dubiously as if she didn't trust it to do the same thing twice; she could barely find her mouth to answer a question.

She found her mouth now. "Nudibranch."

"Nudiwho?"

"Or worm, maybe. Or a mollusk without a shell."

"Banana slug."

She ignored his suggestion, but became suddenly articulate. "It's so strange. I don't remember drawing it at all, it just appeared, the way things kept popping up after I cleared the water, like the champagne cork and the beer bottle. I never even noticed the beer bottle."

"Beer," he said, and went around her to the ancient refrigerator. "Want one?"

"I don't suppose the champagne bottle is in there."

"Dream on. This thing is making slime again."

"What thing?"

"The refrigerator. It's bleeding black slime out of this little pipe."

"Uh."

"The truck sounds like a motorcycle, the refrigerator's falling apart, the rent on the store is going up next month, and you're sitting there reading about naked slugs."

She lifted her head. One eye regarded him thoughtfully between strands of her hair. He saw her lips part, the beginning of her smile. He put the beer down. Her lips tasted of salt; her hair smelled of the sea; her ear was a pale, whorled thing that could only be understood by his tongue. Grazing, he loosened the jewel at her earlobe, swallowed it, and found out much later, as he lay in bed contemplating her other ear, that he had dined on opal and drunk gold.

She was reading again, naked on her stomach, her chin on one hand, absently fingering the remaining earring. She made a sudden sound, a little hiccup of discovery.

"They're not horns."

"I can't tell you how relieved I am."

"They're ears."

"A worm with ears."

"A shell-less snail. Not real ears. Rabbit ears."

"A snail with rabbit ears."

"Little protrusions that look like ears. It's called a sea hare." She paused, reading, frowning. She changed hands under her chin, fingered the other ear. "It shoots purple ink when it's disturbed, it can lay twenty million eggs, and it's both male and female."

"Wow."

"Where's my earring?"

"I ate it."

"No, really," she said, feeling around the sheets. He moved closer, pulled by some strange inner tide.

"You're obsessed by ears," he breathed, feeling the cool drop of gold on his tongue. Then she turned under him, her arms around his back, her head on the open book. He saw the sea hare floating in and out of her hair before he closed his eyes and she pulled him with her long white arms down beneath the waves.

Megan went back the next day to the tide pool. She recognized not so much the pool itself as the bare place among the barnacles where she had sat. The starfish had moved an inch or two; the anemones were closed. There was no sign of a sea hare.

She stood after a while, her arms folded, gazing out past the great rocks strewn along the tide line, where the waves churned and broke, to the vast gray plane of water. She had been looking into tide pools all her life, having grown up in the northernmost coastal town in the state. Drawing the sea, she had slowly drifted south, through small fishing ports and smaller towns where travelers could buy a tank of gas, a hamburger, a coffee cup with the name of the town on it, a motel room that overlooked the sea. Fishers, loggers, retired people lived in those tiny towns; or like Jonah, people looking for a quiet spot to read or dig up fossils for the rest of their lives. Such people clung, barnacle-like, to the cliffs, in houses facing seaward. Others, like the sea hare, traveled through, vanished, having no real business in a tide pool. Some freaky wave had flipped it that far ashore, she guessed, even while a cold, clear voice in the back of her mind said: there was no sea hare in the tide pool. The sea hare crawled into the drawing.

She didn't draw that day; she walked back into town. Though it was still barely spring, the license plates on cars were already migratory: California, Nevada, Idaho, even an Arizona on a Winnebago parked near Jonah's shop. They were wanderers, following the paths of birds and whales, wanting to bring home visions, landscapes, the echo of barking seals, the endless siren song of the waves at the edge of the world. Browsing along the street, they would buy strands of abalone beads, driftwood vases, shells for ashtrays. They would buy canned Chinook salmon at Ernie's Fish and Bait. They would get lost, scowl over maps, throw caramel corn at seagulls, snap at one another and their children. They would eat clam fritters, oyster sandwiches, crab cocktail at Lindy's Cafe. Then they would lean over the sea walls at lookout points, their faces wistful, slightly perplexed, as if they were trying to understand some lost language that they once knew, in a distant time when seals walked ashore like men, before all the mermaids changed to manatees.

What, their faces would ask, do these barking seals, this smell of brine and guano, this vastness no Winnebago can cross have to do with me? Then they would get back into their cars so they could reach the next star on the map before dark. A wanderer herself, Megan knew the lure of the road, the peculiar quest for freedom that had the safe lights of home at the end. The journey was more important than the place; most important was to return home, with crumpled maps, salt and pepper shakers shaped like clamshells, a sweatshirt with whales on it, and to be able to say: I have been there, I have gone on a journey, I have come safely home. The world was a dangerous place for mollusks without their shells, and yet they ventured into it, restless, curious, or maybe following some ancient migratory instinct to return to the place where souls were spawned.

Megan herself wandered into Mike's Twice-Sold Tales, where she browsed among the marine-life books, hoping for some new insight into sea hares. But those she encountered led, it seemed, a life scarcely worth mentioning, tagged onto a paragraph or decorating an illustration of chains of species. Mike, a huge man with a nicotine-stained mustache, as chatty as a sea urchin, glanced up from his antique *Moby-Dick* and lifted a thumb. Translated, it was a greeting, discussion of health, the weather, business, and a general recognition of the species Resident-Who-Has-Shared-Winter-Storms-Love-Loneliness-Stir-Craziness-General-Inbred-Insanity-That-Comes-Before-the-First-Tourist. He was back in his book, dissecting whales, before she could respond.

She went back to Jonah's shop, where he was in much the same position, reading some antique geology book on a stool in a corner, while Jenny gave change and smiled at the customers. He grunted at her, a conversational gambit that said less than Mike's thumb: I'm-Okay-You're-Okay-I'm-Busy-You'll-Be-Busy-Store's-Okay-Okay? He turned a page; she went into the back room to put a pale wash of red across the starfish, and a wash of lavender so diluted it was barely visible across the sea hare.

"God, you've ruined it," Jonah commented later, on his way to the bathroom. She whirled at him, indignant.

"Jonah!"

"How about some tangerine while you're at it?"

She studied the drawing. It did need another color, something neutral. "I'm not one of your customers," she said coldly. "Go crab at them."

"I'm sorry. It hurts my eyes."

"Thanks." She lifted a shoulder as he kissed her ear. "And stay away from my ears."

"A trifle sensitive, aren't we?"

"I spent hours in the cold working on this sketch, and you just walk in and tell me I ruined it."

"It was a beautiful sketch. And then you put those Popsicle colors on it. It's just a matter of taste, that's all. I'm not trying to tell you how to paint."

"You are, too," she said between her teeth. "You have no more sensitivity than a three-year-old."

"Well, maybe you should try some primary colors while you're at it. If that's what's in the sea."

"Maybe you should go look for my earring."

"Excuse me," Jenny said, parting the back curtains. "There's someone here who makes jewelry." She closed the curtains again briskly, leaving an impression on the eye of silver rinse, glittering glasses, pink lipstick, two rhinestone cats on a chain holding her sweater together, a fashion statement that Megan associated with fox heads dangling from your shoulders and circle skirts with poodles on them. Jenny, Jonah said once, was the kind of person who would crochet a Kleenex box holder. But he needed her: she was competent, she liked people, even Jonah, she was unflappable through all his moods, even when she stumbled into a squall.

"That's all I need," Jonah said sourly. "More jewelry." He disappeared into the bathroom and called, peremptorily, "You talk to him. Her. I can't."

Megan stared icily at the curtain, wanting to toss the red wash over the top of it. A coffee wash, she thought suddenly, between the red and the lavender. Cafe au lait. A diagonal line down the rock, spilling into the sand.

She parted the curtains. The jewelry maker stood at the counter, studying what Jonah had beneath the glass. She paused half a step, blinking. There was too much of him for the shop. Too much of him for the town, she thought. He didn't belong in this tide pool. He was quite tall, dressed in black denim and leather; his short hair was whiter than Jenny's. He wore an earring in one ear. He turned at her step and smiled. He smiles, she thought. His eyes were pale green, the misty color the sea got sometimes when the sun broke behind the clouds. She was too amazed to smile back.

"This is Megan," said Jenny the unflappable.

"She'll help you. Megan, this is Adam I-didn't-catch-your—"

He held out his hand, the one without the box in it. "Fin." His hand was broad, strong, gentle. "I've just come into town. I've been showing samples of my work at other shops. They all said I should talk to Jonah. You have some very nice pieces already. Are they local?"

"Mostly," Megan said. She had to clear her throat. "Jonah gets some things inland, when he goes fossil swapping. Where are you from?" In God's name, she wanted to add, and what are you doing here?

He waved a hand in the general direction of Hawaii. "East." He smiled again, showing white teeth, and she laughed a little, because it was so rare, after a long winter, to see a face that wasn't dour.

"That's west."

"Oh, yeah. I'm a little turned around on land. The mainland." He opened his box, a simple rosewood case, beautifully mitered and polished.

He used opal and onyx, all colors of jade, aventurine with gold, amethyst with malachite, pearl and garnet and peridot. Some of the settings looked antique; others were richly barbaric, or as simple and elegant as his box. She lifted her eyes to his face after a while, astonished, and saw in the simple, elegant lines of it something that might, under a wash of gold light, or a subtle change of expression, turn as wild and exotic as his work could turn. She swallowed. "It's beautiful." His face changed slightly; she blinked. "Your work. Do you do your own carving?"

He nodded. She noticed his earring then: an onyx rabbit sprinting, legs outstretched, back arched, a silver quarter moon curved over it, the moon's horns rising out of the rabbit's feet. "I see my own designs like dreams in my head," he said. "I like to make them visible."

"So do I," she said, surprised, and he looked at her. He was oddly pale for an islander, she thought suddenly. Maybe he had come even farther than she guessed: from some ancient, foreign seaport where every language in the world was spoken at once.

"You're an artist?"

"Just pen and ink," she said, suddenly shy, unused to discussing her work with strangers. She made a brief gesture at the far wall. "Just seascapes."

He walked through the shop to see them. People glanced twice at him, recognizing him, and then trying to figure out who they imagined he was. He seemed oblivious of the attention. He studied an anemone attached to a barnacle-covered rock. Its tendrils, open and flowing with the tide, were flushed with a faint green wash. Below it, a pale pink wash spilled out of a starfish's arms, colored some algae, and drained into pearl-pale sand.

"I like the colors," he said, returning. He studied her again, as intently as he had studied the anemone. "Do you do only seascapes?"

She nodded, forgetting her shyness then, under his calm gaze. "Always. I always have. It's all I've ever wanted to draw. I don't know why. Maybe because it's a world I can't enter. I can't belong in it, the way I can belong on land. This is the closest I can get—the only way I have of belonging. Of understanding." She flushed a little. "I can't explain. I can only draw it."

"Yes," he said softly. His eyes held hers a moment longer; she became aware, in the brief silence, of the tide gathering and breaking and spilling across the sand, regathering itself, breaking again. She heard his breath gathering. Then she moved, touching her glasses straight, and his face turned from her as he closed his box.

"I love your work." Her voice sounded odd. "But you'll have to talk to Jonah. It's his shop."

"I see. Then I'll leave this here for Jonah."

"You don't want to take it with you?" she asked, amazed. He put the box into her hands and smiled again, lightly.

"I'm sure it will be safe with you. Jonah has a good reputation. I'll come back tomorrow; maybe he'll see me then."

She watched him through the window as he crossed the street, turned a corner; the smooth satiny wood in her hands seemed still warm from his touch. Jenny, ever efficient, suggested briskly, "You'll want to take that upstairs before someone buys it."

Megan turned her head, stared at Jenny. "What's he doing here? He belongs south. Where everyone looks like that."

Jenny shrugged. "He washed ashore here. You did. Jonah did. Seemed nice, didn't he? More like one of us than one of them."

Megan nodded, her face easing at the familiar division of Jenny's world. "I'm just not used to one of us being one of them."

"Bet," Jenny said, springing the cash register open for a customer, "he was born here. Right here on these cliffs. There you are, Mandy. Enjoy."

Jonah, annoyed by Megan's insistence that he go upstairs and look at jewelry when the last thing the store needed was more, kept to his stool behind the register, answering questions about the fossils now and then when people interrupted his reading. He concluded, from Jenny's sporadic comments, that Megan had been persuaded by some blond in tight black jeans; she had probably not noticed much beyond that. He avoided the back room, not wanting to pick another fight while she laid New Age colors on her perfect drawings. Going upstairs finally, after he closed the shop, he found the rosewood box on the table in the middle of his rocks.

He ignored it, going to the stove where Megan was stirring dill seed into cabbage. The smell reminded him of low tide in mud flats. She wore long glittering strands of jet beads in her ears; he considered them, found them too formidable. His hands were closing in on her hips when she spoke.

"Have you looked at Adam's jewelry?"

His hands curved on air, dropped. "Adam." He wandered away, ate a piece of cabbage. "Jenny says he looks like a refugee from Beverly Hills."

"Jenny did not say that; you did." She added kielbasa to the cabbage. "He can still make jewelry. Go look at it."

"Later." He rummaged in the fridge: no beer. Lifting his head, he saw her New Age washes staining the horizon: pale crimson shading into lilac, where the sun was going down. The close smell of cabbage, the soft spring colors, made him suddenly restless. "Let's go out."

"Now?"

"After supper. There's music at the Ancient Mariner."

"I was going to finish framing the drawings."

"Do it tomorrow."

"Adam's coming back to talk to you tomorrow."

"Funny," he said, munching more raw cabbage, "how irritating some names are. Adam. Nobody's named Adam, except Batman."

She turned slowly, gave him that blank, blue-gray stare. "What are you talking about?"

"You keep saying his name."

She rapped the spoon on the edge of the pan: maybe a comment, maybe just getting cabbage off the spoon. "What do you want me to call him?"

"Bill. Joe. I don't want you saying his name, this blond god from L.A. I want you to say my name."

Her eyes were still blank, cool, but her lips quirked suddenly. "He liked my washes."

"He would. He's from the land that invented mango garbage-can liners. Apricot bomber jackets. They don't even eat things that aren't pastel."

She rapped the spoon again, but the corners of her mouth were still crooked. "He's not from L.A. He's from the east. I mean west."

"What?"

"West. Like Hawaii. Or Fiji. Tokyo."

"That's the Far East."

"Well, maybe that's why he got confused."

"So am I. You're still talking about him."

She sighed, put the spoon down. "Jonah. You're driving me crazy."

"I know," he said penitently. "I'm sorry. Let's go out. I've got cabin fever. Turn off the cabbage. Let's go for a walk. Please?"

They went out the back door, walked until dark, picking up shells, agates, looking for glass floats. The beach was adrift with velella, tiny purple sailboats as delicate as butterfly wings that caught the wind and sailed the surface of the sea. Some storm had tumbled them ashore; dried, light as leaves, they blew across the sand, minute ghost ships lost on land. Megan, digging in piles of kelp, kept mistaking kelp bladders for floats; Jonah walked head down, scrutinizing the tide line for jade, pearls, ambergris. They kissed finally, blown together by random currents, barely recognizing each other in the dark, the kiss cold as wind, salty from the sea.

They drifted home, ate sausage and cabbage, then went down the street to the Ancient Mariner, where a band from up north called Hell-bent tried to prove it. Megan gave up on them early, blasted out the door by the harmonica player. But she held Jonah's hand until then, and she kissed him before she left. Jonah ordered another beer, wanting mindless noise, movement, wanting, suddenly, to be hell-bent himself, as long as he could find his way home safely afterward.

A woman appeared on the stage among the stocky, wild, bearded men. Jonah got a confused impression of her in the smoky light. A guest singer, he heard, from where-did-you-say-you-were-from? Her answer was lost in rowdy cheers. She wore something black, glittering, skintight. The sound system was poor; Jonah couldn't understand her words. Her voice was clear, strong; it moved up and down an impossible range. Her black hair hung to her hips; her face appeared and vanished behind it. She pulled it straight back from her brow with one hand, revealing earrings of onyx and ivory, a fall of overlapping circles, each half-black, half-white, separated by a yin-yang curve of gold that continued around the circle. Jonah, gazing at them, tasted a cool, rich wafer on his tongue. I'm possessed, he thought. I want to eat jewels. Then the woman's eyes caught his, glittering, sea green, and something snapped through him as if the air were charged.

Odd things were happening inside the sound system. Tide flowed through her voice, drowned the music, dragged back into the system on a long, slow sigh. For an instant, before it built again, he heard her voice, high, sweet, elusive. And then he heard water again, gathering, gathering, pulling treasures out of the deep as it shaped and coiled and finally broke with a hollow, powerful moan against land, spilling stone, shell, pearl, spume across the sand. And then her voice came, low now, murmuring through the ebb.

He swallowed dryly, and realized that he heard no other sounds in the world but the singer and the sea. He turned his head to see if the mysterious tide had entranced everyone; the movement brought the bar noises crashing around him: arguments, laughter, the drummer taking a final run down the drums, a cymbal, applause. The singer, her face half-lit, half-hidden under the dark wave of hair, gave them half a smile. Her single eye found Jonah again; she pulled her hair back with her hand and let him see her face, pale as foam, as finely sculpted as any shell shaped through the ages by water and danger and necessity. For a moment, as he stared back at her, he heard, beneath the human voices, the secret gathering of the tide.

Then she stepped out of the light. He stood up, looking for her, not knowing what he was looking for. The bar was crowded; heads were every color but black. He reached the stage finally, saw only rowdy, bearded faces. There was an absence of her in the smoke-laced shadows, the flickering candlelit tables. He veered to the bar finally, ordered another beer, thinking if he waited a little, she might sing again. He downed the beer quickly, ordered another, trying to ignore the feeling that the night had suddenly split itself between the moment when he had not known of her existence and the moment when all he knew was her absence.

He got home late; Megan was asleep. She had left a light on for him, over the table. He stood groggily, blinking at fossils, at the box on the table. Everything looked strange: He could barely remember why the table was littered with stones, what significance the box held. He flipped it open absently, still looking for something, for a meaning in what he felt.

The box full of treasure dazzled his eyes. It must have come out of the sea, he thought crazily, and then saw, lying among the brilliant stones and crystals and metals, the onyx-and-ivory earrings.

TWO

Megan woke at sunrise. A line of gold ran around the curtains. In the distance she could hear the low, lazy tide stirring the sea mosses, sorting shells. She sat up. Beside her, Jonah lay so still he might have been some ship's figurehead the sea had washed into her bed. He was breathing, though so evenly and quietly she had to untangle his breath from the sea. His skin smelled of beer and smoke. She reached for her glasses, slid out of bed; he didn't stir. She pulled some clothes on, wandered with her drawing pad into spring.

She walked a long way, in and out of dispersing mists, half dreaming, looking for a still life along the tide line. But her eye glossed over seaweed, velella, broken mussels, and sand dollars; they seemed an incoherent jumble. I need a bone, she thought. The moon. Something pure and simple. A seal surfaced in the waves to look at her, but did not stay to be drawn. She saw what she wanted then: a line, thin as spider web, cutting through a tendril of mist. She stopped. The line stretched into the tide, pulled earth and water together. A figure, shapeless in fishing boots and windbreaker, held the pole. Against the mist, the figure was a few bunchy lines, male or female, bulky, nearly colorless. Megan opened her drawing pad, pulled a pen out of her pocket. She rarely drew people; this was not a person, this was a sea species, a tide dweller, like the sandpipers and hermit crabs, sending a tentacle into the waves to see what there was to eat. Megan caught the angle of the body and the pole before the fisher reeled in to cast again. She looked seaward then, sketched a quick, feathery breaker. Something small and hard struck her shoulder, and she felt a claw in her hair.

She shook her head wildly; it scratched her scalp. Then she stilled, thinking more calmly: the fishhook. The weight had hit her shoulder; it dangled in front of her, pulling at the hook tangled in her hair. She groped for it. The fisher was walking toward her, reeling in methodically. Megan felt the hook scrape behind her ear; she caught it finally, a clump of hook and hair in her fingers as the fisher reached her.

It was a woman; Megan didn't recognize her. She had long curly iron-gray hair flying out from a knitted cap; her eyes were the same oyster gray as the water. She had a lined, rugged, weathered face, about as graceless as a rockfish. Shorter than Megan, she looked hefty, shapeless under her jacket. She seemed annoyed, as if Megan's hair had crossed her line on purpose.

"Hold still," she said brusquely, and put her pole down. She picked through Megan's hair with stubby fingers. Her voice was a deep growl. "Lost the bait on that cast. At least you don't have a worm in your hair."

"Thanks," Megan muttered. Profuse apologies not being forthcoming, she added, aggrieved, "I think I'm bleeding. You could have cracked my glasses with that weight."

"I could have," the woman agreed with daunting calmness.

"Well, you should learn to cast. The ocean's that way; if you look, you can't miss it."

"I wasn't looking at the ocean. I was looking at you. Why not? You were looking at me. You were putting me down on your paper."

"You could have asked me not to, if it bothered you. You didn't have to throw things at me."

"It doesn't bother me," the woman said, shrugging. "Draw me or not. You caught my attention, and so my hook followed. It happens. Hold still; it's a triple hook."

"Great."

"What's your name?"

"Megan. More to the point, what's yours?"

The woman gave the kind of fat, raspy chuckle Megan associated with chronic smoking. "You going to sue me? Over a scratch? Humans are so delicate. Who do the manatees sue when the speedboat propellers scar their backs for life?"

"What?"

"Who do the canned dolphins sue? Who do the little violet snails sue when, floating upside down on their bubble rafts on the surface of the sea, they run into an oil slick?"

Brother, Megan thought. She said, "All right, all right, just get the damn hook out of my hair."

"Might have to cut it out. I have my fish knife."

"Oh, no. No knives. Just snap the line and I'll cut it out at home."

The woman chuckled again. "Don't be afraid. Anyway, I want my hook back. It's mine, after all. And I want to see what I reeled in. Megan. What do you do with your drawings?"

"I sell them. Ouch."

"One more prong. What else do you draw?"

"Tide pools," she muttered. "Birds. Kelp. Sea things."

"Then why me?"

"I wasn't drawing you. I was drawing a piece of sea life. Something attached to the sea, getting breakfast like an otter or a gull."

The woman gave a short seal's bark. It might have been anger or amusement; there seemed both in her expression. The hook came free in her hand. She looked into Megan's eyes then, her eyes wide, unblinking. "You must look closer," she said. "You must look closer. You don't see anything at all."

"People like my drawings," Megan protested.

"Of course they do. You show them what they expect to see. But you don't see what's really there. You couldn't even see me." She untangled the rest of the line from Megan's hair, caught the weight before it dropped. Megan, irritated by the portentousness, answered, "Of course I see you. You've been in my hair for five minutes. You're in my drawing."

The woman gave her raspy chuckle. She picked up her pole. A toad-woman, Megan thought darkly. Toadfish. And lunatic besides. "Look at your drawing. My name is Doris. Dory, you can call me next time."

"Next time what?"

"Next time you want me." She turned, wandered back along the tide line, pole over her shoulder. Megan watched her, at once cross and curious. She wasn't local, she wasn't a tourist. She was someone's aging, eccentric sea wife, widow, maybe, living along the cliffs, her mind full of scars and barnacles, like an old whale's back, from being too long in the sea. Someone else—husband, son, sister—kept her just human enough. She went behind one of the huge rocks scattered along the beach; she didn't reappear. She must have stopped there to fish, well away from Megan's hair. Megan stooped finally, picked up her drawing.

She gave it a cursory glance. The wave had gotten smudged, but the simple essential lines were unchanged. What she had wanted to say. . . . She gazed at it, pleased, despite the memory of the hook in her hair. The fisher, the line into the sea, the wave. . . .

She looked more closely at the wave. She was aware of her heartbeat suddenly, a little private sound louder than the break and drag of tide. It wasn't a smudge in the wave where the line broke the water and the fishhook disappeared. It was a graceful tangle of tide-tossed hair.

Jonah, rapt, drowning at the bottom of a dream, down full fathom five among the dead men, the rotting spars and spilled treasure of sunken ships, was mildly annoyed when the white arm of a sea goddess reached endlessly and insistently down to pull him up into light. He hid in the coral where the butterflyfish slept, tried to burrow into the parrotfish's nightly cocoon; the hand pursued him.

"Jonah."

He tried to make himself invisible, one of the little ghoulish creatures living in the sea's eternal night. The hand plunged after him, scattering schools of luminous fish.

"Jonah! Wake up. You slept through the alarm."

No, I haven't, he thought, hearing the alarm all around him in the sea. Then he opened one eye, found himself in bed, with Megan, dressed and smelling of tide, sitting beside him.

He moved after a moment, dropped a hand over his eyes. "God," he breathed. "I had the strangest dream. What time is it?"

"Ten after eight. What did you dream?"

"I dreamed I was searching for fossils on the bottom of the ocean. There was a great cliff; I could swim up and down it, picking fossils out. But they weren't bivalves and trilobites—I was picking whales out of the cliff, walruses, seals, manatees, dolphins, sea turtles. Only they weren't big; they were tiny, shrunken things, and in my dream I thought: they've been forgotten; that's why they're so tiny. I'm in the future, and they're in the forgotten past."

"Well," she said comfortingly after a moment, "they're not all gone yet. I saw a seal in the tide watching me watch it."

"Did you go out drawing?" She nodded. "I didn't even know you were gone." He trailed a finger down her arm sleepily. "Did you draw?"

"I did one." Her eyes seemed opaque behind her glasses; they got that way sometimes when she didn't like her work.

"What?"

"Just something. I'm not sure if I like it."

"Let me see."

She shook her head. "Later, maybe. Let me think about it. Do you want me to bring you some coffee?"

"Coffee," he said, as if he couldn't remember what it was he drank a pot of every day. But a bit of his mind had darted off into deeper water, in pursuit of something.

"You know. Black stuff, comes in a cup."

"Uh." He sat up suddenly. "No, I'll get up. I remember now."

"What?"

"Where my dream came from." He swung around, found the floor, and padded out to the dining room, where the box sat on the table among his rocks. He opened it.

"There they are," he said, and there they were: all the great sea animals, tiny carvings of jade, turquoise, malachite, silver, gold. "That's what made me dream." He was silent again, touching moons of black and white, rimmed with gold.

"Do you like his work?" Megan asked.

"Oh, yes," he sighed. "Yes."

Reading on his stool behind the cash register later, while Jenny worked, he kept avoiding sea-green eyes. He studied the antique *Compend of Geology* stubbornly; thoughts crystallized between the lines. All I have to do is sit here until the jewelry maker comes in. . . . "Fossils . . . of extreme interest to geologists, because they reveal the nature of the former inhabitants of the earth." Then I can ask him about the woman who bought the earrings. The woman who sings. ". . . may be defined as any evidence of the former existence of a living thing." He would remember her.

But how well do I remember her? "In some cases . . . even the organic matter . . . is preserved. . . ." Black, black hair, her hand pulling it back. Her voice like smoke, like fire, bright and dark. What she wore, night black, yet sparking light. ". . . more commonly . . . only the shells . . . and of these . . . sometimes both the form and structure and sometimes only the form." Her face, pure and mysterious as a moon shell, turning and turning inward, outward . . . the color of her eyes. The blur of color coming at me across the room, into my eyes, into my blood. . . .

"Jonah, do we have any little cards explaining this one?" Jenny asked, holding up an ammonite. He rocked a little on the stool, jarred by the force of his imaginings, the boundary to another world buckling against the insistence of the real. Jenny's voice, the customer's hopeful face, the preserved form and structure. . . .

"Oh." Both women looked strange, Jenny and the customer; there was only one face his eyes expected. He leaned forward, pulled at a drawer in the counter. "In here, somewhere. It's an ammonite. Mesozoic Period." He pulled out one of the cards, handwritten in Megan's calligraphy. "Here." Holding it across the counter, he looked up into sea-green eyes.

The world stopped. Stopped moving, stopped making noise, twenty-seven billion forms of life stopped breathing air, drinking light. Then it started up again, with a lurch of sound like ground gears.

"Are you Jonah? I'm Adam Fin."

He held out his hand. After a moment, Jonah shook it, wondering how he could have found any similarities at all between the darkly glittering singer and this fallen angel. The green eyes narrowed faintly, a smile glinting through them, contradicting the bland innocence in his face. Jonah half expected the clamshells to clatter together in horror, the *Compend* to disintegrate into a pile of ash, the name to etch itself into the plate-glass window. Then he thought: this is ridiculous, I'm having a bad case of spring fever, I'm hallucinating.

"Fin?"

"One *n*. Like a fish." He smiled again, this time with teeth. There seemed a lot of them, white as fish bone and predatory. That, Jonah remembered, was the fashion in places where people paid attention to fashion. "So you like my work." His voice seemed deceptively gentle, silky. Jonah expected to see brine running out of his smile, as if he had just taken a shark bite of something.

"Yes." He dared not ask, he decided, which of the three women had told him that. Then, abruptly, frowning, he did ask. "Did Megan tell you that? When? I only looked at it last—this morning."

"No."

"No." He drew breath, his eyes sliding away from the chilly, smiling eyes. "Not Megan."

"I haven't seen her yet this morning."

"She's probably on the beach, drawing," he said inanely, and then, too late, heard the undercurrent beneath Adam's words. Adam simply nodded.

"Then I'll look there for her."

"Why?"

"Why what?"

"Why do you want Megan?" Jenny turned to look at him, hearing the sharpness in his voice. Adam's blank, surprised expression mirrored hers. Jonah shifted, feeling somehow foolish and threatened at the same time. He said, without waiting for an answer, "I'll have to take your work on consignment."

"Fine with me," Adam said mildly. "Which pieces do you want?"

"I'll have to go upstairs and get the box."

He found it where he had left it, closed among his fossils, and brought it down. He opened it on the counter. Jenny joined him, making vague, appreciative sounds, filling his own silence as his eyes, flicking across a pirate's treasure of metal and jewels, found nothing. They must be there, he thought incredulously, the yin-and-yang wafers of onyx and ivory. They had to be there, hidden under a gold whale, under a polished black starfish. "I'll take these," he said, breaking his awkward silence, shifting jewels. "These."

"What about the black cats sitting on the fishhooks?" Jenny suggested. "I love those."

"Right. And this."

"And the sea-otter pin, with the tiny abalone shell on its tummy."

"Fine." He picked up a sea-turtle pin, its back malachite, its head and feet paler jade, jointed with silver. "This."

"And this little pink-jade octopus; it looks like a flower, the way its arms curve like petals."

"Fine." He swallowed. "Jenny keeps the shop going; she knows our customers. There was—I thought I saw—"

"Yes?"

"We couldn't possibly have lost them—if so I'll pay for them—"

"What," Adam asked, "are you looking for?"

The world seemed to quiet again. Jonah lifted his eyes, feeling naked, vulnerable, pleading silently for mercy. "I saw a pair of onyx-and-ivory earrings. Overlapping circles, dark and light divided by gold. I don't know what happened to them."

There was no mercy in the fine, dangerous face.

"You only thought you saw them in the box," Adam said gently. "But you recognized my work. I made them for my sister."

Upstairs, Megan laid two drawings on the floor and sat cross-legged, studying them.

Sea hare, she thought.

Sea hair.

Something is happening. Something very strange is happening. Things are drawing themselves into my drawings. Or am I drawing them without realizing it? But that old woman caught my hair on her hook, and that's my hair there, floating like a mermaid's in the surf. How would I have known to draw it?

She hugged her knees, staring at the drawings.

"Well," she said finally, a little wildly, "there's only one thing to do. Go back and draw again, and see what else turns up." She got up off the floor, leaving the drawings there, the beginning of some story without words that she had to pull in the shape of fish and shells and seaweed out of the sea.

She went out again, feeling a touch lunatic herself. She hadn't showered; breakfast had been a cup of coffee with Jonah before he went down to open the store. They hadn't talked much; he seemed dream-fogged, and she was dumbfounded. She walked to the beach again, hair flying, pocket full of pens and pencils, her drawing pad under her arm, her eyes wide behind her salt-flecked glasses, determined to make the mystery reveal itself or vanish.

The tide had turned; most of the tide pools were underwater. She sat on a wedge of boulder, watched the tide bubble around it. She drew the rocks in the distance, rising above the surf like the craggy towers of some forgotten kingdom. Sea palms on lower shelves of rock curled under the tide, then popped upright, shaking their fronds. She added a cluster of them, and three pelicans, time-warped from another era, that flew along the breakers. She studied her drawing. Nothing, she thought grimly, that shouldn't be there. She added a fishing trawler crawling along the horizon, and a couple of men casting off the top of a rock. There was more impulse than art to her composition, but she began to enjoy the randomness. Everything about it was unexpected, so nothing could surprise her.

"Megan?"

She looked up, surprised. Adam Fin, looking more homogeneous in blue jeans and a windbreaker, smiled down at her, then glanced at her drawing. She, who hated people looking over her shoulder, shifted to reveal more of it to him. "Hi," she said, and patted barnacles. "Sit down."

He did so, ignoring the hoary teeth pushing against his backside. He watched the water a moment, eyes narrowed against the wind, then said, "I talked to Jonah. He took some of my work."

"I knew he would."

"Is he always so intense?"

"Pretty much. He says he likes rocks better than people." She added a bit of cross-hatching to the rocks, then looked up again to find Adam's profile, turned seaward, still as marble, hair pushed back by the wind, a quarter moon glinting in one ear. For just a moment, she envisioned that profile superimposed on her sketch, as if he were dreaming the rocks, the pelicans, the kelp and tide. Light sparked across the silver quarter moon in his ear; the onyx rabbit seemed to sprint across the wind toward the tide.

"Does it mean something?" she asked curiously. "The black rabbit? Is it lucky?"

His stillness broke; he touched it, smiling a little. "I don't know. Sometimes yes, sometimes no. In old tales, rabbit is a trickster. It changes sex, it changes shape; it lures you this way and that; it steals power and gives it away; it changes the path under your feet, and in the end, it changes what you think you want into what you are really looking for."

"All that," she said, marveling.

"Sometimes it just plays tricks."

She watched it rocking under his ear, the moon caught in its paws. Her eyes strayed again to his profile. "Jenny thinks you were born here."

"She does?" There was a touch of humor in his gentle voice. "Why?"

"She says because you're more like one of us than one of them."

He still looked seaward, but the shadow deepened under his cheekbone. "One of us," he said, amused. "One of them."

"Were you?"

"Born here?" He leaned gracefully, catching a trail of foam between his fingers. "Yes. Here. Jenny's right."

"But you traveled."

"Now I'm back." He flicked the foam into the water. "You weren't born here."

"I was born—"

"In Port Jameson. Jenny told me. Up north."

"You know it?"

"I know all the towns along the coast. I'm part salesman, remember?"

"But where do you live now?"

"I'm staying with some people," he said vaguely, "until I find a place."

"You're going to stay?"

"For a while. Maybe longer. Who knows? Long enough to make some things, sell some things, make a little money."

"That's all there is around here," she commented. "A little money."

"People bring it in from up north, down south. Seattle, San Francisco, Los Angeles—"

"Jonah thinks you're from Beverly Hills."

He laughed at that, noiselessly, still watching the tide. "Jonah has too much imagination."

"I always thought he didn't have enough."

He leaned back, hands splayed among the barnacles, his eyes on the water, but she felt his attention shift to her. "Why do you say that?"

She shrugged. "He likes to classify things. He's very cautious. He hates the color in my drawings; he thinks it's commercial. He has good taste, but he can be rigid about some things. He didn't even want to talk to you at first; he wouldn't look at your jewelry, even when I told him how beautiful it is. I don't know why he changed his mind. When he finally looked at it, he dreamed about it."

He was silent a moment, absolutely still, the way the waves were still sometimes, just before they began to gather and turn again. Then he said slowly, "He locks up imagination maybe, frees it by night. Some people do that. Their lives are rigid, but their dreams are full of poetry. Monsters. Things rich and strange. Imagination is dangerous. It changes things. You think you know what the world is and where you are in it, and then you walk out the door, and the storm clouds are a migration of great white whales, and the moonlight on the water is a stairway down into the sea."

"A stairway into the sea," she repeated, and saw it suddenly, in her mind, moonlight and pearl, beginning just at the edge of the tide and running into the deep. She shook her head, laughing a little, and Adam's eyes turned away from the sea to her.

"What?" he asked, smiling.

"Nothing. I just saw your stairway. I've never thought that way about the sea. I've always drawn what I saw, and I never imagined anything that wasn't real."

"Pretend it's real," he suggested lazily. "What's it made of? Your stairway?"

"Moonlight. Pearl. Something dark, blue-black, like the underside of mussel shells."

"Where does it begin?"

"Just there. Where the outgoing tide draws back the farthest from the land."

"If you could—" He looked at her again, still smiling faintly, his eyes seeming at once opaque and full of light. "Would you?"

"Go down the stairs?" She nodded, pushing her hair out of her eyes to contemplate imaginary stairs. "Now I can only go as deep as a tide pool. If I could stand on the bottom of the sea and draw all the little luminous fish in the dark . . . draw kelp, looking up toward light . . . I could draw these things from photographs, but I never wanted to. Anyway, Jonah would hate that more than he hates the colors."

"He hates the sea?"

"Oh, no," she said quickly. "He loves it."

"And he loves you."

She glanced at him silently, saw only a waning quarter of his face. "He's crotchety," she said slowly. "Hard to please, sometimes. But then, so am I. We're alike, in a lot of ways." She paused again. "I've never—"

"What?"

"Talked like this to anyone. I don't usually. About my drawings. About Jonah."

"Sometimes it's easiest to talk to strangers."

"Do you love anyone?"

His expression didn't change, but she had surprised him: he stopped breathing; again his body grew still. "No," he said at last. "Not for a long time. And even then, not for very long."

"It was like that for me," she said with sympathy, "before I met Jonah. It seemed—just luck, that we met. An accident."

"Maybe," he said gravely, "one of these days, I'll have an accident."

She leaned against her drawing, studying him as she studied tide pools. "You'd more likely have a collision," she said, and saw his teeth flash.

"Why?"

"Because you seem more dramatic. Exotic. Jonah and I belong in a tide pool. You belong in the great deep. Among the whales and dolphins—"

"And sharks?"

"No," she said indignantly. "Of course not. A narwhal. That's what you would be. Something real, but not quite believable."

He looked at her, the expression in his eyes unfathomable.

She wondered suddenly if she had hurt him. But he only said lightly, "Jonah would put me among the sharks."

"Jonah would not. Barnacles don't know sharks."

"And where would Jonah put you?"

She chewed the end of her pen, studying the drawing for whales. "Jonah doesn't think that way. He sees everything in black and white."

He chuckled, amused by something. "That's a perilous way to think. One day color will wash across his eyes and he'll be in a world where nothing is familiar anymore. Not even you."

She looked at him, blinking. "That's an odd thing to say."

"I see odd things," he said lightly, and leaned forward to study her drawing. "It moves," he commented. "It's hard to catch the sea moving, since the drawn line freezes it. But I can hear your sea."

She flushed, pleased. "I was just doodling. Just—something odd is happening to my work. It's going through some kind of change. I don't—I don't quite know what to expect from it now."

"In what way?" he asked gravely. She was silent a long time, while he waited; she shook her head finally, pulling her hair tight with her hands.

"It's hard to describe. I just have to keep at it until I know what it wants—what it wants to tell me."

He made a soft sound. "You draw the sea. Maybe it's the sea you're trying to hear."

She looked at him again. "You sound like that old sea witch."

"Who?"

"A woman I met this morning. She cast her hook in my hair and reeled me in like a fish. She's rude and crazy and ugly, and she changed my drawing."

"How—"

"She just did. She walked into it and changed it. Old barnacle." She could feel her face frowning and smiling at the same time. His face changed slightly; a shadow passed over it, or light. She asked, surprised, "You know her?"

"Oh, yes," he said softly. "Dory. The Old Woman of the Sea." He stood up suddenly, as if he finally felt the barnacles. "That's what we always called her."

"Is she crazy?"

"No," he said simply. "But sometimes her sanity is terrifying." He stepped off the rock, into fingers of tide. He turned, gave her a smile. Tide washed away his footprints. She stopped watching him after a while and studied her sketch for changes. Boat. Rocks. Birds. Sea palm. Waves. Fishers. No mystery. Just land meeting sea. Birds diving out of air for food, plants growing up out of water for light. Humans hunting fish, eating from the sea.

Normal. She closed her pad and leaped onto dry sand. She picked up half a Styrofoam float that had rolled in on the foam, and a small opaque bottle with something inside it. She stuffed them in her pocket and headed home.

Jonah found them on the table among his rocks when he came upstairs after he closed the store. Megan's drawing was propped against the toaster; he studied it a moment. Birds. Fishers. Rocks. Trawler. It lacked the precision of her underwater drawings, he decided, but the lines were good. He wondered where she was. He drifted over to the table, vaguely annoyed at her absence, as he would have been vaguely annoyed by her presence. He transferred his annoyance to the junk on the table that was littering his orderly mess. He tossed the float at the garbage can. Rim shot. It bounced to the floor and slid under a cupboard. He gazed at it, motionless, a glittering shadow, a smoky cadence trailing through his thoughts. He turned restively, picked up the bottle. Something shifted inside it. He held it up to the light, looked into it.

He was standing with the bottle upraised, shaking it now and then to shift the flickering, unidentifiable lights in it, when Megan walked in. He grunted, too absorbed to speak. She set a bag of groceries on the cupboard, then turned. She pushed at her glasses hesitantly with her forefinger, her brows going up behind them.

"What are you doing?"

"There's something in this bottle."

"What?"

"I don't know. I can hardly see. . . . Where'd you find it?"

"It washed ashore in the tide. What is it? A message?" She reached for it. "Let me see."

"Wait—" He held it higher. "I'm looking."

"Is it treasure? I found it. It's mine."

"Salvage belongs to the government, who shall apportion its value." He turned the bottle; weight shifted; something rattled faintly.

"In what country?"

"Florida, I think." He caught a reflection, a memory in the glass that might have been opalescent walls, windows, a tower. "Can I break it?"

"It's probably sand."

He upended the bottle, shook it over the floor. A drop of water trembled on the lip. Megan watched it, as mesmerized as he was. "Not sand. I can't tell what kind of bottle it is. Steak sauce, or something. It's not antique, is it?"

"Probably. It's been floating around in the ocean for a hundred years, waiting for someone to find it and break into it. Now it's more valuable than what's inside." She watched him patiently. "Can I see?"

"Castles," he murmured, watching the shifting lights. "Luminous fish. Reflections. Dreams. Rhinestones from Woolworth's." He yielded the bottle finally. She held it to the light a moment or two, motionless, not breathing. Then, abruptly, she dropped it into the sink and tapped it once, twice, with the marble rolling pin.

"Be careful," he breathed. The glass shattered on the third tap.

They gazed at the pieces. Megan stirred them with her finger. Jonah picked up a shard, held it to the light. She watched him. He shook his head finally. "Nothing." He drew a long breath, looked at her. "But there was something."

"There was," she said in a small voice, "until I broke it." She stirred the pieces again, her eyes wide behind her glasses. Then she began to gather the shards methodically.

"Wait," Jonah said quickly, before she threw them out. "Save me a piece. I can look at it through my hand lens."

She gave him that flat, incredulous stare before her face loosened and broke into a smile. "Oh, Jonah. You can't see it that way."

"Then what was it?" he demanded.

"Something." She tossed the pieces in the garbage, then removed her glasses and drew the back of her hand over her eyes wearily. She blinked at him, half-blind; he wondered suddenly what she was seeing. "It's like the sea hare."

"What?"

"I thought it was over, but I guess not." She put her glasses back on, began to unpack groceries.

"What's not over?"

She didn't answer, just took eggs out of the bag, then an eggplant, which he hated and she loved, and chicken livers, which she hated and he loved. She wasn't going to answer, he could tell. When she opened the refrigerator, she let her hair swing in front of her face to hide it. He opened his mouth, impatient, wanting answers. She straightened abruptly before he could speak, and pointed out the dining-room window, where the lights of the town were streaking the twilight. "Look. That's what you saw. You held it that direction. You said they looked like lights."

"There was weight," he insisted, astonished. "Something rattled."

"A broken shell. Something that went down the drain."

"Sure."

Her mouth tightened. She unpacked cereal, milk. He went to her, put his hands on her shoulders, felt the tension in her. "What about the sea hare? What does that have to do with a bottle?"

She shrugged his hands away, swung the cupboard door open, narrowly missing his head. "Nothing, probably. I can't explain. I saw Adam today. He said you liked his work."

He folded his arms, backed against the counter. "You saw him today where?"

"At the beach. He stopped to watch me work."

"You never let anyone watch you work."

She shrugged. "I let him. He's an artist. He knows the sea."

"He's a hustler."

She turned to stare at him, stunned. "He's an artist. He's nice."

"Nice." He reached past her, pulled a box of crackers out of the bag. "Jenny is nice. Baby llamas are nice. Adam Fin is a barracuda."

"You are so critical." She slammed the cupboard door so hard beer in the bottom of the bag clinked. "It's a wonder you even like me. If you ever stopped, who would there be left in the world for you to like?" He stood still, blinking, hearing thoughts inside his head clink like the beer bottles. He wondered if he held one against the window, would it reflect another world, or would it simply gather into itself the lights of the world he knew?

There was something in that bottle, he thought stubbornly. And there is something else in Adam Fin. But he didn't speak. He moved into her silence, put the milk and the beer away, matching her mute arguments with his own.

THREE

Megan sat on the floor in Mike's bookstore, her back against history, surrounded by ocean. It was a slow morning. The bell on the door had rung three times. Rain tapped against the windows, wandered off, came back, tapped again. She was aware of someone circling her now and then, but she refused to look up. No one came to Mike's for history. The books she heaved onto her knees were massive, colorful, precise. They measured the mountains beneath the sea; they plumbed the abysmal waters. They told what the narwhal ate, how the male seahorse gave birth to its young, how the sea cucumber, which flung its inner organs at its enemies to confuse them, contained a chemical that might combat cancer, and that the homely hagfish had three hearts, and what orchestrated the beat of a hagfish's hearts could also steady a human heart. They knew, from the great blue whales to the one-celled algae, who ate what. They had counted the millions of eggs an oyster might lay in a year, and the number of rhymes in the song of the humpback whale.

But they hadn't read the message in the bottle.

Nor, she decided, surfacing to the gray light, did they know that a sea hare could crawl out of the water and turn itself into ink. Or that an old woman could cast a line into a drawing of the tide and catch a human on her hook.

She leaned back against the shelves, drew her hair out of her face. She must have sighed: Mike, on his stool, lifted his unkempt head, to which air moss and air snails probably clung, and turned an eye in her direction.

It was a question, his attention. He didn't care that she was littering his floor with herself and his books, but that she hadn't found what she wanted in them. No one turned a page or breathed among the stacks; the place was empty but for them.

She said wearily, hardly expecting Mike to offer much more than a crooked smile, "I keep finding odd things in the tide. But those books don't say anything about them." He was motionless, still listening, one finger marking the line he had read. She went on, talking to herself more than to him. "Yesterday I found a bottle with something in it. Something that shifted, something shining. . . . When I broke it open, nothing was there. But there had been something. These books are full of such strange things. Did you know that they made cloth of gold out of a fiber secreted by sea pens, and that sea pens look like long, feathery underwater quills? Maybe you could write a message with them. But these books don't say anything about what I need to know. They explain everything. They don't see anything that's maybe there and maybe not. It's like Jonah wanting to look for a mystery under his hand lens. It won't be there. But it was there."

She stopped talking. Mike was looking at her with as much expression as an oyster, waiting patiently for her to quit making conversation so that he could get back to his book. Then his backbone straightened a little. He drew in air, a long tidal gathering through his nose. Expression, subtle as color in a kelp leaf, passed through his eyes. "Yeah," he said, and Megan stared at him in astonishment. "I know." He set his book down carefully and collapsed a little into his bulk to rummage under the counter. "I found one, too."

"One what?" she whispered.

"One of those things. One of those things that don't fit." He lifted it gently off a shelf, set it on the counter, then stilled again, gazing at it, unblinking.

Megan got to her feet, not easy after being weighted with the cumulative knowledge of the sea. The thing on Mike's counter looked like a broken roof tile. It was flat, black, square but for a corner bitten off. As she looked more closely, she saw it was latticed with fine and intricate lines that revolved, at the corners, around tiny scallop shells. Latticed, it wasn't black, she realized, but blue so dark it melted toward black. Then all the lines flowed together; it was flat, black, solid. And then latticed again, the scallop shells a faintly paler blue. And then flat. A piece of black tile.

"What on earth—"

"Nothing," Mike said simply. "That's what I figure. Nothing on earth." He touched it gently; lines flowed under his fingers. "I found it washed up in a pile of kelp. Moves like water. Like something opening and closing to water."

"Yes," she said, entranced. "It would, I guess, being underwater."

"You figure—" He hesitated, then became expansive. "You look at it maybe from their point of view. For millions of years, the sea was like those books to them. Everything's explicable, expected. Fish bones, kelp leaves, pearls, whatnot. Then odd things start drifting down.

They've seen wood floating, so they're not surprised by ships, cloth of gold they can guess at, and pearls they know, and the little octopus can live in porcelain teacups. So they think: this is how humans live, floating on the water, coming apart now and then, and they learn to recognize clothes, and flesh, and then, after the fish feed, they recognize bone. But now . . . think if you were living down there, finding beer cans. Barrels of chemicals. Styrofoam coolers. Flashlight batteries. Plastic baggies. Maybe TV sets off sunken fiberglass boats. Refrigerators. Old socks. Tangled-up fishing line. If you didn't know, if you lived maybe inside a glint of light, what kind of bizarre world would you guess was falling apart and drifting out of the air down into the sea?" He turned his finding; the other side was pale and luminous as pearl. Megan stared at him, mute. "So I look at this and wonder what's down there, breaking up, washing ashore." He looked at Megan, shrugged his bulky shoulders a little. "Makes you wonder. At least it does me." Someone pushed the door open; the bell rang. He slid the finding back under the counter. Megan opened her mouth, closed it. Mike gave her his crooked, one-sided smile, then went back to being a walrus on a stool reading a book.

Jonah, taking a day off, had driven the truck to a cove north of town, to putter along the cliffs. Worm tubes and the occasional crumbling fossil clam were all he expected to find, though that morning he thought vaguely of shark teeth, or the ancient tracks of rain. Except for a couple from a camper picking through the treasures along the tide line, the cove was empty. He walked around the south arm of the cove, close to the water, where tide pools formed in the sandstone, and the cliffs were sliding shard by shard into the sand. There he picked among the broken pieces, occasionally helping the cliff down by poking into its side. The sandstone yielded easily, revealed little except the unmistakable tracks of other fossil hunters. Still, he was content in the gray, damp winds, with the roiling sea at his back, and the seagulls crying overhead.

He and Megan had mumbled back into one another's good graces; by midnight he had forgotten the color of the sea and remembered only Megan's eyes, their intentness, their sudden smile. He had been cured of earrings; Adam Fin, from wherever, was not a barracuda but harmless as a harp seal. He crumbled mud around what looked like a brachiopod, whistling. The ghost of the brachiopod itself crumbled away, left him a handful of nothing. He let it fall, still whistling, and eyed the tide. It had moved farther out, giving him a chance to clamber along the edge of the cliff out where it dipped down into deep water, and then over to the other side, which was usually tide-bound. He dropped his finds into his windbreaker pocket and began to climb.

Fifteen minutes later he was picking his way across what looked like giant ribs or backbones, partially submerged in sand, polished by the waves. There was a cave on this side of the cliff, with nothing much in it but the usual barnacles, starfish, anemones, hanging like some kind of weird living wallpaper down from where the tide stopped rising. But farther back from the water, around the outside of the cave, he had once found a perfect bivalve half the size of his palm. He went back there.

He heard the whales sing then.

He recognized them from some old record of Megan's: a flute player jamming with whales. It sounded more like whooping jungles to him, creaking timbers, demonic foghorns, than song. There were vast, deep notes that blew through him like breath trembling through a reed. I shouldn't be hearing those notes, he thought, shaken. They move through the deep sea, the leviathan call across hundreds of miles.

His eyes fell on the backbones and ribs of rock he had walked across.

They seemed to be arched in a dive through time, a sea mammoth caught and frozen like a little trilobite in the floor of the ocean. But this isn't the floor, he thought, then: it was underwater once. I'm at the bottom of a fossil sea, hearing the ghosts of whales. They were all around him, the voices of the sea, whistling, scraping, ratcheting, whooping, booming. He stood stunned by noise, trembling in currents of sound. What is happening? he thought. Something is happening.

Then there was only one sound: a song so faint he could barely separate it from the gentle splash and sigh of water within the cave.

It was a human voice; it was the sea's voice. It flicked away foam, wandered over stones, lingered in the anemone's tendrils. It turned over a shell, scattered agates. For a moment, as the sea idled, it ranged free, sweet, deep, then impossibly clear and high. He recognized it.

He took a step toward the cave, feeling his heart beat in his throat, his lips. The cave emitted a breath of brine and guano, then cool, rainy wind. He took another step, another. A wave rolled over his footprint. The voice grew louder. His eyes stung with salt, with sweat. There was no language in his head, only the tide and the voice and the wind. He reached the mouth of the cave.

Water ran past him, lapped the mossy walls, almost reached the shadows in the back. A gentle note filled the cave; he breathed it like air. Something at the back of the cave moved a little. It was slick, glittering, a mass of green and black, that melted into shadow, into stone. The voice sighed through the cave; tide pushed him forward. Again he smelled brine, guano, salt, death. And then the sweet rain. The shadowy mass stirred; a pale stone took shape, then a long, straight fall of shadow. The tide ran around his knees. He tasted the song, felt it in his throat, in his blood. Water splashed among the stones; he heard a light laugh melting in the foam. The sea wrapped itself around his thighs.

A gull cried overhead. He blinked, found himself standing at the empty, shallow cave he recognized, one with no depth for shadows. The sand at his feet was barely damp; the tide was still working its way across the tide pools. He listened for the song. Then he realized he was listening, and tears broke like a bone in his chest because he had heard the sound of fossil rain, he had seen the mermaid's hair.

A few miles to the south, Megan walked the tide line like a scavenger, head down, ignoring the sea, intent only on what the morning tide had pushed up on the beach. Other dedicated scavengers, who had found plastic bleach bottles or gallon milk jugs washed ashore, had cut holes in them to drop in whole sand dollars, blue agates, bright pieces of mother-of-pearl. Megan, frowning at the sand, narrowly avoided collisions. She had nearly walked into surf fishers' lines a couple of times; she barely heard their warnings. Now and then she stopped, shifted kelp with her toe, nudged a jellyfish over to see what it might be hiding. She was putting a magnifying glass to the mystery, she knew; if she looked at it directly, it would be somewhere else, behind her back, or where her shadow began. Like light flickering on water, it would never be where she had seen it last.

But still she searched for the pearl in the kelp, the bone made of coral. She filled her pockets as she walked, hardly seeing what she put into them, plastic, metal, cork, Styrofoam, tin, until her jacket swung bulkily at her hips and rattled when it hit her. She was absently trying to shove a wet towel into her bulging pocket when she ran into someone not quick enough to get out of her way.

It was Adam. He had his hands on her shoulders, steadying her as she raised her head and pulled her mind up from where the clams were blowing bubbles. She pushed her glasses up, and saw him from behind a brine-flecked mist. She pulled them off, began wiping them on the towel.

"Here," he said. "Let me." He took them, wiped them carefully on the underside of his sweatshirt. Then he slid them back on her nose, gently adjusted the earpieces under her hair, an oddly intimate gesture that made her aware suddenly of the muscle beneath the sweatshirt, the height and weight of the body blocking the wind. She shifted her own weight a little, backing a half step. He dropped his hands, looked down at the torn, sandy towel she dragged.

"Going swimming?"

"No, I was just—I was—" She paused, drawing hair away from her eyes. What had she been just? Trying to stuff a towel into her pocket. His expression changed.

"Is something wrong?"

She shook her head, sighing. "No. I was beachcombing. I got a little carried away. There's so much junk."

"Most people," he pointed out, "pick up shells."

"I'm not looking for shells."

"What are you looking for?"

"I don't know. Secrets. Mysteries. Pearls and ambergris and black coral. But I keep finding garbage instead."

He shrugged lightly. There was no expression on his face. "Just leave it. The tide will pick it up again. Anyway, you didn't put it there."

"Right," she said dourly. "That's toddler mentality in a nutshell. I didn't put it there, and anyway, Mom will clean it up."

He smiled. "Now you remind me of Dory. Never satisfied with the world. Grumbling and snorting and talking to yourself, trying to stuff all the garbage in the world into a grocery bag."

She shook her head. "I'd use a leaf bag. Thirty-nine gallons, made of recycled plastic. Drag it behind me down the tide line. Or a shopping cart. I'd wheel that along the wet sand and throw cans in it, and get snarled up in fishing lines and dead kelp."

"And then you'll get annoyed at the kelp. All those untidy piles the sea drags up and leaves lying around like laundry. You'll throw that into your shopping cart."

"And what about the dead jellyfish?" she demanded. "Talk about untidy. And the crab backs from molting crabs? Not to mention all those empty shells. I'll have to buy a coat with pockets as big as the sea."

"What have you got in your pockets?" He prodded one, marveling. "Anything good?"

"Actually," she admitted, "I'm not sure. I was looking so hard for something I wasn't paying attention to what I picked up."

He made a dubious sound after a moment, his eyes still smiling a little, the opaque milky green of bottle glass tossed around in the sea for a century. "Then how do you know you haven't picked up what you were looking for in the first place?"

She was silent, looking at him. "I don't know," she said at last, and laughed a little at the thought. "Maybe I did."

"Maybe you should look."

She went up to where the sand was dry and sat down. She realized then how far she had walked, almost beyond the boundaries of the town. Great jutting curves of cliff hid the harbor; the houses on them were sparsely scattered. She had left even the fishers and the beachcombers behind; they were alone but for flocks of gulls and sandpipers, and footprints wandering in and out of the tide. Adam sat beside her, watched her pull things out of her pockets. There were beer caps, a sardine tin, a Tinker Toy wheel, a baggie full of wet sand, a Styrofoam bait carton with a couple of dead worms in it, a fishing weight, a wool glove, a baby's teething toy, a tennis shoe.

She stopped when she saw the shoe. Adam was stretched out on his side, leaning on one elbow. His eyes, flicking from her face to the shoe, found nothing wonderful in it. She said, her voice sounding oddly high, "There are still things in my pockets."

"Take them out."

"But there's not room for a shoe in my pocket."

"It was in there," he said irrefutably. She reached into both pockets at once, pulled out an empty pickle jar, a film canister, a plastic glass with Ronald McDonald on it, the lid of a Ninja Turtle lunch box. She got to her knees, still pulling things out, her eyes wide, incredulous. Adam watched silently. She dropped a piece of a child's chalk board, a length of picture wire, a diving mask, a bicycle chain, and a fan belt before she stood up. Adam didn't move, except his head, lifting a little to see her face.

"What is this?" she breathed. "What is all this?" Still things came out: a jump-rope handle, a hairbrush without any bristles, the plastic nozzle of a vacuum cleaner. "This is not what I was looking for."

"It's what you found."

She stared at him. Expression had finally surfaced in his eyes: a sorrow as deep and complete as if, she thought, he were watching the world die.

And then she realized he was.

A wave fanned across the sand, spilled around him, began to tug the bottle caps, the Styrofoam back into the sea. It tugged at Adam, who lay in water as easily as on sand, indifferent as a seal to the turning of the tide.

She began to tremble, feeling the weight in her pockets and knowing that there was not time enough in the world to empty them. She whispered, "What are you?"

Jonah drifted back home at twilight. He moved, he felt, through the evening tide. It sang in the back of his mind, insistent, pervasive, the way the sound of the sea seemed ingrained in the floorboards of the apartment. No window could shut it out, no dream. He found Megan sitting idly on a kitchen stool, gazing at nothing, a peculiar, distant look in her eyes. He went to the refrigerator, got a beer, and glanced at her again.

"Did you draw?"

She shook her head. "No. I just walked."

"Oh."

"You?"

He nodded. "Same." He added, making an effort, "I found a couple of things."

"Oh." She drew a breath, subsided. He glanced out the window over the sink. Twilight drew a thin line of sapphire above the sea. He watched it darken, forgetting the beer in his hand, following the pale, elusive frills of foam as the black waves broke. A star moved over the water toward the harbor: a trawler coming home. He drank finally, and remembered Megan, so silent he had forgotten she was there. She got that way sometimes, chewing over her work.

He moved, touched the cold stove. "I'll cook." She murmured something. "What?"

"Okay." She added, after a moment, "I'm not very hungry."

"I'll cook that frozen tortellini."

"Okay."

He opened a cupboard, rattled a pot loose from a clutter of lids. He said without looking at her, "That Adam. The jewelry maker." She made another noise. "Where does he live?"

"He does—he said—" He looked up then; she shook her hair over her face, finding words. "He said he was with some friends."

"What friends? Where?"

"He didn't say."

He grunted, kicked the cupboard door closed. He set the pot in the sink, ran water into it. "Reason I ask," he said to the water, "is Jenny thinks we should get a few more pieces from him."

"Oh."

He set the pot on the stove, turned on heat. "Did you buy sauce?"

"No."

"You know how to make it?"

"Yeah. You get out the butter."

He gazed into the water, stirred it aimlessly for a while with a wooden spoon. "Then what?" he asked, rousing. "After you get out the butter?"

"That's it. You toss some butter and salt and pepper in the tortellini and it'll be fine."

He blinked, pulled earthward by a vague sense of incongruity. "Do we have butter?"

"No," she said after a while.

He turned the water off, looked at her. She was hunched, her face a quarter moon within her hair. He couldn't find an expression, let alone read it. He set the water aside, pulled a frying pan out of the stove drawer. "Eggs, then. Scrambled?"

"Fine."

"Did he leave a number with you?"

"What?"

"Adam Fin. A phone number?"

She shook her head, straightening a little; he heard her sigh. "No."

"Well, then how do I get in touch with him?"

"I guess you'll have to wait until he finds a place to live."

He cracked an egg against the pan with more force than necessary. "That's it? Just wait until he wanders back in? It could be days!"

"It could be. So what?"

So, he wanted to shout, I have to wait days to find out if the woman singing in the bar he says is his sister is the woman who sang to me in a cave, or if I just dreamed their voices were alike and that there was the shadow of her long black hair against the rock? His mouth felt dry. He dumped eggshells, knowing suddenly how an oyster felt, waking up to a grain of sand in its bed, trying to live around it, only to find it growing larger, luminous, more insistent the harder the oyster worked to ignore it.

"I think," he said finally, "I just think it's odd he left all that with us and not even a number where we can reach him. It's expensive stuff."

"I guess he trusts us," she said wearily, and added after a moment, "I don't know why. Anyway. You don't even like him."

He didn't answer. He stirred eggs, pushed a couple of pieces of bread into the toaster. He found himself staring down into it, watching the flush of heat along the element. He looked up to find Megan watching him, her eyes speaking suddenly, but nothing he could decipher. Do you? they asked. Have you ever? Would you believe?

"Jonah?"

"Huh?" he said, and then, "Oh, shit, there's no butter for the toast."

"There's some diet margarine."

"I hate that stuff. Tastes like salad oil." He got a couple of plates, spilled egg onto them, added dry toast. He handed a plate to Megan. She looked at it bewilderedly, as if wondering what he expected her to do with yellow lumps and a piece of cardboard. He lifted his own plate, eyed it, and set it down abruptly.

"I'm going out."

He felt her watching him until he closed the door, but she did not even say his name.

His feet led him to the Ancient Mariner, where he bought a beer and hunched over it, listening, beneath the sounds of the jukebox and some weird woman haranguing the bartender, for an echo of the voice in his head. He upended the beer, drank half, and fell deeper into the music, chasing a spindrift song through the caves in his head. Finishing the beer in another burst of energy, he found the woman eyeing him.

She looked, he thought, like an oyster. Lumpy, gray, with a ruffled and colorless shell. The bartender, Sharon, who was married to Marty down the street who ran the arts and crafts gallery, lifted an eyebrow at Jonah.

"Another?"

"He'll have one," the older woman said. "I'm buying."

"No, I have to—"

"Name's Doris. You can call me Dory." She brought herself and her glass over, sat down beside him. "If you can hear that much beneath the music."

"I can hear," he said, despite Aerosmith going at it from the jukebox. She fixed him with her oyster eye.

"Sing me what you hear."

"I can't sing."

"You'll have to, for her. You'll have to wring music from your bones." She shoved his beer at him. "Drink it."

He could not, he thought, drinking with impolite haste, have heard what she said. He put the glass down, and smelled it suddenly, from the woman, from a crack in the wall: brine, guano, new rain falling in a new season. He closed his eyes, felt the sting of brine behind them. The woman was saying something else.

"There's a price. Everything has its price."

"Beer?" He reached into his pocket. "I've got it."

"Money's not worth much, down there. Gets old and crusty, hidden under kelp; coral grows around it. Coral likes money. It's hard, you can build on coin. I've seen gold like eyes peering out of coral skeletons. No. The price wouldn't be coin. You won't want to buy what that coin makes, the way it ends up down there."

"What?" he said, mildly buzzed and not having the foggiest notion what the old bivalve was talking about. "What ends up down where?"

She joggled his elbow crossly. "Down underwater. You should see what crawls out of those rusting barrels. It's an army of ghosts that eats everything in sight. Eats coral, eats the little plankton, eats the chemicals drawing one fish to another, so they can't breed, and if they do, it eats their eggs. You think you see everything, with your lenses, your this scopes and that scopes, your radars drawing pictures of sound. You don't see what's not there anymore. It makes things disappear." She turned to Sharon, called in her rattly voice, "He'll have another."

"No, thanks. I've got to go."

"He'll have another." Her hand clamped on his wrist; he saw her eye again, fierce and gray as a gale. "You'll stay. I know what you want. I can hear the singing in your head."

He stood still. His mouth was very dry. He reached for his bottle; it was empty. He waited while Sharon, looking amused, brought another.

"Where's Megan?" she asked, throwing the name at him like a lifeline from another world. It was too short and too late.

He gulped beer. "Megan? Doing some drawing. Or thinking about it. I'm looking," he said to both women, "for a man named Adam Fin. Tall, blond—" They were both nodding. "He left some jewelry with me," he added, and saw the oyster eye narrow in a smile. "But no address, no phone."

"And you want," Dory said, chuckling, "a certain pair of earrings."

He had to breathe twice before he could answer. "Yes. You know him."

"I know him." She drank her own drink, sea green and rimed with salt. "I know her. They're mine, him and her. My first and greatest and most wild children."

FOUR

Megan dipped her hand in the tide, drew the shining out of the sea.

It flowed like gossamer from her hand, cloth woven of foam, of light. In the bright morning it was barely visible, yet of substance: wind stirred it, or invisible tides. She draped it around her neck; it wound itself through her hair. She continued walking. Long ribbons colored like mother-of-pearl floated in on a breaking wave, lay in the wet sand like reflections of sunset. She picked them up, wrapped them around her wrist; they streaked the air behind her with changing shades of blue. The next wave brought her a living crown.

It was a band of giant, irregular pearls hung with a net of tendrils to which seahorses clung, and tiny sand dollars, delicate, feathery worms, minute, transparent fish. She put the crown on her head; the net fell over her shoulders like a cloak. Now, she thought, I must have my scepter, and the sea rolled it to her feet: a stark white bone with a starfish impaled on its pointed tip. She raised it, and felt the net wrap around her so tightly a seahorse embedded itself in her cheek.

She sat up. She was tangled in sheets. Jonah, uncovered beside her, mumbled something and groped. His hand found nothing; one eye opened, thoughtless as a fish's eye. She felt her cheek, shook him until the other eye opened.

"Jonah. There's a seahorse in my cheek."

He squinted at her. "There's no seahorse in your cheek."

"Are you sure? I can feel something scaly."

"There's no seahorse." He yawned. "That's a baby starfish." He rolled out of bed, padded to the bathroom. Megan, rubbing her cheek with one hand, untangled herself with the other. She reached for her glasses.

When she put them on the world turned to water, and she saw it, washed with moonlight and foam: the stairway down into the sea.

She woke up. She was tangled in sheets; Jonah was gone. Then she realized he hadn't been there. It was still night, and he had never come home. She pulled herself across the bed to peer at the luminous dial on the clock. Five minutes to three in the morning. She dropped back, her eyes wide in the dark, remembering. He had left his scrambled eggs on the counter, gone out abruptly. She had scarcely noticed; all her attention had been on Adam, lying in the surf on the kitchen floor. Maybe, she had thought after a while, Jonah had gone for butter. She got up finally, scraped cold eggs into the garbage, and made a tuna sandwich with the toast.

She had fallen asleep listening for him.

She put her glasses on, turned on the lamp. She went into the kitchen to see if he had left a trace of himself: a beer bottle, a fossil. Then she looked among his rocks to see if he had left a note. She flicked on the bathroom light: no message on the mirror. She sat down on the bed, hugging herself, feeling a hollowness in her bones, as if she were blown out of glass and the blow falling at her out of the dark would shatter her.

She whispered, "Jonah."

She heard his key in the lock then. The door opened. She went out to meet him, found him standing in the doorway, blinking at all the lights. He held the doorknob with one hand, and the door frame with the other; seeing her, he swayed in surprise and would have sat down on the floor if he hadn't been hanging on.

"It's you," he said.

"I live here," she said a trifle crossly. "I'm Megan. If you're looking for someone else, you got the wrong apartment."

"How did you know?"

"How did I know what?"

"That I'm looking for her?"

She felt herself grow rigid with shock. Her mouth shaped words; no words came for a moment.

"Who?"

"Who?"

"Who her?"

"What?"

"What her are you looking for?" It came out, to her ears, all in one word. He blinked, swaying again, then deciphered it.

"Her."

Her voice rose. "Her who?"

"The singer."

"You met a singer?" She covered her mouth with her hands. "You met a singer with that band that night?"

"No." He shook his head so emphatically his glasses nearly fell off. "I haven't met her yet. I can't find her."

She felt an absurd urge to laugh and cry and throw a brachiopod at his head at the same time. "Jonah, what the hell are you talking about? You have a crush on some singer in a band? Is that where you've been? Listening to her?"

He blinked at her again, his eyes round and heavy behind his glasses. "It's not a crush. It's an obsession."

"For a woman you haven't met?"

"I knew you wouldn't understand."

"What," she said tightly. "Don't. I. Understand."

"Obsessions. They don't have anything to do with what's real. This doesn't have anything to do with you."

"Jonah, it's three in the morning and you're shitfaced! Don't tell me this has nothing to do with me. You're obsessed with rocks and you leave them all over the house—"

"Fossils."

"Don't tell me that has nothing to do with me when I step on a worm tube getting out of the bathtub! Where are you going to put this obsession? On the kitchen counter?"

"In my head," he said, and she made a sound she had never made before. He let go of the doorknob, raised a hand, and lurched a half step. "Now," he said. "Now. Now."

"Don't 'now' me."

"She's a dream—"

"I gather."

"I mean in my head. I think. That's where she sings. In my head."

Megan closed her eyes, wondering if she were dreaming Jonah. But he was still there, breathing fumes and gazing at her hopefully. "Jonah."

"Megan."

"What are you talking about?"

"Well, she sang at the bar, too."

"Uh-huh."

"And then in the cave."

"What's that? Some jazz club?"

"The cave," he said patiently. "Around where I was looking for fossils. She sang. And whales sang. Maybe they sang because she drew them there—"

"Did you dream this?" she asked sharply. He shook his head again, top-heavy.

"I thought yes. Then no. That's why I have to find Adam Fin."

She felt her throat close; her hands closed over her arms. "Adam," she whispered, and heard the sound of water, running into dark, secret places. "What does this have to do with Adam?"

"Adam," he mocked. "Adam. You keep saying his name. I don't even know her name. The old oyster wouldn't tell me. 'Ask her,' she said. 'Ask her. She'll tell you the price of her name.' So I have to find Adam Fin. I was just out asking people."

"Why?" Her voice jerked. "Why Adam?"

"Because he knows where she is. When she walks on land. He knows her."

She felt the blood run cold and thin under her skin. The stairway, she thought, out of the sea. She went to Jonah, took his arm very gently away from the door frame, and locked the door behind him, though she knew that in the end, no door would keep out the sea.

Jonah, bleary-eyed and stubbled, sat behind the shop counter the next morning, his eyes on the *Compend*, which was written in some troublesome language of which he only understood a word or two here and there. The conch shells and big cowries and the chambered nautiluses on the shelves sang faintly to the rhythm of the waves. Their music, delicate as notes played on a glass, kept drifting between his eyes and the page. He listened as intently to the bell on the door, to the quality of voices, though they all spoke the obscure language of the *Compend*. Jenny, cheerful and efficient, only disturbed him when she had to; she seemed to sense how he needed to seep, fossil-like, into the wall, while he waited for Adam Fin's pale, calm face, his mocking eyes.

Finally, after hours of listening for a voice that never spoke, he despaired, snapped the *Compend* shut with a sound that made Jenny start.

"I have to go," he said.

"I'm just about to leave for lunch, Jonah. You seem a little under the weather. Have you caught a bug?"

He smiled a little, crookedly. "Some kind of a bug, yeah. Megan's upstairs. Call her and she'll cover your lunch break. I have to get out of here."

"Well," she said, her voice mild, innocent of subterfuge, "I hope you feel better soon." She reached for the phone. She had never heard the music of the chambered nautilus, Jonah guessed. She had never wept over a darkly glittering shadow, a scent of brine. For a moment he envied her.

He drove the truck to the cove again, knowing he would find nothing. He wanted to stand at the mouth of the cave, just stand there, in the place where she had been, not hoping she would be there, but to feed his heart with memories. The tide was coming in, but he climbed along the side of the cliff anyway, then around its face. Tide licked at his heels, as he made his way across the long bones of rock. Ruthless afternoon sunlight scoured the cave clean of shadows; the rough, exuberant waves shouted but refused to sing. Still he stood there, staring at the sea life along the cave walls and trying to find the mystery behind the barnacles.

The sea poured around him suddenly, hit the back wall; it echoed laughter as the wave withdrew. He grabbed at rock, cut his palm on a crusty barnacle. He waited for the powerful drag on his body to end, then slogged back over the whale bones between waves, wet to the crotch. Hugging the cliff above the deep water, where the lip of rock was narrowest, he came face-to-face with Adam Fin.

He was laughing the deep booming laughter in the cave. He didn't cling to the cliff, he leaned gracefully into it, so finely balanced that Jonah might have knocked him off with a pebble, except that he had no desire to see what Adam Fin would do in water. Dissolve, grow a fish's tail, turn a seal's face up at Jonah, or worse—whatever it was, he might not be found easily again. His teeth seemed even sharper in the sunlight.

"Got a little wet," he commented. "Didn't you." He reached out suddenly, caught Jonah's wrist. Jonah, hanging on by one hand, nearly fell. He pushed himself back against the cliff, panting, and found Adam looking at his hand. "Cave bite?"

"Barnacle," Jonah said tersely. There was another wrench at his precarious balance; Adam twisted his hand back, held it over the water. Three drops of blood fell. Jonah turned his face into the cliff, swallowed a taste like iron in his throat. He forced himself to speak.

"She said—Dory said—there is a price. Is this part of it?"

"No. I'm just being perverse." He laughed without sound at Jonah's stare; his eyes were cold as rime. "What is it you want, Jonah?"

"I want—" He stopped at the edge of saying, drew breath. He said to the barren cliff, "You know what I want. You knew before you laid eyes on me. She's your sister. That's all I know. But she's nothing like you. She's timeless, and she is the face of the sea, all its beautiful shapes and colors and all its songs. I don't even know her name. She haunts me and she won't let me find her. Help me. Tell me her name."

"Storm," Adam said. "Undertow. Rapture of the deep." Still he held Jonah's hand over the sea, where green water weltered against stone. "You know her. She has shown her face before, rising in the wake of wrecked ships, singing to the doomed. Turn your face to land again, where you are loved. You could never pay her price. And the price you will pay will be too high."

"What price?"

"Megan."

Jonah blinked at the word. It seemed incongruous, irrelevant, like an apple tree growing placidly out of the middle of the sea. "Megan. This has nothing to do with her. She'll understand. And she can take care of herself."

The grip on his wrist tightened; he wrenched at it, then caught wildly at Adam's wrist to keep from falling. They stood poised like dancers on the fine edge between land and sea. A high wave spun against the cliff's edge; brine fanned into the air, flecked their hands, Adam's eyes, Jonah's mouth with bitterness.

"You don't know her," Adam said.

"I don't know who? Megan? Of course I know her." He stopped, blinking at another flick of water; his eyes narrowed, searching the pale, sea-washed face for a hint of expression. "You." He tasted brine again, and spat. "You follow her. She lets you watch her draw. She talks to you. It's you she wants, not me. So why are you throwing her name at me? You take care of her. Until this is over."

"You think you can walk on water to return to land." Still his face held no more expression than a clam.

"I am walking on water," Jonah said tightly. "That's all I can see, all I can hear. Tide and her voice, calling. Tell me where I can find her."

"What if I offer you something instead of her?"

"There is nothing." He swallowed, his throat tight. "Nothing instead of. Nothing without."

"What if I offer you freedom?"

"Freedom?"

"From her."

His eyes widened; his hold tightened, as if the cliff had shifted beneath him at the words. "No."

"Look at yourself," Adam said softly. "You can't even see out of your own eyes; you can't remember your own past. You are already adrift in the sea, without enough sense to be afraid. You're a stranger in your own life. The only voice you hear is hers, and she's not even human. I'll tell you how to stop that voice in your brain, in your blood. I'll show you how to return to land before she pulls you underneath the waves."

"No."

"I warn you." He spoke softly but very clearly through the tide spilling around them and the gulls crying overhead. "You will find her price too high."

"She can have whatever she wants," Jonah said wearily. "Just tell me. Tell me where to find her. I'll give you what you want for that. Anything."

The familiar cold, mocking smile surfaced finally in Adam's eyes, like a shark fin cutting the calm surface of the sea. "You are so reckless with your promises, you humans. Don't you pay attention to your own tales?"

"I can't pay attention to anything," Jonah whispered. "I can't see words anymore. I can't even think. You offer me something I can't refuse, then you laugh at me because I can't refuse it. Just tell me where I can find her."

"You can find her where land touches sea, where lost ships founder against the siren's song, where the last light of the sun and the first light of the moon touch the sea." He dropped Jonah's hand, and added, as Jonah groped wildly for him, "Or you can find her at the Ancient Mariner Friday night. She'll be singing then."

He slid out of Jonah's grip like a fish. Jonah turned his face to the cliff. He heard the splash a moment later; the sea reached up to touch his cheek.

Megan, haunted by the dreams and shadows of memory cast up out of forgotten places in her brain, spent a frantic hour or two in Mike's bookstore after Jenny came back from lunch.

"They," she demanded of Mike. "Who are they? Where do they live?"

Mike wrapped his book around a thumb, sank his head onto one fist, and tapped a tooth meditatively with a forefinger. He removed the finger finally and said, "If you want names, names are in mythology."

"Mythology. But that's not real. This is real."

He gazed at her so long she wondered if he, too, were about to change into something unexpected: answer her with a sea lion's bark, or show her the webs between his fingers. He said finally, "There is the Kingdom of Ys, the beautiful, drowned city haunted by its princess, who sings to mortals and drags them down under the sea when they come to her. Someday, it is said, Ys will rise again. There is Sorcha, the sea kingdom of the selkies, the enchanted children of the king, who can live in the sea and on land, and who are tormented by their longing for both. There is Tir na n'Og, Land of the Forever Young, one of the Isles of the Blest, which appear out of the sea mists floating on the waves just long enough for mortals to see their unattainable richness and magic before they sink back down beneath the waves.

There is the Island of Glass, with its castles of light and crystal that you might glimpse within the weaving strands of sunlight on the sea, if you don't look directly at it. There is the realm up north, ruled by Sedna, whose temper is terrible and whose looks can kill, who watches with her single eye over the mammals of the ocean. There is Fata Morgana, the dream palace made of clouds that appears in the first misty light of morning, or in the last light over the sea before night. But." He shrugged a little. "None of that will do you any good."

A couple of browsers, who had never heard him speak more than dollars and cents, gave him scattered applause among the shelves. Megan, entranced by glimpses of the hidden realms in Mike's head, pleaded, "Why not?"

"You said it. Mythology is what was real. What's real now is for you to see. For you to say. That's why it's nowhere in here." He opened his book. "But go ahead and look."

So she did, and found water kingdoms everywhere under the sea, but all safely bound between the lines of language, all belonging to someone else. She found the seals who walked ashore in human form and the sea goddess named Doris, who had fifty children, and the sirens who sang so sweetly on rocks that they lured sailors to their deaths in the sea. But the sailors were trapped in the amber of tales, safe and unchangeable. None walked around now, drunk on secret music; none felt pain or gave it. Jonah, she thought, and felt the nick at her heart of fear and betrayal. Would he wreck his boat on the rocks or could she rescue him? Did he want to be rescued? Would she bother? And the sorrow in Adam Fin's eyes was not a yearning for human love, but grief for something else. He had not filled her pockets with pearls, but with the broken pieces of the world she knew.

But what was his world? A glint of light in a wave? In a bottle? Or was it more accessible? She closed the books and went out to where the true sea blew spindrift at her glasses and flowed over her feet, drowning her footprints as she passed. Mike had found a piece of it; there must be other pieces she could puzzle together, as they might puzzle, trying to fit together a jump-rope handle and a vacuum-cleaner nozzle and a bicycle chain. This time she ignored her own world; she let the garbage lie, and the agates and even the perfect sand dollars. Her pockets empty, she looked for nameless things to put in them.

The long walk wearied her; her thoughts drifted, unmoored. The warm late afternoon light worked its odd magic on familiar things in her path. Her eye, persistent in its quest, transformed them. The sand dollar, whole and white as bone, was distinct as a moon on the wet sand; the world was upside down. Great ropy tangles of kelp with their dark, scaly leaves were mermaids, their thick golden hair coiled around them as they slept. Agates and sea glass shone like jewels; horses, white as foam, rode the waves, manes streaming behind them as they raced along the border between worlds, then vanished back into their own. Song drifted endlessly from the waves, luring, coaxing, pleading, in some forgotten language. The dead jellyfish had been a tiny, delicate floating kingdom of glass; the purple mussel shell a flake of dark castle wall; the white seal lying just beyond the surf was a man.

She stopped, seeing the seal again, long, pale, and graceful. And then Adam. He turned seal's eyes to look at her. And then they were sea eyes, foamy green. He was sunbathing. He was pale everywhere, sleek and muscled, a swimmer. He wore bathing trunks, but the way he looked at her, he might as well have worn nothing.

She swallowed. Light lay between them, a curl of water. She took a step back. He was on his feet then, a movement too quick for the mortal eye. He stood in front of her, wordless, insistent, his skin speaking, luring, coaxing. His eyes promised knowledge, promised gentleness.

She drew breath, loosed it slowly. She put the back of her hand to her mouth, and took another step away from him. She whispered, "Jonah."

He spoke her name; a pearl dropped out of his mouth into his hand. He touched her then, took her hand, smiling gently. He laid the pearl on her palm and closed her fingers over it. Light or sea ran between them; when she blinked he was gone.

The Ancient Mariner was crowded when Jonah walked into it on Friday. The musicians were still setting up. Whoops and crackles and other underwater noises came out of the sound system. In the dim light, faces looked unfamiliar, oddly shadowed. No one had the long dark hair he remembered. He went to the bar, ordered beer. He didn't recognize the bartender.

"Where's Sharon?"

The bartender, a slender, bearded young man with a shell in his ear, gave him a cheerful smile, but seemed not to hear his question. Jonah swallowed beer, feeling light-headed, edgy. He looked around more carefully. Faces crowded into the shadows, talking, laughing. She would not be laughing, he thought. Her face would be calm, mysterious as the moon, until she sang. But he did not see her.

He finished the beer quickly; the bronze fixtures along the bar gleamed with a mellower light. The bartender passed him another. A familiar gravelly voice caught his ear; he ducked behind his bottle, upending it.

He found someone at his elbow; he thought he recognized her, and then didn't. There were a number of strangers, friends of the band probably, from other little towns along the coast. Here and there, at the candlelit tables, was the well-dressed tourist, wearing a skirt, heels, a tie. The band had changed; instead of being Hell-bent they were the Undertow. There seemed a lot of them, as they moved around the stage, and they all seemed to look alike. Jonah, finishing his second beer, decided that was a trick of the lighting.

Dory jostled along the bar, moored herself beside him. "So you've come," she said.

"Where is she?"

"She'll be here." She sipped her briny drink and surveyed herself in the bar mirror. She touched her wild hair approvingly, widened a crepey gray eye, then settled into her normal expression of mingled crankiness and amusement. "She's looking for Adam."

"Last I saw," he said sourly, "he was feeding my blood to the sharks."

She chuckled. "He has his ways." She touched her glass rim, licked salt off her finger. "He'll be back."

"I can't wait."

"He went looking for something, he said, along the tide line. Something he said you gave him."

"I didn't give him anything," Jonah said shortly, raising his empty bottle at the bartender.

"You gave him something. You must have. You wouldn't be here for free."

"Oh." He ran a hand over his face, felt the stubble on it with surprise. He caught a glimpse of his own face in the mirror. It seemed ghostly, unfamiliar, the hair too long and fiery, the face gaunt, chalky. Can't be mine, he thought. Dory was gazing at the face, too, curiously.

"What did you give him?"

He shook his head. "I don't know. Whatever he wanted." He turned restively toward the stage. Lights flickered; something else flowed, glittered, just within the door beside the stage. He watched it, thoughtless, entranced. Dory's voice jarred him again.

"Don't you want to know?"

"What?"

"What you gave him?" He looked at her, wondering what she was talking about. She gave her rumbling, bitter chuckle. "What do you think he wanted from you? A fossil? A pair of earrings?"

He turned impatiently, seeking the glittering shadow. "What does it matter? What in my life is worth anything to me anymore? Is that her? Is that her in the doorway?" He felt her: the undertow in his thoughts, in his blood. He didn't hear Dory's answer.

He didn't see anyone as he crossed the room, only the fine, star-shot shadow, shifting between dark green and black. The musicians, tuning, taping cable down, ignored him. He reached the door, stepped into the dark and heard the hollow, crashing boom of the tide.

Cool, briny wind blew through the passage; an invisible breaker, flooding the shadows, flicked seawater on his lips. The narrow strip of light from the open door slanted across a still, pale face, a single pearl in an earlobe, dark hair falling over a dark fall of glittering fabric spilling open above a foam-white breast.

He heard his heart pound. He made some noise, some movement; she lifted a hand, long and pale and as delicately jointed as coral.

"Not yet." Her voice, light, murmuring, was barely audible above the invisible tide. The hand moved out of the light; he felt it, touching his mouth. He lifted his hands to catch it, his lips parting as her finger traced them. Her hand slipped through his like water; in the light, he saw her eyes smile, an alien, luminous smile.

He swallowed, his throat parched, lips burning, as if he had drunk seawater. "I don't know your name," he whispered.

"My name is Nereis." A secret wave gathered and broke; she swayed a little as if it swirled around her; the glittering, tide tugged, parted between her breasts. He didn't know he had lifted his own hand until he saw it in the light; his fingertips barely grazed cloth before she caught them.

"When?" he demanded, and didn't recognize his voice. "You call me and I try to find you, and you vanish, and now I've found you, you can touch me, but I can't touch you—" He felt her tongue slide between his clenched fingers, and his voice broke. He stumbled forward, brought himself up against the blank wall.

"Jonah." She spoke from where he had stood near the open door, her face in shadow now. "I am very old. Older than the little fossils you pick out of cliffs. Older than the cliffs themselves. And I am very dangerous."

He swallowed again, gazing at her, pushed against the wall as if by some churning onslaught of water. The water loosed him finally, pulled him off balance, a step toward her. He couldn't see her face, but he saw, where her hair was swept back, the pearl a shade paler than her earlobe, that would be small and hard and silken against his tongue. He closed his eyes against it, pleaded, "Why? Why did you come to me in that cave?"

"Because you heard my voice. I sang to you and you stood in the ancient seas and listened." He felt her fingers again, light and quick, a touch of spindrift against his chest, and then the tide rising, flowing around his thighs, idling a moment, soundless and full, before its strong, churning pull away from his body. "You listened," she said again, as he opened his mouth, drew breath, sagging against the wall. "And you love the forgotten sea. Jonah."

"Yes," he whispered.

"Do you want me?"

"Yes."

"Then you must find me."

He opened his eyes again. "I have found you."

"In your world," she said, "but you must find me in mine. I cannot stay long on land. I am too ancient, too tide-drawn. You must come to me. If you want me."

"I want you," he whispered, swaying in the invisible tide. "I want you at the oldest place under the sea. The place where fossils and time began. But how can I live under the sea? I'll drown, loving you. All through history, people have drowned, loving you." The tide, playing around him, ebbed slowly, pulling him into its long, powerful embrace; he fell to his knees at her feet. He gazed up at her, saw her face in shadow, and then in light as she bent suddenly. Her fingers tangled in his hair; she drew his head back, kissed his open mouth, and he felt her breath flowing into him like tide, full, relentless, endless, until he heard his own blood sing with her voice. Then the tide turned; he felt it drawing back around his face, his groping hands. It dropped him, receded into shadow, into silence. He lay stranded, beached on the floorboards, swallowing the pearl she had left in his mouth.

Memory burned his lips as he rose; he gripped the door a moment, blind. He made his way out as unobtrusively as possible, clinging to the shadows, looking at no one, until he found the bar and leaned on it. He lifted his eyes then, saw the room behind him in the mirror.

He stared at it senselessly. It was made of pearl, of glass, of light. Moonshells crawled across the floor; bubbles drifted, popped, spoke words. He turned abruptly. On a stage of crystal, the musicians played strands of light. Fish darted in and out of the strands. The musicians' hair drifted, full of colored snails, brilliant, rippling ribbons of sea slugs. Their faces were so translucent he could almost see the fine bones beneath the skin, as if they were related to the strange, luminous fish in the deep of the sea. Pearls floated from their mouths as they sang, clustered on the rocky ceiling above their heads. The listeners, with hair and beards of sea moss, foam, the gold secretions of pen shells, lifted hands drawn long and fine by endless currents, and sipped from mussel shells as blue-black as their eyes.

"What?" Jonah whispered; a bubble escaped him, joined the pearls along the cave roof. He felt a touch and whirled. Starfish clung to the bar; a fish swam under his nose. He felt his knees give, and clung to the bar, feeling sea life stir under his grip. Something rippled between his hands, a solitary, shell-less wanderer. He remembered it swimming in and out of Megan's hair: the little sea hare in her drawing.

He inhaled a great breath of water as easily as air. "Megan." Her name choked him, turned his chest to fire. Adam, polishing an abalone shell behind the bar, smiled.

"Welcome," he said softly, "to the belly of the whale."

FIVE

Jonah had vanished.

Megan, white-faced and stunned, searched the town for him; no one had seen him. She went to the Ancient Mariner; no band, she was told, had played there recently. She tracked Hell-bent down in a nearby town: they had never, she was told, had a female singer. No bodies clutching fossils had been dragged to shore by the tide. He was in love with someone; he had run away. That was obvious, she told herself, as she stared, numb and mute with shock, at the blank wall of his absence. Still she looked for some hint of where he had gone, some aberration of his life among his socks, something peculiar among his rocks, a message between the lines of the *Compend* he had left lying open on his stool in the shop. And even while she searched the obvious, the impossible fact of where he had gone lay stark and clear as the moon in the dark of her mind.

He had fallen in love with a mermaid and had gone to live in the sea.

He had, it seemed, taken all the mystery in the world along with him. She could find neither Adam Fin nor Dory. Even Mike had forgotten how to talk. When she asked about the Otherworld, the Land Beneath the Waves, he only grunted, his eyes on his book, and pointed a finger at the shelves. She spent days sketching, hoping that her pen would reveal some message of him, but the sea told her nothing; her sketches remained stubbornly unmysterious.

So she changed them, sitting for long hours on the sand, drawing feverishly, desperately. She drew roads of light leading to palaces of cloud and glass rising into the morning mists. She drew underwater creatures: angelfish with legs and rippling wings and narrow, delicate fish faces; butterflyfish that flew in great clouds of color above the water; goatfish with slitted yellow eyes and slender, hooved legs that galloped along the sea floor, herded by the damselfish and her dogfish. She drew a seal with Adam's face; she drew his body with a seal's face. She drew Jonah, with his long red floating hair and his glasses, and a scaly mer-tail, sitting at the bottom of the sea on a giant clam, reading. She was crying long before she finished it; the lines of his body were starred with tears of sorrow that he had gone, tears of fury that he had left her for another woman, tears of helplessness because the sea showed her only its flat blank face and would not speak to her.

She left Jenny to run the shop, except at lunchtime. Jenny, worried over Megan's hollowed, white face, said, "He'd never have just left you, the store, everything. You should call the police."

"He left me," Megan said crossly, "for another woman."

"What other woman? You know all the women he knows. You are so close; why would he have left you for someone else?"

Megan, practicing at the register, which she loathed, banged the drawer shut. "Well, he did. Maybe he'll be back, maybe not. I'll just have to keep the store open until we run out of things to sell. Jonah handled all that."

"He'll be back," Jenny said, with her exasperating optimism. People, Megan decided dourly, existed in different worlds at the same time: the people who inhabited Jenny's world never ventured farther out to sea than the surf for a little fishing, and if they were lured out of that world into someone else's less predictable world, they probably did come back. "Anyway, he'd never have left his fossils."

Megan's mouth tightened; a tear fell, in spite of her, among the register keys. He vanished, she thought, into a drop of water. Into light. And Adam Fin knows where he is. And Dory knows. But they won't tell me. And I don't know why they took him. She said, punching keys, "He told me he was obsessed by another woman. Some singer. He said it didn't have anything to do with me. How he figured that, I don't know."

"Who is she?" Jenny asked, startled. "Where does she live?"

"I don't know. He didn't tell me."

"Well," Jenny said practically after a moment, "he has all his money tied up in the store. He has to come back and deal with it. Don't you think?"

"I don't know." She folded her arms against the register, dropped her face against them. The register made a noise; the drawer sprang open against her ribs. "Don't hold your breath."

She walked on the beach later in the dark, dry-eyed, pleading silently for a hook to fly out of nowhere and catch her by the hair. Or for Adam Fin to appear in her path. Maybe he would have taken me where Jonah is, she thought wearily, if I had wanted him. But I didn't want a mystery. I just want Jonah back, leaving rocks all over the place, and cooking for me, and criticizing my work. I want his bony body and his cobalt eyes behind his glasses, and his mouth nibbling the earrings out of my ears if I forget to take them off. She tripped over something and kicked it irritably into the surf. What could they want with him, anyway? He's crotchety, he sits around reading all the time, he complains about everything, and he hates meeting people. But he loves me, and he feels like smooth wood in my hands. And he loves my art, and he loves the sea.

Too much, apparently, she thought, and felt the sting of salt behind her eyes. What if he doesn't want to come back?

She sent another bit of something in her way flying into the waves, touched her glasses back up her nose, her eyes wide. He's human, she thought, not fish. Not whatever they are. He can't live in their world.

Seven years, the tales said. Seven years, and even then, some mortals did not want to return to the real world.

So, she thought, dry-eyed again, her hair wild in the wind, whipping across her mouth. I'll find him and ask him. I'll know, then. I'll know. But how?

She stopped, staring out at the vast, restless dark. If I find Adam, she thought, maybe we can bargain. If he wants me. But I don't think that's what he wants. I don't think that's what he wants at all. But maybe, when I see him, he'll tell me what he wants for Jonah. Or what she wants.

She.

A face sketched itself in Megan's mind: a model's face, with wide-set, sea-green eyes, hair black as the sea on a moonless night, cheekbones that could cut. She shivered. She wrapped her arms around herself, felt the hollows between her ribs.

Or me. With my hands colored with washes, my glasses sliding down my nose, my big feet. I can't sing a note to save my life. Even if I do find him, will he want to come back? But if I don't find him, I'll never know. So I'll find him.

But how? The waves took up her question, curled it under them, withdrew on long sighs of *how*? She stood a long time listening, but they never answered.

Jonah sat against the figurehead of an ancient wreck. Her hair was green with moss, her smile was sweet, distant, the only thing visible in a blind, green face. He leaned his head between her breasts, his back against her fishy waist. She was the only mermaid he had seen down here; he found her smile wry and oddly comforting.

The wreck lay on a shelf of rock that plunged into shadow. Or it lay in a room so vast the ship seemed simply a piece of décor: a graceful pile of worm-eaten wood, out of which a skeletal hand waved now and then. If he looked for it, he saw the structure of the room, great walls of pearl and watery light, windows of thin sheets of mother-of-pearl through which water moved like air. If he looked hard, he saw the people in the room, glints of light forming faces, shimmering garments. They took more human form to look at him, as if he were some kind of mirror; even then their faces, like living fossils, were disturbing. They were immortal, and as old as water; they could resemble what they wanted. They could wear periwinkles for eyes on a kelp-leaf face. When they took human faces, their beauty could be inhuman.

So far, only Adam had spoken to him. Others brought him things to eat and drink; what, exactly, he refused to guess. Everything tasted strange, briny, wet; he might have been eating jellyfish or sea slugs, for all he knew. Eating was one of the two preoccupations in the sea. If he looked straight into it, huddling close to the figurehead, he saw the lovely anemones turn into mouths surrounded by fingers with which they stung and guided their food. He watched starfish cling to clams, force them open little by little, suck out the helpless inhabitants from their homes. He saw the sea cucumber extend a sticky finger to dredge plankton from the sea floor; the great-eyed, luminous dragonfish jut out its spiky lower jaw to pin and take in prey larger than itself. He watched the squid rise up from the deep waters below the cliff, pass silently as a nightmare on its way to graze the warmer, livelier upper regions. He watched the sperm whale dive past him as silently to search for the leviathan that never showed itself above the dark; he watched sharks eat the whale, leaving him in a cloud of blood that he could taste. Nothing scented him, though; he left no more trace of himself in the water than if he had been a dream.

Sometimes he would find the entire sea mating around him. Then some undulation of a great fish's tail would bring him a memory of the curved, darkly glittering mass in the shadows of the cave. He would grow blind and deaf as the figurehead with desire, and find, when the urgency around him faded, only Adam's mocking face.

"Where can I find her?"

"She'll tell you where. She'll tell you how." He cracked an oyster between his fingers, drew out the pearl and ate it, amused at Jonah's expression. "Be patient. Here, only the fish hurry."

Jonah dropped his head back against the mossy breast. "Am I dead? In my world?"

"This is your world."

"You know what I mean."

"You're not dead. You are living in the great whale's eye. You have become something rich and strange." He tossed the oyster in the path of a passing starfish. "Strange, at any rate. Your eyes are haunted; there are little snails in your hair. You should have stayed with Megan."

"Megan." She was another life, the Otherworld of air and light.

"Remember Megan?"

"Of course I do," he said irritably.

"You vanished out of her life. She stands at the edge of the sea and mourns."

"She knows?" he said, so startled he nearly became aware of the water in his throat. "She knows I'm here? How could she possibly?"

"We gave her pieces; she put them together."

"But why?"

Adam shrugged a little. In the sea, he wore a sort of bodysuit of a glistening, fish-scale blue that covered everything and hid nothing. He looked, Jonah thought sourly, like something out of Action Comics: Aquaman, hero of the deep, capable of tying the giant squid into knots while processing oxygen out of water in his lungs to share with the beautiful, unconscious scientist with one foot caught in a giant clam. Except for his eyes, which viewed Jonah with as much tenderness as a shark. "She'll tell you."

"Who? Megan?"

"My sister." He touched the figurehead lightly; for a moment he wore its sweet, human smile. "She chose you." He pulled moss off the face, bared one worm-eaten eye.

"She said for me to find her, in her world. I'm here. She brought me. As if—as if she might have wanted me. I mean—" He swallowed, touched his glasses, across which a minute snail was crawling. "Maybe all she wanted was another set of bones."

"No."

"I mean, what am I? Some long-haired, short-sighted bookworm whose idea of a good time is picking brachiopods out of a cliff. And she—" He loosed the word again, on a long, slow whisper, trailing bubbles like tiny pearls that caught in the mermaid's moss. "She. . . ." He stirred restively, blind with the memory of her kiss, of the swelling tide that had touched him everywhere. "How could she want me? She just brought me down here to torment me, the way she tormented me in my world."

"My sister never takes what she doesn't want. The sea changes itself at every touch of light, but it is never false."

"Then where is she? Is there another price to pay for her? What more can I pay than this?"

"She'll tell you," Adam said equivocally. "And you still owe me."

"I know," Jonah said indifferently. "But what have I got left?"

"Your ears. Your eyes." He flashed his teeth at Jonah's horror. "Time. Your fingers. How can you feel stone with no fingers? Your teeth. You have a lot that you don't seem to value. Your voice. Shall I take away your voice in return for my sister?"

"What," Jonah asked tersely, "do you really want?"

Adam pulled more moss from the wooden face, uncovered a pearl in its other eye. His face changed. Jonah, watching in astonishment, felt his own face melt into expression. He lifted one hand after a moment, caught what fell from Adam's eyes and floated down as pearls.

Maybe, Megan thought, standing on the cliff above the tide pools, I could get there by drowning.

The tide pools were appearing and disappearing under the rush and drag of water. Barnacles opened and sent out feathery legs to catch at food roiling over them. Anemones' graceful tendrils stunned the minute transparent animals tumbling past, who were themselves filtering the rich brine through nets of mucus in their mouths. The feeding frenzy, invisible to Megan's eye, yet vivid to her mind's eye from all the books she had been reading, made her wonder what Jonah ate. Sushi, she decided morosely. If I throw myself into the water, maybe they would rescue me, guide me into their world. Or maybe they would just let me drown.

Then she snatched at the word, remembering it from half-forgotten tales. Guide. I need a guide.

She sat down on the cliff, flung a pebble into the water instead of her body. What could possibly guide her from the wonderful yet predictable sea, where nothing was left uncounted, undissected, unexamined, and ultimately uneaten, to that world where the sea sang with a siren's voice and the wild breakers blowing spume changed into the white horses of the king? Something had led Jonah there, where his mermaid languished and blew bubbles and showed him, no doubt, how to make love to something whose appropriate parts resembled a tuna fish. But she walked, Megan remembered; she had legs when she walked on land.

She sighed, and tossed another pebble.

How had all this begun? she wondered. There was a time before the singer, and a time before Dory and before Adam Fin. When there was no magic, just Jonah and me living together, and the shop, and my drawings. Then one day, then once upon a time, then something happened. . . .

The sea hare crawled into my drawing. The sea hare brought the magic.

She contemplated that, frowning. Follow a sea hare into the sea? It would be akin to following a slug through a forest. And she had found the sea hare in her drawing, not in the tide pool. She would have to walk through that sea of paper and ink to follow it.

Gulls along the tide line began shrieking, bickering over something edible that had washed ashore. Burrowed beneath their feet, the clams siphoned water through holes in the sand, filtering out microscopic suppers. She and Jonah ate the clams, except when some pesticide dump contaminated them. Then the plankton ate the pesticides, the clams ate the plankton, someone else ate the poisoned clams. So far, always someone else. Not, she remembered sadly, that it mattered anymore. Not to Jonah, who had been eaten by the sea.

Is he still alive? she wondered, chilled. Did they leave his bones somewhere so deep he'll become a fossil before he ever gets washed ashore? Jonah, lying in the dark abyss, slowly covered by a constant fall of sea debris. . . . "No," she whispered, shaking hair out of her face, "they didn't take him to kill him." She thought of Adam, lying in the surf, watching her pull garbage out of her pockets, the look on his face as if he were the one dying. . . .

She stood up restively, frustrated by so many pieces that didn't fit. Adam. Dory and her fishhook. The singer. She had never met the singer; she had spent five minutes with Dory; Adam she knew a little better. . . . She began to walk along the cliff, toward town. Adam had watched her draw. Adam had watched her recognize him as something more or less than human. Adam had stood in the tide, willing her to touch him, and then he had turned her name into a pearl. She had put the pearl in a little box with her grandmother's gold wedding band, a tiny perfect sand dollar no bigger than a nickel that Jonah had given her, a fossil shark tooth she had found, a dried rose from some forgotten dance, the opal-and-gold earring that Jonah hadn't eaten.

She began to walk a little faster. From the time after the coming of the sea hare, there were her two drawings, and there was Adam's jewelry. She hadn't looked at either for some time; for all she knew, the sea hare had crawled back out of the picture carrying all of Adam's things. If not, maybe there was some clue, somewhere. An inky arrow, a dotted line, a trail of earrings showing the way. Follow the yellow brick road, the path of the setting sun, take the road not taken. . . .

At home, she checked her drawings first. The tide pool, matted but not yet framed, still held its unexpected visitor. Her hair still floated in the tide, tangled in Dory's hook. She went downstairs, into the shop, where Jenny was wrapping a necklace of moonstones for a customer. She went behind the counter, gazed down through the glass at the shelf where Adam's jewelry was displayed. Jenny turned to her as the customer left.

"He's selling very well," she commented. "Don't you think we should get a few more pieces? And we have some money for him he never picked up."

Megan, finding no messages in the gold spirals, the penguin pin of moonstone and onyx, made a noise. She straightened, her eyes still on the fine work. "I don't know where he is."

"He must have left a phone number."

"Not with me."

"An address?" Her white brows rose above her glasses. "He must have given Jonah some idea. . . . Now where did Jonah put—" She opened a drawer or two, then lifted the phone and removed the address book beneath it. "What is his last name?"

"Fin." Megan slid her hands over her eyes, feeling a sudden urge to laugh. "Adam Fin."

Jenny ruffled pages. "Well, he's not under Fin. Maybe Adam?"

"I don't think even Jonah knew. He asked me once where Adam lived."

"He never left a number?"

"No." Her voice came out unexpectedly husky; she bent over the counter again, swallowing past the burn in her throat. "He didn't leave anything. Except these."

"Well," Jenny said again, blankly. "That's odd. He'll be back, sooner or later, to check, I'm sure. I've sold at least one thing every day. And someone said she'd think about the penguin pin. Someone bought the sea-otter pin just yesterday—I told Jonah to take that. And the blue-whale earrings got snapped up right away."

Megan, chin on her palm, swiveled to look at her. "What else?" she asked dully. "Do you remember?"

"Of course. I made a list. How else would we know what to pay him?"

"Oh."

Jenny smiled a little and produced it efficiently from the drawer beneath the register. "The sea-turtle pin. The cats-on-fishhooks earrings. The bracelet of silver dolphins. The rabbit-moon earrings."

"Which?"

"The black rabbits running under the quarter moons."

"But I remember—" She moved abruptly; her elbow slid jarringly off the counter. "But Adam was wearing one when he first came."

Jenny shrugged. "He must like them. The gold-and-amethyst pendant—"

"Hare."

"What?"

She was staring at Jenny. "Hare. Not rabbit."

"Well," Jenny said tolerantly, "whichever." She went back to her list, while Megan, gazing at amethyst and moonstone through the glass, followed the trail of the sea hare into her life.

Jonah, left alone for a long time under the mermaid's smile, was driven finally, by her blind stare of pearl and wormwood, to leave her for something that could see him. He moved easily, he found, through an element that seemed to shift constantly between air and shadow, water and light. Sometimes he saw clearly how he wandered, along with whale and mackerel and jellyfish, through rooms whose walls were living coral, with ceilings of pearl and gold, or walls of giant kelp rising open to the light, jeweled fish darting among the leaves. Occasionally figures passed him, so vague he barely recognized the sudden sketch of color, the swirl of water, until he felt their eyes, their attention. Once or twice, he followed more familiar forms, humans of a dreamlike beauty, long hair bound with pearls and cowrie shells, slender feet disturbing not a grain of sand. These he would have expected, if he had ever thought about such a place. They would melt away eventually, reappear with hands of scallop shells and jet-black eyes that never blinked. Sometimes they followed him; he would feel their eyes and turn, and find something part kelp, part luminous, and always with those intense, unblinking eyes. They never spoke. Once, compelled to turn, he found a tiny purple animal rippling after him, leaving a glistening trail that hardened into mother-of-pearl. He recognized the sea hare. Something that looked like a fat gray cucumber flowed up behind it and ate it. He heard Adam's laughter.

He began seeing odd human things: bits of time frozen on the ocean floor. Some he expected: the pirate's chest sagging open, spilling coins and diamonds; the marble head of a warrior gazing pensively at a brain coral; a gold goblet; a steel buckler lost in some sea battle; cannonballs, like the eggs of some huge sea turtle, scattered in the sand. These lay where they had fallen, in the midst of gardens blown of glass, in hallways, on tables, in fountains that spilled air instead of water. In one of the gardens, where colorless roses glistened like ice around him, and he walked a path of darkly gleaming fish scales, he heard the faint, gentle song that haunted him.

He stopped. It came from everywhere. The light changed, or his vision became unearthly for a moment: the shining towers of light and gold, the gardens spun of glass, the windows of every fish's color, were of such loveliness he knew he had stepped beyond his world. A pearl fell from his eye. And then the vision was gone, leaving him alone, neither of one world nor another. But the song, stealing like rapture into his blood, was unchanged, and it beckoned now from one fixed place in the sea.

He moved again, more quickly. The sea itself lured him: a leaf traced his lips with its fine edge as he pushed through a stand of kelp; others clung briefly, intimately, like hands. He found a path of soft white sand or crushed pearl beyond the kelp; the song, flowing on its own warm current, grew stronger. He followed the path, tripped over a wooden mast with a rotting sail, then climbed over a cargo of burst oak barrels. Within the slats of one barrel, he saw the mad, bald, old-man's face of an eel; it chilled him, but did not notice him. Something nibbled delicately at his ear: a tiny fish grazing as through the inner whorls of a shell. The path vanished under a huge tangle of cable; he climbed it, and then what looked like a jungle of plumbing pipes, scarcely noticing what he picked his way over, intent only on finding the path again. He found it, meandering like the song into a garden whose walls of coral and anemone and stone rose higher than his head, lining the path. Pale anemones opened slowly as he passed, showing him their hungry mouths. The path veered sharply, ended at a wall. He stopped; the song beckoned on the other side. He retraced his steps, turned a corner, another, and was stopped again by a solid mass of crimson coral. The song, stronger now, came from beyond it. He stood a moment, bewildered, while small fish darted through his floating hair. And then he recognized the maze.

He gave a cry of frustration and longing; all around him coral polyps snapped shut. But the singing, deep, languorous, soothed him, coaxed him to turn, try again, turn down the next branch, where the singer would be, pale as pearl, sleek and naked as a fish, her long black hair jeweled with bright anemone; there, she would be, not there, but there, not this turning, but that, or most certainly that. She would be there, singing, her long fingers gently sliding over, under an oyster, feeling for its pearl.

He reached the end, found not a mermaid, but a little ivory door set in a vast black wall that cut across the center of the maze. There were no more choices to make, there was only the closed door, and the singing on the other side of the wall. He opened it, resigned to finding the other half of the maze. The singing drifted over him, through him, murmuring, enticing.

What lay before him stunned him.

He closed the door after a long time, stood with his face against it, trembling. Still the singer called to him, the haunting voice of the siren, with her hair of drifting kelp and her icy fingers of foam: Come to me. Come. I am all the beauty in the sea, leave your mortal world and come. . . .

He felt someone beside him, knew without looking who it was. He whispered, "That's death in there."

Adam leaned beside the door, his own face carved of ivory, as colorless and hard. "You see."

She was still singing, still pulling at his heart, his bones. "Why? Why there?"

"She is waiting for you," Adam said shortly. "That is where she chooses to wait. You followed her between earth and water to find her. You wanted her that badly."

He stared at the door, as if he could see through it across the dark and terrible waste, to the luminous tower at its heart. "I can't." He swallowed; there was a pearl caught in his throat, pearls trapped behind his eyes. "I can't fight my way across that."

"Then find your own way back to your world," Adam said. His eyes were deadly as the eel's eyes; his voice colder than the abyss. "This is her price: you will find her in that tower. This is mine: if you refuse, you will stay here forever, between earth and water, neither of one world nor another; you will never die, and you will never cease to hear her sing.

"Choose."

SIX

Megan gazed into the tide pool, looking for the sea hare. She had brought her drawing pad, to try to coax it back into the world. The anemones were still there; the starfish had crawled away; the chiton, nibbling pink algae, had turned pinker. She dipped her hand into the pool, stirred the bottom. Nothing popped to the surface; nothing shifted itself beneath the sand into her hand. She dried her hand on her knee, leaning over to watch the water still. It reflected the blank morning mists, the shadow of her face.

She whispered, "Adam."

And he was there, looking up at her, through her dark reflection.

She jerked back, with a cry. He lifted his hand above the surface of the water, seized her wrist. He didn't pull her, just held her: an arm coming out of a circle of rocks holding eight inches of water. She felt like a shrimp grabbed by an anemone.

He said nothing; his face, colorless, expressionless, beautiful, seemed hardly human. He wore something that looked like fish scales; a tiny sand dollar, like the one in her box, clung to his hair. A basket starfish, its intricate arms weaving and branching, spread itself across his chest.

She was shaking with shock, with his sudden unfamiliarity. She found her voice finally. "I was—I'm looking for Jonah." Still he said nothing, his face underwater rippling a little, as the wind brushed the pool. She heard her heart pound, in his silence. "Can you help me?"

He spoke finally. "There is a price."

She nodded, hardly hearing, so relieved that he still spoke, and in a language she understood. "I'll pay it. I just want Jonah back."

"He does not know his own way back."

She nodded again, jerkily. "So. Then I'll come for him." She paused, her eyes on the unblinking, sea-green eyes. "But will he—will he come with me?"

She got no answer for a moment. Then, in a swift, graceful seal's movement, he had slid out of the pool to the rocks beside her, so effortlessly she never felt his weight, just the altered position of his hand. He seemed camouflaged against the rocks, almost invisible; his scaly garment had changed color to suit his background.

"I don't know," he said. He shrugged lightly. "He's drifting like a ghost between worlds, neither here nor there, enchanted by a song, afraid to reach the singer. When he cries, he cries pearls; sea mosses drift against him and cling. He won't die there, but it's not much of a life."

Her eyes were huge behind her glasses. She opened her mouth; words stuck, burning. "Pearls?"

"It's pointless, crying tears in the sea."

"Jonah—Jonah doesn't cry."

He looked at her; something behind his eyes—ice, a smile—made her shift. "He learned."

She drew breath through her open mouth. She said somberly, her eyes on the line where the pale mists touched the sea, "I'd better go and get him."

"If you want him. Why would you? He left you."

"You took him," she said, and glanced at his fingers on her wrist. "You wanted him. I don't know why. That little sea hare in my drawing that was you. You make the rules."

"Still," he answered softly, "he may not want to return. I can't promise that he will."

"Well." She withheld tears stubbornly, turning her face to let the wind hide it beneath her hair. "What if he does want to come back and he doesn't know how? I can't just let him float around like a kelp leaf, dropping pearls and wishing he had something to read."

He smiled slightly. "You still love him? In spite of her?"

"Maybe, maybe not. I don't know. But I can't leave him there with nothing human to talk to." She lifted her head, shook hair out of her face. "How do I get down there? How did he find his way down?"

"He was seduced by the sea."

She blinked. Then she met his eyes and felt the blood burn in her face. "That's how."

"That's one way."

"Well." She licked her lips. "What are the other ways?"

His smile deepened. "I could take you there. Why don't you let me? It is the simplest way. Like falling into a dream. You take me in, I take you in. Simple."

"I know, but—"

"Why? Jonah was unfaithful to you. He can't expect you to be faithful to him."

"Yes, but—"

"Am I so unattractive to you?"

"You're beautiful, but you frighten me. Jonah, I know. And you'd make it easy for me to get into your world, but how easy would it be for me to get back? Nobody told Jonah how to get back."

He made a soft sound, and loosed her wrist finally. "Shrewd. You want to get there and back again."

"With Jonah."

"If he chooses. It will cost you," he reminded her.

"Yes."

"Yes, what?"

"Yes, whatever it will cost."

"Not so shrewd."

"No," she sighed, "but I don't know how to bargain for Jonah. I don't know how to say, you can have this for him, but not this. I don't know what he's not worth because right now he's costing me everything. So take what's left. What do you want?"

"I'll tell you when you find me again."

"Where—" She reached out then, to hold him, but he was sliding back down into the tide pool. "Wait! Adam!" She plunged her hand in after him, caught his hair; it turned into sea moss and left a tiny sand dollar in her fingers. She flung it in despair back into the pool. "Adam!"

Three bubbles surfaced, floated a moment, and then popped, one after another, sending words into the air. "Draw," they said, "the stairs."

So she opened her drawing pad and sat there, drawing the stairs she remembered from her dream. They began in the tide, each ebbing wave revealing another step, and then another. As she drew, the mists overhead blew inland and sunlight streaked the water. She made the steps out of pearls and kelp leaf, coral, scallop shells, the first step visible where the first wave broke, and the others sloping down, while the waves scrolled above them. As they descended into deep water, she drew kelp forests and seals and perch, sharks, the great winged rays, the whales that swam along her path. On the top step, she drew the sea hare.

She looked up then, and saw the light glistening, breaking, glistening on something that the waves, stroke by stroke, were excavating like a lost city from the sand. She dropped paper and pen and ran, leaping off the rocks into the shallow surf, splashing through the tide, deeper and deeper until she reached the first white step. She looked down and saw them unfolding endlessly down, so far that the creatures of the deep swam, as she had drawn them, in vast cliffs of water along the stairs. She went down one step, a second, a third. Just before the walls broke and flooded together over her head, she saw the gold towers shining at the bottom of the sea.

Jonah, left alone, stayed for a long time beside the door, sitting on the pearl path, his ear to the ivory, as close as he could get to the ancient and beautiful face of the singer. Twice, he rose and opened the door. Twice, he closed it, sat back down, unable to enter, unable to turn away from the woman for whom he had swallowed the sea. Finally he rose, drifted through the coral maze as if he were following the halting, incoherent pattern of his thoughts. He turned a corner at random and found Dory unexpectedly, pruning coral with a parrotfish.

She wore a long, flowing pale green garment; but for the fish in her hand, she might have been some Victorian dowager tidying her garden. Her wild gray hair was being tidied by tinier fish, who picked the bubbles and dead plankton out of it as she worked. She glanced at Jonah before he could back out; he passed her, his shoulders hunched a little, against the hooked barbel of her derision.

But she said only, "You're not the first."

He stopped. "The first what?"

"The first to look at that and turn away." She gestured with the fish. "Sit."

He did, on a ledge of dead coral, grateful beyond words that she deigned to speak. He asked uneasily, "What happened to the others?"

"Adam keeps his word. They've faded by now, overgrown with mosses, barnacles. They haunt the pilings of rotting piers; they fling themselves into every tide, hoping to be cast ashore."

"Did anyone—did anyone ever try to cross the waste?"

She scratched her head with the parrotfish, thinking back. "A few," she said, "but that was before it got so bad."

"Before—"

"The waste changes, grows like some living, malignant thing."

"What happened to them?"

"I don't know. They never came back out, that's what I do know. Whether they reached Nereis or not, they never returned through the maze."

He watched her shift the parrotfish along a branch of coral. The graceful, flowing tendrils of the open polyps turned dark, in his mind's eye: a long fall of shadow down a shell-white face, the single, glistening pearl. She had watched the first creature secrete the first shell, wrapping itself in delicate armor; she had watched it settle in the mud, the preserved form and structure; millions of years later, she had watched Jonah searching for it in cliffs formed after she was born. His back was to her; she sang, so that he would turn and face the living sea. "But why?" he whispered desperately, seeing the waste again. "Why?"

Dory shrugged a little. "She's untamed, like the sea. No one questions her; no one questions the spindrift, or the shark's tooth. It's there, that's all, to be dealt with or not. My other daughters—they've done their share of mischief, following ships, singing sailors overboard on a whim. Some mortals lived to tell about it; others didn't. Some even coaxed my children ashore, for a time. But Nereis—she makes her own rules. What she wants, she takes, for her reasons, and there's always a reason, for she rules the sea. She taught the great whales how to sing; she rides the dolphins as they leap. She set the spirals in the narwhal's first horn, turning and turning with her hands. She is the restless eye of the sea; all its living things swim through her mind. She took you for a reason."

"Why?" His voice had no sound.

"Ask her." He did not answer; she shrugged again, shifting the parrotfish. "Then what will you do? Drift between earth and sea until you become a shadow, a ghost, a reflection of yourself, always wanting her and always afraid, mourning what you might have had, but never certain exactly what it was you lost, because you never had the courage to stare that darkness down?"

"It's more than dark. And it will take more than courage. I never had much to begin with. Or I never had to think about it."

"Adam told you your future: the open door or the closed door. There is nothing for you out here. No hope. No chance of escape. He won't bargain with you. He knows all the faces of the sea, and all her moods. He takes for himself where he can, when he wants. He teases humans and sets them adrift in their own desires; sometimes he sees them safely back to shore. But, serving Nereis, he is implacable. She sets her terms; he won't oppose her and he won't help you."

"No mercy."

"As much," she murmured obscurely, "as you give her."

He stirred himself to ask, then didn't. Mercy, like courage, was one of those nebulous words contingent on action; he preferred going through life without needing to use them. He sat silently, hunched over himself, feeling his hair already drifting like moss. The siren song melted through him again, dark, husky, tender; he closed his eyes, felt the singer's hands, the wild, roiling embrace of the sea, the pearl that had slid between her lips into his mouth. It's simple, the song said. Just open the door and enter and come to me. I'm here in the tower, waiting for you. The rest is unimportant. Shadows. Dreams. Ignore them. I am the only reality. Nothing can keep you from me. I am the Queen of the Sea, and I am all the beauty in the sea, and more beautiful than any tale. Come to me. Come.

He drew breath; pearls slid down his face. Dory glanced at him, a quick, sidelong question. He said, "After all, I never thought I could breathe water, either. I've already done one impossible thing."

Dory nodded vehemently, disturbing the little fish in her hair. "Yes."

"I'll die in there."

"Possibly. "

"But there's an end to dying, in there. There's no end out here. Just that song in me producing an inexhaustible supply of pearls. And Adam's pitiless eyes."

"They are pitiless, aren't they?"

"His laughter's worse."

"Worse. Much worse."

"And I might not die."

"No."

"And if I don't die, I'll see her face instead of his."

"Much more preferable."

"I remember her eyes, the first time I saw her sing. In that noisy, smoky bar. She met my eyes and I felt like I'd swallowed a lightning bolt. Did you ever feel like that?"

"A hundred times."

"Even if I die, even if she's cruel enough just to lure me in there to watch me be eaten, at least the song will stop."

"Is it so terrible?"

"Oh, yes." He felt the pearls brush down his face again. Dory turned; he met her eyes and let her see the new pearls forming. "Anything that beautiful is terrible. Because it's outside of you. It's not you. You'll do anything to make it part of you. You'd eat it, drown in it, kill it, let it kill you. Anything to stop it from not being you." He rose. "Even this."

"Wait," Dory said quickly. She collected the pearls he had wept, put them in his pocket. "To remind you," she said obscurely. He said nothing, waited, his eyes on the wall beyond the maze, until her busy hands found the last pearl, and she let him go.

Megan reached the bottom of the stairway into the sea. The steps vanished, she had noticed some time back, one by one as she left them behind her. The ocean flowed tumultuously around her, behind her, overhead, but it never touched her. In this world she had entered, the ocean was the dream. The delicate walls and towers shimmering in the timeless golden light of a gentle summer afternoon were more substantial than the school of mackerel overhead. Was it Ys? she wondered. Or was it Tir na n'Og, Land of the Forever Young? Or were all these just human dreams, and this the land beneath the sea that had no human name? Or maybe, she thought uneasily, it was simply what she expected, and the truth lay beyond her eyesight, beyond human imagining.

The last step vanished; she stood on a path of moonstones that led to the closed gate of the palace. The gate and walls were of crystal and glass, outlined in gold. Within, she could see a garden blown of glass: roses, hedgerows, stately trees whose great ridged leaves resembled kelp. She saw no one.

There was a glass bell beside the gate, she saw as she came closer. A little glass hammer hung beside it. She wondered, as she lifted the hammer, if the entire world of glass would shatter around her when she struck the bell, to reveal the wildness behind its pristine face.

Not even the bell cracked, but the deep sound that came from it, reverberating through the palace, seemed to shake even the light.

The gate opened immediately, on its own accord, or by invisible hands. Megan stepped into the garden. She waited. No one came. What is this? she thought. This isn't Adam's world. This is like my drawings. This is some story out of a book. Where is the man who slithered up through a tide pool like a seal, with a starfish riding on his chest?

She said aloud, tentatively, "Adam?" No one answered but the trees, their glass leaves ringing like small bells.

She wandered through the garden, saw glass sea anemones among the windflowers; both moved gently to unseen currents. There were glass benches here and there among the trees, and statues of animals with fishtails: a mer-lion, a mer-peacock, a mer-swan, a mermaid. She looked closely at the mermaid. Its hair coiled over its shoulder like flowing honey; its brows slanted over wide-set eyes; the icy contours of cheekbone and jaw were seal-sleek and beautiful. Megan's glasses misted suddenly. She touched them, swallowing, and forced herself to move.

Maybe, she thought, all this is just a way to cushion the fact that Jonah wants to stay. A consolation present for Megan. She saw a door into the palace in the distance, the color of pale coral, limned in gold. As she neared, it opened.

She stepped into a vast hall. Soft corals grew in pots, fanned gently by air or water. A grove of giant kelp stretched from floor to ceiling in one corner. Light from stained-glass windows drenched it; the colors danced like fish among the leaves. There was a wainscoting of white scallop shells along the walls; the shells were taller than she. Above them, more beasts frolicked in the sea: mer-unicorns, mer-dragons, mer-wolves, mer-elephants, even, Megan saw with astonishment, a mer-sphinx. Looking more closely at a mer-dragon, she realized it was alive: the walls were coral and all the vivid sea animals formed of coral polyps, pulsing gently to invisible tides.

Am I in air or water? she wondered. She spoke Adam's name again, watching for a bubble to form in the air. The name only dwindled in the silence.

A door opened across the room, inviting her. She didn't argue. Someone was thinking all of this, but why and how were beyond her speculation. The door led her up a spiral staircase. The tiles lining the steps were black, dark blue, and white, with tiny scallop shells at their corners. Colors changed; the lines in them opened and closed as if to the flow of water. There was a tile missing on one step. She knew, before she studied it, that a piece of one corner would be still embedded in the step.

Maybe this is Mike's palace, she thought. What he dreamed up, around the tile, when he thought about it.

The door at the top of the stairs opened to a bedchamber. It was a tiny tower room, with a bed and a chest, and windows that looked out over other gardens, other towers. She couldn't see beyond the palace; the light was too bright. The bed was carved of oxblood coral; ropes of kelp hung in a canopy over it. The chest was a giant clam. It opened as she looked at it, revealed a dark, shimmering, close-fitting dress of fish scale and black pearl. It weighed nothing in her hands. Beneath it was, she decided finally, a net made of jellyfish tendrils. Beneath that was a cloak made out of starfish. Beneath that was a glowing ball of glass filled with water and tiny, luminous lantern fish. Beside that was a trident as long as her arm. It was made of bone and its three points were barbed.

She touched a point, uneasy again. I can ignore all this, she thought, and tried to close the clamshell. It would not close. Nor would the chamber door open, no matter how she tugged.

"Fine," she muttered finally, dourly. "Fine." She pulled her clothes off, tugged the scaly garment over her head. It had a light, papery feel, and it glittered silver-dark. The black pearls at sleeve and hem weighted it. Shoes had fallen out of it when she unfolded it; reluctantly she discarded her Reeboks. Shod in thin fish-scale slippers, she felt suddenly vulnerable. What, she wondered, am I supposed to do with a trident while I'm practically barefoot? To placate the clamshell, she tossed the cloak and the net over her arm. When she picked up lantern and weapon, the clam began to close.

The chamber door opened.

She went back down the stairs. A different door opened; she entered another huge airy room with a long table in the center of it. A single chair fashioned of mother-of-pearl stood at one end of the table. As she looked at it uncertainly, she smelled clam chowder.

She pleaded, "Adam, I don't want lunch, I want Jonah."

But silent, invisible servants entered, carrying a formidable array of dishware and flatware; it arranged itself with precision in front of the chair. Chowder was ladled into a clamshell; steamed scallops appeared on a scallop shell; boiled lobster was served in its own shell on a bed of tiny shrimp. Her chair shifted back, waited for her.

She felt a moment's revulsion, as if she were being served fillet of merman's tail. But the smell of the chowder made her feel hollow. Everything eats and is eaten, she thought. I'd eat this at home. Except the lobster; we can never afford lobster. She sat down tentatively, ate a scallop. Nothing happened. She picked up one of three spoons, dipped into the chowder. Her goblets were filled: white wine, champagne, water. Somewhere above her, music began to play softly.

This, she thought after a while, when the lobster was a litter of shell and she was finishing the champagne, is what they do to the condemned. Feed you all your favorite things, then send you out to die.

She lowered her glass, and found a merman sitting on the other end of the table.

She jumped, splashing herself, before she recognized Adam. It wasn't so much the long, graceful, darkly glittering tail that disguised him, as his expression. He seemed remote, as he had in the tide pool: a wild, beautiful, unpredictable creature shaped by water and tidal forces, ruled by nothing human. She was surprised that he didn't speak in bubbles, or in the language of whales.

He said, "The dress and the starfish cloak are camouflage. You'll need the lantern; sometimes the water is dark. The net and the trident may come in handy; I don't know. No one has ever used them before."

"For what?" she whispered.

"You want Jonah. For whatever reasons. You must ask the Queen of the Sea for permission to take him back to your world. You will find her in her tower, singing to him."

"Where—" Her voice jumped.

He looked behind him, at a little ivory door that had just unlatched itself and begun to open. "Through there. If you must have him. If he wants you."

She tossed back the champagne and rose. "Come with me," she pleaded suddenly, glimpsing the darkness behind the door. "Adam." He didn't respond. Perhaps, she thought hopelessly, he had discarded his name along with his humanity. She bundled everything into the net. She touched her glasses straight, looking at him uncertainly, then walked without looking at him into the dark beyond the door.

Jonah stood in the ivory doorway, looking out over a wasteland.

It reminded him of videos of a war zone at night, flashes of light revealing an indecipherable landscape, or of some dim, barren planet that was a constant open sore of volcanic activity. It was a sullen, mutant sea around the beautiful tower, and it seemed to have created its own crazed life. Dark, bulky scavengers patrolled the waters; their skeletons, like those of the tiny fish in regions light could not reach, were luminous. Figures that looked almost human, glowing eerie, phosphorescent colors that might have seeped out of rotting chemical barrels, prowled through the debris at the bottom. There were great, nightmarish piles of it, junk that cascaded in sudden avalanches to resculpt the shape of the waste. Ghostly jellyfish trailing endless tentacles bobbed like underwater torches around the distant black hillocks of debris that rose between Jonah and the tower. A step sideways would have hidden it from him, but not its gentle light, nor the mermaid's voice.

He realized that the prowling, phosphorescent figures were turning faces in his direction, scenting him as nothing else did in the sea. He ducked, moving as slowly as everything else in the strange, motionless water, as if it were heavier than the flowing sea beyond the door, or slightly viscous. He crawled, a bottom fish, hiding behind debris, behind dead coral colonies, within stunted, pallid kelp that grew no higher than his head. Once he saw eyes, a face drifting at him out of the murk. It was only a sad-eyed manatee. Its front flippers had been mangled; its back was badly scarred. It moved past him slowly, using its tail, to nose at some pallid sea grass. Things crept through the debris around him, showing a claw now and then, a glassy carapace over bright organs. Once the tentacles of a massive, glowing jellyfish touched a huge, upraised claw. In the electric flash, the scavenger was illumined. It was longer than Jonah.

Some vast slanted wall appeared in front of him as he rounded a pile; it hid the tower. He recognized it finally, from old World War II movies: a sunken vessel lying on its side, crusted with gigantic mussels. It seemed safer to drift over it than go around; he clung close to it, guiding himself up across the deck from mussel to mussel. He peered over the top, saw other huge old scuttled ships like toys on the sea bottom. Liquid seeped slowly, constantly from their holds, turning the mussels vivid colors; whatever had been buried inside them wasn't staying put. Jellyfish swimming through the seepage occasionally sparked flashes along their tentacles. One spark shimmered back down the seepage into the hold near him. He heard a muffled explosion. Mussels bounced off the side of the hulk, followed by a stream of black liquid.

The mermaid's song, low and gentle across the terrible waste, coaxed him; he gazed at her tower awhile, delicate and pale in the distance, ringed by a moat of empty water. Finally he pulled himself down the side of the ship. The ships lay end to end in a jagged line; he found only more debris in front of him. He crouched under the keel, watching for movement, then slowly crept forward. He found a huge turtle lying on its back, little more than an empty shell but for its head and the plastic bag over it. He shook the shell; the fragments floated away. A dark shadow looming overhead snapped up the head in its wrapper. Jonah dove under the shell. But the shadow had lost interest in food; it thrashed away, drawing the attention of crabs hidden around Jonah. He huddled under the shell until the shadow finally stopped writhing and drifted to the bottom. The crabs moved then, shifting out of the debris, rising out of the sand; one crawled out of an old bathtub. Jonah, turned turtle on all fours, snuck away under the shell while the crabs fed.

He saw a pale, webbed foot and froze, clinging to the shell. Other mottled feet stalked past him on both sides. He felt a thump on the shell and waited in terror, for the kick that would wrench the shell from his grasp and leave him as defenseless as the turtle. But the ghostly mer-demons passed him silently. He moved finally, crawling over a lead pipe that must have bounced off the turtle's shell.

Another enormous shadow passed overhead, sending a plaintive moan reverberating through the water. Only an explosion within one of the sunken hulks answered it, as a passing jellyfish ignited something volatile. That silenced the whale briefly; Jonah heard the siren's voice again, light, drifting, soothing, and he wondered for a moment which of them she sang to. The whale answered her, and then passed on, silent again, a solitary Ancient Mariner searching for its kind.

Moving closer to the tower from garbage heap to garbage heap in his undignified scuttle, he began to hear the song more clearly. Sometimes he thought he understood a word, though the language she sang was older than the human voice. It enraptured him, her closeness; her voice teased his attention from the dangers of his journey; it seemed a caress of praise, of pride at his courage. I'm coming, he told her, picking his way past what looked like a demolished building tossed into the sea. He dodged pipes sticking crazily out of lumps of concrete and rounded a toilet standing upright with a baby crab's eyes peering over the rim. I'm coming. . . . He saw the glistening rain of tentacles sweeping toward him half a second before they hit.

He froze in horror. They struck; light flashed down them, hit the turtle shell, and then his face. He flinched, trying to scream, and nearly inhaled a tentacle. They kept coming, dropping down around him, surrounding the turtle shell. He cowered beneath it; pale ribbons massed against his face. Something bounced against the shell and rolled into the pile of tentacles. He tried to crawl; the tentacles had tangled around the shell. He shrugged the shell away finally, started to rise, and slipped into the massive body of the jellyfish.

It was dead. He stood up, staring at it, picking tentacles away from his body. It had been alive, charged, when it hit him. But he had never felt the shock. The jellyfish, it seemed, had not been so fortunate. Then he felt the shock of illumination throughout his body.

It touched me and died, he thought. I killed it.

He stared at it, then lifted his head at a movement, and found the eerie waste guardians gathering around him. He tensed, searching wildly for escape. But they came so far and no farther, just stood, scenting him, their blurred faces rippling with undecipherable expressions.

They backed away from him slowly, left him to his kill.

He gazed after them, bewildered; they glanced back at him now and then as they scattered, disappeared behind the debris. For a moment, his astonishment overwhelmed even the siren's song.

They're afraid of me. I wonder why.

Then the mermaid's song whispered through him again, and he pushed blindly through the ruined sea toward its heart.

SEVEN

Megan walked into a sea of dreams.

It was very dark at first. The light from her living lantern revealed a great forest of mer-trees, the tall, gently swaying trees of glass she had seen in the garden, though these had fish-scale bark and leaves of kelp. Fish, shining like jewels in the dark, browsed among the leaves. She stopped there, laid her bundle on the sea bottom and drew out the starfish cloak. She put it on, trying to remember what ate starfish. Something slow-moving, she hoped, and small.

She picked up the net again, and the trident of bone. The lantern, caught in a current, or unbalanced by some inner tumult, rolled away from her through the trees. She followed in a slow-motion sprint, the long gown flowing, the starfish a glowing, undulating wave behind her. The lantern was always ahead of her groping fingers. She had almost caught up with it when a mer-lion leaped out from between the trees and roared.

The roar was a splash of light. Its tail was gold, its mane adorned with beads of tiny cowrie shells. Its teeth were shark's teeth, huge, primitive, irregular. She hiccupped a bubble and dove under the starfish. After a while she lifted a corner of the cloak. The sea was dark again; the lantern had stopped moving. Still huddled, she crawled closer to it. It stayed still. She gripped it tightly and stood up.

She walked into a storm of minute, glowing things as intricately formed as snowflakes. They whirled around her, a blizzard of light, then swarmed away. Something else flowed after them, leaving an impression on her mind's eye of a flock of startled mer-ravens, with black wings and scaly tails. She stood still, uneasy in the quiet water, waiting. A great mer-unicorn bounded through the kelp trees, moon white, with a narwhal's spiral horn and a fish's tail that propelled it up through the water as its forefeet touched bottom. A small trident sped after it, touched its flank. Megan dropped again, but not before she had seen the wild hunt that chased the hind: the riders blowing conches, the pack of dogfish, the seahorses striving under the urging of the intent, beautiful, merciless hunters fitting tridents of fishbone into their bows. She hid, a mound of starfish, while the seahorses, their manes and tails elegant masses of colored filament, bounded through the water above her head.

The sand settled; the water was finally still again. She rose, her eyes wide, her hair drifting around her, catching the interest of the tiny jewelfish, who darted through it as if it were seaweed. She went on through the forest. Now and then she caught the flash of gaudy wings as parrotfish and cardinalfish swam into her light, but nothing more disturbing. Finally she reached the edge of the forest and the water began to brighten.

She stood among the trees, looking out over the edge of a cliff. Far below she could see the land beneath the waves. It was not made of glass, but of pearl and coral and pirate's gold. Its banners were flying fish, its gate was the bone of some great fish's mouth. The road leading into the gate was paved with scallop shells. She could see where it ended, but not where it began, nor how she could get from the top of the cliff to the city below.

I could float down, she thought. Just step over and drop.

But what rules prevailed in that mer-world she was uncertain.

Things mirrored the earth too closely, and even covered with starfish, she was reluctant to fling herself over a sheer wall of stone. Besides, what might they make of her, the avid hunters with their bows and tridents, seeing her drift down, a trespasser without a tail? They might make target practice of her.

She pondered, kneeling at the cliff's edge, watching tiny movements, flickers of color within the city walls.

Is Jonah in there? she wondered, her eyes on a tower taller than the rest, made out of moon shells, with round windows like portholes ringing the top. Adam said he was wandering around with snails in his hair, crying pearls. Is he with the sea queen now? Did he weep enough pearls?

She stilled her thoughts, leaned over the cliff edge, straining to catch a note or two of the song that had lured Jonah out of the world. But she only heard the distant voices of whales.

She rose after a while, walked slowly along the cliff edge, watching the road below for the hunters. The road was swallowed by forest before she saw them return on it. She wandered on. The cliff began to slope; the kelp trees thinned; bushes of coral grew among them: sea fans, mushroom coral, fire coral, oxblood coral, angel's skin. She saw an angelfish overhead, its tail a pearly white, its wings of delicate, feathery tentacles. Its face resembled Adam's. She stopped, wanting to speak to it, but its eyes were closed, as if it prayed.

She closed her own eyes, briefly. What is this world? she thought. Where am I really?

When she opened her eyes, she saw a flock of goatfish gamboling along the cliff, pausing to eat eelgrass and sea cucumbers. She waited for the damselfish who herded them, but the goatfish, black and amber-eyed, were apparently wild. They cast slitted glances at her starfish cloak, but did not come close. As they browsed through the coral, they startled butterflyfish, who swarmed up and darted toward the kelp forest.

She continued along the slope. It leveled for a while, into a meadow of grasses and sea lilies, but it was high above the floor where the city stood, and still she saw no way down. Beyond the meadow stood another dark kelp forest. Leaning out over the cliff as far as she dared, she saw the wall of rock stretch into the distance, with not a hint of road winding down from it. She had left the city behind. All she could see of it was the high tower made of pearl; the rest was hidden by forest, and by the misty shadow of the cliff.

Now what? she wondered, sighing. Turning, she saw a rabbitfish on the meadow grass.

Its back to her, it nibbled something between its paws, balanced on its green mer-tail. She felt something in her grow focused, very still. For this, she had the net. For this, she carried the trident. To pin down the changing sea and look into its eye to see what it truly saw. She crept up behind it so quietly she thought it must hear her stillness. She held out the net, weighted it with her body, and fell with it over the sea hare.

It struggled beneath her; she held it tight, and felt it change. She clung fast, spreading the net with her hands, gripping the tail between her knees. It stopped moving then. She felt a face against her face.

She angled the trident swiftly against his throat. She sat up carefully, keeping him tangled in the net: the merman caught by the fisher, the hare caught by the hunter. She said, "You must be worth something. A wish or two, at least."

For a moment he was silent, looking at her out of alien eyes. Then he surrendered a human smile of acquiescence and amusement. "Only if you drag me out of the sea into your boat and threaten to cast me ashore."

"Can you make an exception?" She was smiling now, for he had never really left her alone in the sea: he had given her the net and himself to catch.

"Perhaps. For you. What do you wish, mortal maid?"

"I wish, merman, for you to guide me through your sea."

His smile faded; he considered her wish. He lifted a finger through the net, shifted the trident from his throat. "You don't have much to bargain with. And you already owe me."

"I'll pay you later. This sea is full of human words."

"So humans made it."

"I want to see your sea. Out of your eyes. I want to see what you are made of, what you are behind all your faces."

"Why?"

"Because," she said softly, "you came into my drawing for a reason, and you haven't told me what it is. All you've given me is what I've read about, what I've drawn."

He was silent again; nothing of the smile lingered. "It costs," he warned her. "More than you can imagine. It may cost you your heart."

She held his eyes. "I'll pay it," she said recklessly, not sure any longer what her heart was worth in the sea. He shook off her net and rose.

"Come."

Jonah stood in a snowfall of plankton.

He assumed it was plankton, vaguely recalling pictures in Megan's books. Microscopic plants and animals with intricate, transparent structures: They looked like lilies, or space stations, or roulette wheels radiating strands of light. Alive they floated on the waves; dead they drifted down until they were eaten, or until they reached the sea bottom. These were drifting, but either he had shrunk or they were huge as cars. Some had legs, some had chambered shells, some carried a Catherine wheel of filaments. They bounced down around Jonah, stirring up storms of sand and mud. Caught in an open ring between the tower and the ships and piles of debris, he dodged them wildly. There seemed no end to the fall. He crawled finally beneath what looked like an egg, heaving one bulky, liquid side up, as if he were trying to lift a water bed. Whatever had been growing in it was dead, chewed apart by something dark and cloying inside.

After a long time the drift came to an end. He crawled out. The crabs were beginning to move among the plankton; their great claws mowed a ragged path through it. Jonah, finding it easier to dodge them, shifted to let them pass, then followed after them. Others came up behind him, surprising him, but they seemed uninterested. Withdrawing their eyestalks, clicking claws at him, they scuttled away sideways. He moved among them, barely noticing their cleanup operation, only that they were clearing his way to the tower, which always, he noticed, was farther than it looked, as if perspective changed constantly in that fluid world. He was working his way toward it patiently when the water became very dark.

All around him the scavengers began to scatter, crawling over one another in their haste. Jonah, staring upward, found the night falling into the sea. He clambered over the scavengers, sliding on their slick shells, riding them until they bumped him off. Finally the darkness hit. A solid wave of sand roiled over him, blinding him, throwing him down, nearly burying him. Sounds too loud to hear reverberated through him. The sand kept coming, churned up, throwing him when he tried to stand. Something else sagged over him. Trying to flee the sandstorm, he tangled in it and fell. Struggling, he only drew it more tightly around him.

A net, he realized finally, as cord pulled across his face. He was caught in a net along with some writhing, bellowing sea animal who was flailing on top of layers of crushed crab and monstrous plankton.

He could see little in the gritty water, but he guessed from the sound and the fury that he was caught in a net with one of the great whales. He clung to the net to keep it from cutting into his face, and rode out the storm until the wild thrashing eased a little. Trying to grope his way out, he hit something sharp, hard, at his back. He felt along it, recognized it finally as a shard of squashed crab shell. He loosened it, and, bringing his arm up as far as he could in the tight embrace of the net, he began to saw himself free.

By the time he finished, the whale only shook itself from time to time, thrashed a fluke, stirred up sand; he escaped while the sand was settling. He had to stumble, half-blind, through cloudy water, tripping against busy crabs and decaying plankton, before he saw the tower again.

He could make out details by then. The tower walls spiraled with grooves like a narwhal's horn; a single window glowed, darkly translucent, over an open doorway. Tears stung his eyes at the sight of the open door. He caught them, put them in his pocket, as Dory had done. He sat down to rest a moment, gazing at it, hearing the mournful cries of the whale mingling with the mermaid's song. Nothing moved between him and the tower except a strand or three of sea grass. The waste was empty, littered with broken shell. He rose, pulled onward, tide-drawn, driven, like a turtle to its island, a whale to its mating ground, a salmon to the river of its birth.

By the time he reached the tower door, he barely knew what he was: a man swallowed by the sea, who had swallowed the sea. The light, sweet voice drew him up winding stairs inlaid with starfish; walking on them, he hardly knew if they were alive or dead. He had no idea, by this time, which he was, nor did he care, as long as he saw the dark glittering at the top of the stairs, and the long dark hair, and the pale, slender hands reaching out to take him to the peaceful place on the other side of mystery.

He heard a muffled thud; water spiraling up the stairs pushed against him, jostled him up the last few steps. The door below had shut, he thought, and then reached out to cling to the doorposts at the end of the stairs as the water began to swirl. Or was it the tower revolving, as if it were caught in some vast whirlpool? It shook him loose, flung him across the little chamber at the top of the tower. He hung against the wall, his back to it, his eyes closed, unable to move in the force of the spin. He felt something dragged out of him by the roots, and a hollow where his heart had been.

The song had stopped.

"Jonah."

He looked into the center of the maelstrom, into the mermaid's eyes.

On the cliff, the merman disappeared.

Then the cliff beneath Megan disappeared. The city below peeled away like wrapping paper; all the human language—mer-lion and goatfish—left the sea. Megan, losing track of her own shape as the water jerked her fourteen ways, pulled hair away from her eyes, looked frantically for Adam. He was beside her, in a streak of light. And then he was gone. And then there again, his eyes of water and light, his skin foam, sand, light. Around her the sea lilies curled into balls, and the giant kelp bowed to the wild currents.

"What is it?" she cried. "What's happening?"

He didn't answer. She felt an arm drawing her upward; the rest of him was barely a reflection in the water. A school of anchovy darted by, turned molten silver, flashed away the other direction. A kelp tore loose from its mooring, a swirl of leaves and yellow bladders that clung to Megan, laid rubbery leaves against her face. She pushed at it, found a cloud of bubbles where Adam's face should have been.

"Adam?"

They broke the surface. He turned to foam then; spindrift shaped him in the wind, then fell back into the waves. She heard a sound as if the world was being sucked down a drain.

She saw it then: the end of the world. It was a gigantic maelstrom, the eye of the sea, a vast, revolving hurricane of water that whirled around its own deep funnel. She made a noise on an indrawn breath that scraped her throat.

"Adam!"

He found his mouth finally. "It's my sister."

"What do you mean, it's your sister? That's your sister?"

He nodded. The sea around him turned green as his eyes; for a moment all she could see of him was his eyes, and the heave of green water. Then foam shaped his mouth again. "One of her faces."

She stared at it, horrified, fascinated. Then she heard the maelstrom's singing, deep, wild, beautiful, and she felt her heart turn to ice. "Adam!" She tried to grip him, realized that her own hands were foam. She was drawn and shaped like light across the surface of the sea. Her mind remembered a body; the need, answered a moment later, found her fingers again, white as foam, but solid. "The same sister? Jonah's singer?"

He developed an ear and a profile; she had a disconcerting feeling that the other half of his face was missing. The profile nodded. Its mouth was set, unamused. "The sea queen. In your words."

Her voice vanished; somehow he heard her anyway. "Where is Jonah?"

"With her, I would guess."

She stared at the edge of the world again. Gulls, bits of blown white paper, circled above, as if the deadly current were reflected in the wind. Cold tears of brine struck her face. "Is he dead?"

"I don't think that's what she had in mind."

Her voice tore out of her then, shrieking. "Well, what did she have in mind?"

"Let's find out."

"Where?"

"Down there," he said simply. Kelp rope circled her wrist, tugged, and she scattered water and foam and seaweed hair. She felt the relentless tide of the maelstrom.

Fish rode the maelstrom with them: tuna, whales, octopus. She saw the great white shark so close she looked for her reflection in its eye. It was cold, dead space, that eye, a piece of the abysmal sea. Schools of small fish, clouds of shrimp blew past them like leaves. Soft coral, starfish, sea urchins, an old boat hatch, a smiling figurehead, whatever wasn't nailed down to the bottom of the sea spun in the current, dredged up to be sucked down again. She felt the current quicken as they grew closer to the funnel. An improbably long, graceful, pearly head followed by an interminable length of legs slid past her for some time: a shy giant harried out of the deepest waters.

She heard her voice again, rising against the mermaid's voice. "Why him? Why Jonah? He always had his face in a book or a cliff."

"He turned his back to the sea," Adam answered, out of some configuration of light.

"So? Why didn't she take somebody off one of those floating factory ships that can take an entire whale apart and package it before lunch?"

"Maybe she tried. Maybe they could never hear her singing."

Megan was silent. They were spinning near the edge of the funnel; she could see one part of its narrowing wall, things flashing through it too fast to recognize. She said, "I'm going to die."

"No."

"I can't survive that."

"Give me your wrist," he said, and wrapped a kelp-leaf hand around it. They skimmed the edge of the mermaid's song. And then they dropped, whirling so fast down one long note that Megan could barely separate water from light, or her body from her terror, except for the kelp wrapped around what she assumed was a piece of her.

The world drained into a dark and silent sea.

Megan, drifting, hit bottom and found her body again. She raised her head, stared through the murky waters. Something crawled here; something thrashed there; a dozen derelict ships bled swamp-gas colors into the water. She felt a touch, found herself eye to eye with a giant crab. Its shell was so thin she could see through it.

She whispered, "Adam." The crab veered nervously. There were people in the distance, naked, faceless, their skin glowing odd, sickly colors. They seemed to sense her, but, like the crab, shifted uneasily away from her attention, withdrew behind the oddly shaped mounds rising all around them. Something crawling near the top of one of the mounds near her lost its hold, came down in a wild slide of incongruous and familiar shapes. She watched, motionless, incredulous, as a Formica table with no legs careened to a halt against what looked like an enormous flattened bubble with a broken shell inside. She almost recognized it, decided not to. Coral skeletons, hard and bare, shimmered ghostly white in the eerie light; the stunted kelp, the few blades of sea grass alive in the deadly water, were colorless as the coral.

Her throat constricted; she heard herself make a little whimpering noise of fear and bewilderment. "What is this place? What is this terrible place? Where did all the bright fish go? Where are all the colors?"

Nothing answered her but the great thrashing shadow, a deep, tuneless mourning that sounded to her ears like the last voice left in the sea. Turning toward the only sound, she saw the tower beyond it, a delicate spiraling thing, luminous and perfect, all the beauty in the waste.

She heard the mermaid's song.

She felt her eyes grow wide, aching and heavy with pearls. It was the pure voice of the nautilus shell, the sound of limpid water wandering from chamber to glistening chamber. It sang to Jonah, that voice, lovely, husky, haunted with storm and spindrift, but quiet now, the ebb tide, or the full tide idling a moment, at rest before it turned, dragging hard across the sand, flooding back into foam. It was singing to Jonah now, from within the tower, where he listened, in that private world, safe from the dark and ruined sea around him, safe from any human eyes.

The pearls slid down her face at last; she felt the dark, lifeless waters seep into her heart, into her blood. She brushed the pearls away; more fell. Jonah was inside the narwhal's horn, among the glinting lights inside the bottle. He had locked her out, left her stranded in a dead sea with only a dying whale to sing to her. She heard her own voice making human noises of grief and desolation. She couldn't move except to brush at pearls, which drifted slowly to her feet. She would root herself there, she thought, become a skeleton of coral, because there was no path out of this waste; she would carry it in her heart wherever she went, on land or in sea, so it did not matter anymore what she did, where she went. . . .

The whale stopped singing.

The heartbeats of silence were so unexpected that she lifted her head, shaking away pearls, to stare at it. It moved again, finally, and made its ratcheting noise, but more weakly. She watched it shudder from fins to flukes, and then call again. There was no blood, that she could see, no reason for its agony. But something made it cry sorrow, or perhaps for help in that bleak water. She moved finally toward it, feeling that if it died of sorrow so would she; alone in this waste, she would dwindle into something pallid and stunted and unrecognizable. Around her, the crabs were feeding on what looked like enormous, decaying plankton. Some circled the whale. Its flukes, driving down hard, scattered them; so did Megan, moving among them on what felt like a layer of broken glass. They were shell fragments, she realized: the broken crabs the whale had crushed in its thrashing. And then she saw the net.

One corner was torn; the rest was tangled securely around the whale, tightening as it struggled. The whale was huge and had teeth; that much she could make out in the dim sea. It raised clouds of sand as it struggled, but, as far as she could tell, not blood. She edged past its flukes, her hands sliding over broken shell. She nicked her finger on a piece, lifted her head sharply, still, as if her silence could hide what a drop of blood revealed of her presence in the water. But no mutant, glowing shark nosed her out. She tugged at the net; it might as well have been wrapped around a submarine. She picked among the shell fragments, found a razor-edged shard, and began to cut.

The net, rotten with brine, parted easily. She walked along the whale's side, slicing her hand sometimes, and the whale's scarred back at other times, feeling its dull roaring vibrating through her bones. She still dropped pearls, but she didn't notice them; instead of making the scratchy, reedy sound that had come out of her at first, she whispered, hardly hearing herself, "This can't be real. Is it the future? Where will you go if I free you? Is there any sea left beyond this place? It's so dark. So terrible. So dark. . . ."

She climbed the net up to the whale's back, to cut above its thrashing flippers. It heaved, feeling the net give; she lost her balance and fell, caught herself in the net. She worked her way back up, kept cutting, clinging to one side of the tearing net so that when the whale broke loose, she might be thrown free. It lay quietly for a few moments. It's dead, she thought starkly. It finally ran out of air. And then it arched up, tearing at the net, a frenzy that made her lose everything—balance, shell—except her hold of the net. It tore further under her weight. She hung on, her face pushed against the whale's side, not daring to fall so near its heavy, rolling body. And then she fell, down into a roil of collapsing net.

There was something softer than crab shell under her. She opened her eyes and found Adam, head and flukes still caught in the net, his face pearl white, his skin grazed by her shell. He opened his eyes. She stared at him, pearls falling silently down her face. He lifted his hand to catch one. And then, as his arms slid gently around her, and she eased against him, she knew that she had lost her heart to the sea.

Jonah stood inside the mermaid's song.

It was wild and bitter and desolate, a song without words, of spindrift whipped from heaving water washed with colors not even Megan would use; of the cries of battered seals, wind-battered birds screaming over great schools of fish, blind and still, sliding like leaves across the surface of the storm; of the voices of whales and porpoises as they fled the relentless stalking shadows above them that tracked their every move. Brine lashed his eyes, his mouth; kelp torn from the sea bottom tangled around his hands; barnacles and starfish struck him, clung. An empty moon shell, tumbled through the water, caught painfully over his ear; even in its pale, lovely hollows he heard the mermaid's storm.

He had no idea where he was; now and then he glimpsed, behind a wash of green and foam, the tower's white wall curving around him, and knew he still stood in the mermaid's eye. And then the sea would change around him, so that he saw it from the fierce and hungry gull's eye, as it swooped over the sickly waters, or he would be tossed among the frantic whales, buffeted by their voices. Every fish he saw, dead and alive, seemed to have the mermaid's eyes.

He began to hear her speak, perhaps out of the moon shell, or perhaps she stood in front of him, in the tower, while the storm raged through his head.

"You saw what had killed me. You could have buried it before it killed again."

A sea turtle slowly sank through the turbulent waters, a plastic bag twisted around its head. He could not see its eyes, but he knew they would be hers. He whispered to it, "I'm sorry."

"You saw what mangled me."

The manatee, with its torn flippers, pushed by every wild current, struggled for balance with its tail. He saw the crosshatched scars of propeller blades on its back. It looked at him as it passed, not with the patient, wistful gaze he remembered, but with the sea's icy foam-washed green.

"I'm sorry." His hands were clasped in front of him, bound with kelp; he bowed his head, a prisoner of the storm, the moon shell still caught against one ear. A barnacle clung to one lens in his glasses; he dared not lift a finger to move it.

"You gave the manatee a human face for centuries, and yet when you finally see its true face, you have no pity for it."

"It was your face we gave it," he whispered, remembering her from another life.

She answered sharply, "Its face is my face. And this was my song."

He heard the whale again, crying for help as it struggled in the net. His head sank; the sound reverberated through the moon shell. "I'm sorry. I didn't think. All I thought—all I heard—you put such beauty in front of me, you told me to find you; you were all I could see."

"Yes! All!" He glimpsed a curve of wall behind a wave, and then a dark glittering whirling away from him. He watched it numbly until it changed into a fish's receding tail. "The dead coral, the crabs with their shells grown thin and fragile in those waters, the poisoned grasses and kelp, the jellyfish that died because you kill everything you touch—I am all that you see here, and I am that dark and barren sea."

"Yes." He cleared his throat, found his voice again. "I'm sorry. It was—I didn't recognize you."

"No. Nor did you recognize yourself reflected in the waste."

"How could I? I wasn't looking for myself. I was only looking for you." He saw her face briefly then, foam white and wild, and beautiful as the secret, inward turnings of a shell. The image turned to foam and swirled away. "Your singing was so beautiful," he said helplessly. "It made me blind, it made me stupid. You made me hunger for you, and told me how to reach you. How could I have stopped to listen to any other song? I'm no different from all the ancient sailors who flung themselves into the sea, following your song, and drowned. I didn't drown, and I did find you, but I didn't know that I was never what you wanted."

"Yes, you are." Her fierceness startled him. "You loved me. You loved my past. But how else could I draw your eyes to my living and endangered sea except to show you what you expected to see? You saw this face. You felt these hands. These you wanted."

"Want," he said without hope. He shook his head a little; the barnacle floated free. "I'm only human."

"You must be more than human."

"How?"

"You must be part of me. You owe me. I want your life."

He swallowed nothing, felt the blood beat in the back of his throat. For a turtle? he wondered blankly. For a whale's life? He moved finally, reached up to touch his glasses. "Yes," he said with an effort. "Alive down here? Or do you just want me dead?"

She was silent; finally he saw all of her, the pearls in her sea-tossed hair, the flowing, tide-swirled garment that constantly shifted, revealing, concealing. He watched, mute, while she considered. "If I let you choose," she said at last, "which would you choose? A life in this waste, cleaning my sea with a shell, or death?"

He started to speak, stopped. She watched him, her face as hard and cold as Adam's, while the sea showed him a quarter moon of breast, a slender knee. "Was what I did that terrible?" he asked helplessly. "Just following your song? We have always loved the sea. We leave ourselves in you constantly. A sunken galleon, an amphora, a billion barrels of oil, our bones. We can't separate ourselves from you. You still flow in our blood. You feed us. You rage at us, wreck our cities, drown our children, and still we come past safety to stand at the edge of your fury to watch all your deadly beauty. Without you, we will die."

"You are killing me."

"Then we will die. And I will," he added on a breath, "here, now, if you want. Or I will clean up the waste with a snail shell if you promise me—"

"I will not bargain."

"No. But I can ask. If you will sing to me. The way you sang in the cave. As if the world had begun in that place, and I was listening to the first song ever heard. As long as I can listen to you, I would choose to live."

Something happened to her face, and to his: he felt it, a tear that was not a pearl, and saw on her face the faint suggestion that it was not carved of stone. He began to hear the song again, faint, mingling with the currents within the moon shell. He met her eyes, saw the storm in them, as ancient and as new as tide, as her song, as all her intricate faces. He whispered, "You choose my fate. It seems fair. We have shown you yours."

"Yes," she said, and turned her head, as at the touch of an unexpected current moving through the sad, dark waters.

Megan walked into the chamber.

EIGHT

Her eyes were red, her hair was full of pearls, she wore gleaming fish scales and thin slippers of scale. She cast an eye at Jonah almost as cold as the mermaid's; her glance snagged on the moon shell, on the kelp rope around his wrists. She tried to turn away from him, then saw the expression in his own eyes. A tear fell from him, and then a pearl. He whispered, stunned, "Megan?"

She stopped. He saw her swallow, saw the red deepen around her eyes. Then she shook her hair over her face, and turned away from him to the sea queen.

She had vanished, leaving only a dozen bright butterflyfish that had been clinging to her hair startling through the water. Jonah said again, "Megan?"

She folded her arms tightly, showed him a white, set profile, and then three quarters of her face. Then she showed him her full face, for nothing about him had the look she expected, of a man fed oysters and pearls from the sea queen's fingers, who could barely remember the unenchanted world. "You look awful," she said abruptly. "You look as though you drowned. You're growing moss in your beard. You're growing a beard."

"I should have used a razor clam," he said weakly, feeling human tears sting again. "You look beautiful. You should always wear pearls in your hair."

"They're tears," she said stonily, and twitched behind her hair again. He watched her, wanting her familiar thin, secretive face, the blue-gray eyes, lovely and easily startled, behind her glasses. She came out finally, frowning at the kelp.

"What's that for? And why are you wearing that shell on your ear?"

He lifted his hands, removed it finally. "There was a storm—"

Her eyes widened a little. "I know. I saw it. Adam said it was her doing it. She." Her hands tightened a little on her arms. "Your mermaid."

"Adam."

"He showed me how to get down here."

He blinked, aware suddenly of some shark-shadow of danger. "He did." Her eyes challenged him; he drew breath, asked anyway, "How did you get here?"

"I walked," she said stiffly.

"What do you mean, you walked?"

"I drew the stairs into the sea and walked down them. Adam told me to do it that way."

"In return for what?" he demanded. "He doesn't hand out things for free."

"You have some nerve asking. Walking is not how you got down here."

He was silent, remembering: a kiss, a pearl. "No," he said softly. "I followed the siren's song. I'm sorry."

"For what? That you followed it? Or for me?"

"I couldn't help it," he pleaded. "That's why it's called a siren's song."

She was silent then, feeling the blood gather again behind her eyes. She whispered finally, "I know. I heard it."

"You—"

"Out there. In that terrible sea. I was out there, alone, and you were in the white tower with the sea queen singing to you, and you didn't know I was out there, and I knew you wouldn't have cared."

"Oh, Megan." He held out his hands, trailing kelp leaves and yellow bladders. "Look at me! What does this look like?"

"Something kinky," she muttered darkly. But she frowned at him uncertainly, more puzzled now than angry. "If—" she said finally, "if it wasn't for that, then what? What did she want you for? Didn't you make love to her? Isn't that what mermaids do? They drag you under, into the magic sea, and trap you there, if they don't kill you first." Her face smoothed suddenly, froze; she took a step toward him. "Jonah?"

"Yes. That's pretty much how it goes."

"Wait—" She stared at him, breathing quickly. "Wait. She trapped you in this tower? She can't want to kill you. That doesn't make sense. Adam said—"

"Adam," he said between his teeth.

"He said I had to ask permission from the sea queen to take you back with me. If I still want you. He wouldn't have said that unless there were a way."

"Do you?"

"What?"

"Still want me?"

"Oh, Jonah, I'm here. What do you think?"

For an instant, he was uncertain. The shadow loomed overhead, turned toward him with sleek, deadly grace. Then it swam out of eyesight. He bowed his head, said bleakly, "I don't think she'll let me go. I've promised her—whatever life I have left."

She put her hands over her mouth. "No," she whispered.

"That sea out there." He paused, swallowed, still staring at his hands. "I didn't recognize her."

"What?"

"She—there were things I could have done. Should have done. Things I should have realized. She brought me down here to see, and I couldn't see anything at all, only her. I hardly even heard the whale, and it nearly fell on top of me. I just wanted it to be quiet so that I could hear her song again. Did you see it out there? The whale?"

She nodded jerkily. She was crying suddenly, noiselessly, her eyes wide behind her glasses, her mouth still hidden behind her hands. "Yes. I saw it."

"She's very angry with me. That was her song, too, she said. The whale's song. I just—" He shook his head slightly, dislodging a tiny snail. "I just wasn't listening. I wasn't seeing. All I could see was this tower. All I could hear was her voice. So." He drew a long breath, looked at her finally. "You might have made a trip for nothing." He paused; she still gazed at him wordlessly, weeping tears from one eye, pearls from the other. He added, "But thank you," fixing her in his memory one last time: her long pale floating hair, her lean body, mysterious beneath its dark shimmer of fish scale. "It was more than I deserved. Considering."

"Oh, Jonah!" She had crossed the distance between them suddenly. "Why didn't you help the damn whale?" Her fists pounded at him a moment. "It wasn't that hard!" She stopped beating him, and pushed herself against him, her arms around him tightly, her face against his neck. "She can't keep you. It's not fair. Maybe there's some way—" She drew back abruptly, tugged impatiently at the kelp around his wrists, unweaving the long golden ropes, while he stared, his face still, at the top of her head. "Maybe if I talk to her. Or Adam does. He told me to come here and ask, so I'll ask—Where is she, anyway?"

"What do you mean," he asked slowly, "it wasn't that hard?"

"What?"

"About the whale. You said it about the whale."

"Oh. I just used a piece of broken crab shell. It cut like a knife. And there. . . ." Her voice faltered oddly. "And it wasn't—it wasn't a real whale. I mean, it was until I freed it. And then it changed."

"Into what?" he whispered. She lifted her head after a long silence, met his eyes.

"Adam."

He closed his eyes. When he opened them again, he saw Adam standing beside his sister.

They did look alike, he realized numbly. Some of Adam's wildness shaped her beauty; some of her ceaseless, desperate love for her realm shaped his. Nereis put her hand on Adam's shoulder, said to him as the butterflyfish darted back into the tendrils of her hair, "You did well. Far better than I did."

"You sang far too well," he said gently. Megan, startled, had turned in Jonah's hold. For a moment, her eyes clung to Adam, until he gave her a smile, bittersweet and without malice, that amazed Jonah. Then her eyes moved to his sister.

Staring at the ancient, sea-formed face, she said, "Oh," soundlessly; the word, caught in a round bubble, floated upward. She shifted closer to Jonah. "You're not," she said shakily to Nereis, "at all what I thought you would be. I thought you would be more human. If I had—if I had known—I would never have dared come for him."

"If I had known him better," Nereis said, "I would have sung to you instead." The sharpness in her voice sent a tremor through the water; the butterflyfish swarmed and flashed uneasily.

Megan felt the tremor pass through Jonah. She drew breath, said helplessly, "I think I've bargained away everything I own to Adam. But if I have anything left—anything worth Jonah's life—it's yours. Adam told me I could ask you to free him. If you would let him return with me. If he wants to come. If you will free him. I'll give you what you want."

"Why?" Jonah whispered. "Why, Megan? I vanished out of your life to follow a singer. A song. Why did you come for me? Why did you bother?"

"You were part of a puzzle," she said without looking at him. "The sea came into my drawings, it walked into your store, it flooded into my life and it took me like it took you—I wanted to know why. And. Because. I missed you." She looked at him finally; her voice softened. "I missed you. I thought you might be missing the world. In tales, people do."

"In and out of tales," he said starkly, "people die in the sea. I won't let you sacrifice anything more for me. I've already promised my life to the sea. I won't bargain away that promise."

"That," the sea queen sighed, "is the first sign of hope you have given me. I want both your lives." Adam glanced at his sister swiftly; she read his thoughts. "No. She is not for you. She is for me."

His mouth tightened a little. "You're sending them back."

"How else can they help me?"

"Can I bargain with you?"

"No. You are far too subject to whim to make any human happy. Unless you want me to give you up, send you with them to live and die among humans."

He opened his mouth to answer, then hesitated. Megan was stunned by the expression on his face; so, it seemed, was the sea queen. Jonah's hand closed suddenly on Megan's shoulder. They said, the three of them, before Adam chose, "No."

He blinked, as if some chasm had opened and then vanished again in front of him. He looked reproachfully at Megan. She said, her eyes stinging in the brine, "You already have my heart. You'll forget me long before I forget you."

"Perhaps," he said softly, "you are right. But watch for me anyway in your drawings. I have a very long memory."

"And you also will leave your heart in the sea," the sea queen said to Jonah. "You will return to land, but your eyes and thoughts and your life belong to me. I am dying. You saw that. For the rest of your life, you will stay within the sound of my voice, the sound of the changing tide. Your life is linked to mine. As I die, so will you; as I become stronger, so will you. You must help us both. For so long I watched you caring about the lost, forgotten life of the sea, when I was young and all life came from me. I sang to you because I need you to see me as I am now. You must find ways in your world to help me. I am no stronger than the most minute life in the sea. If you kill that, I begin to die. The smallest thing you can do to help me will give me strength to live. My song will be in your blood, in your dreams, in your past and future. If my life is short, so will yours be. When my voice stops, so will your heart, for I hold your heart in mine for the rest of our lives."

Jonah bowed his head. He heard her song again, sweet, haunting, within the sound of the tide; beneath it, within it, he heard his own heartbeat. He whispered, "You hold all of our hearts in your heart."

Water shaped itself against him; he felt her, the intimate tide, her song flooding around him until he could no longer stand. His mouth filled with her; she caught his swaying body, dragged him deep into foam and brine, a churning rush of water that slid over him, under him, searched him for buried treasure and fought him for his bones, and cast him finally, with a wild plunge and roil of froth, piecemeal on the sand, where he lay with his lips to the receding tide. Megan, borne ashore on a silken wave of foam, felt its pale fingers everywhere before it loosed her reluctantly to land.

She rolled onto her back, heard the seagulls cry. She felt Jonah's hand groping, touching hers. After a wave or two, she slid her fingers into his; their hands locked. After another breath or three, she opened her eyes to the cool purple and gold of the setting sun.

Jonah raised himself on one elbow, put his arm around her, gathered her as close as he could, until only the most persistent waters came between them. Something cold touched his mouth; he stirred finally, opened his eyes.

A black rabbit running under a quarter moon of silver hung from her ear. She heard his breath still, and raised her face blurrily. Salt was drying on her glasses; he had lost his. She pulled hers off, dropped them in the sand, and saw his eyes, turned seaward then, haunted, troubled, as if he were losing some great treasure beneath the waves, and would bail out the sea with a scallop shell to save it.

The expression faded; he crossed the distance, came back to her. She kissed him swiftly, knowing he would be possessed, he would leave her like that, again and again, as long as she stayed with him. He kissed her back, awkwardly, tentatively. He shifted suddenly, as something hard met bone; he loosed her, turned a little, to push one hand into his pocket. He brought out a handful of pearls.

"To remind me," he said finally, a little bitterly, as he looked at them. She nodded.

"I know. I have one, too." She slid one of her fish-scale slippers off, shook it. A pearl, large and slightly misshapen, glistening with grays and purples, dropped between them; she picked it quickly out of the foam. She turned it in her hand, watching the colors change, for a long time before she felt his eyes.

She met his gaze, saw him unsure, this time, what he had lost, or if he had lost anything at all, or everything. She smiled a little, unsure herself, half-human, half-mermaid with her pale wet hair, her legs gleaming darkly with fish scale, curled gracefully under her. Then she tossed the pearl back to a receding wave.

"It was just a gift," she said. "Like yours."

He blinked, his face easing, and leaned forward to kiss her again, before he said, "Mine are tears."

They rose finally, walked hand in hand out of the tide. He looked back once, and so did she, seeking the place where steps might have begun that led down to the land beneath the waves, where a sea hare might wait for her, carrying a dark pearl between its horns. She saw a little ribbon of foam, headed back to sea, turned purple by the dusk.

Writing High Fantasy

The formula is simple. Take one 15th-century palace with high towers and pennants flying, add a hero who talks like a butler, a wizard with fireworks under his fingernails, and a Lurking Evil that threatens the kingdom or the heroine, and there you have it: high fantasy in the making.

And there we have all had it up to the proverbial "here." How many times can you repeat the same plot? But how can you write high fantasy without the traditional trappings, characters, and plot that are essential for this kind of fantasy?

So I am forced to ask myself the same question when I begin a new fantasy: How can it follow the rules of high fantasy and break them at the same time?

THE HERO

In writing the *Riddle-Master* trilogy, my impulse was to be as deliberately traditional as possible: a ruler leaves the comforts of his castle to learn from wizards how to fight a Lurking Evil that threatens to destroy his land. The hero, the magic, the danger are after all elements of fantasy as old as storytelling. But how do you give the Generic Hero—who only has to be high-born, look passable, and fight really well to be a hero—personality?

I discarded quite a number of auditioning heroes before settling on Morgon, Prince of Hed, ruler of a tiny island, who liked to make beer, read books, didn't own a sword, and kept the only crown he possessed under his bed. He did not talk like an English butler, he knew which end of a shovel was up, and only a penchant for wanting to learn odd things kept him from being a sort of placid gentleman farmer. That small detail—among all the details of a prosaic hardheaded life that included farming, trading, pigherders, backyard pumps, and a couple of strong-willed siblings—became the conflict in his personality that ultimately drove him from his land and set him on his questing path.

Before I let him set forth, I placed him against as detailed a background as I possibly could. I wanted the reader to see the land Morgon lived in and how it shaped him before he left it and changed himself. So I let him talk about grain and bulls, beer and plowhorses, and his sister's bare feet, before I let him say fairy-tale words like *tower, wizard, harp,* and *king,* and state his own driving motivation: to answer the unanswered riddle.

THE HEROINE

In *The Sorceress and the* Cygnet, my questing hero found himself falling literally into the path of my questing heroine. She is, in one sense, the princess in the tower whom my hero eventually rescues; in other words, she is very much a piece of the familiar storytelling formula. But she has imprisoned herself in a rickety old house in a swamp, trapped there by her own obsession with the darker side of magic.

As she defines herself: "I have been called everything from sorceress to bog hag. I know a great many things but never enough. Never enough. I know the great swamp of night, and sometimes I do things for pay if it interests me." She has pursued her quest for knowledge and power into a dangerous backwater of mean, petty magic, from which, it is clear to everyone but her, she must be rescued. The language she uses, like Morgon's, covers a broad territory between palace and pig herder's hut. Her wanderings have freed her tongue.

In the same novel, I also used a female point of view—that of a highborn lady—to contrast with the more earthy, gypsyish, view of my hero. She is a female version of the "friend of the hero"; she frets about the sorceress, gives advice, and fights beside the sorceress in the end. She is perhaps the toughest kind of character to work with: genuinely good, honest, and dutiful. Making a point-of-view character both good and interesting is a challenge. Traditionally, a "good" character has a limited emotional range, no bad habits to speak of, and a rather bland vocabulary. As the "friend of the heroine," she is also a sounding board for the heroine's more colorful character.

I deliberately chose that kind of character because I wanted to see how difficult it would be to make her more than just a device to move the plot along its necessary path. She turned out to be extraordinarily difficult. I wanted her to be elegant, dignified, calm, responsible. . . .

To keep her from fading completely into the plot, I constantly had to provide her with events that brought out her best qualities. Keeping her dialogue simple kept her uncomplicated yet responsive as a character; it also moved the plot forward without dragging along the unnecessary baggage of introspection. She is meant to observe and act; the language should not be more complicated than she is.

THE LURKING EVIL

Traditionally, the Evil in fantasy is personified by someone of extraordinary and perverse power, whose goal in life is to bring the greatest possible misery to the largest number of good honest folk. Sauron of the *Lord of the Rings* trilogy, Darth Vader of the *Star Wars* trilogy, Morgan le Fay of *Le Morte d'Arthur* are all examples of social misfits from whose destructive powers the hero and heroine must rescue humanity and hobbits and the world as they know it.

The problem with the Lurking Evil is that as social misfit, it might become far more interesting than the good and dutiful hero. Yet without proper background and personality, the Lurking Evil becomes a kind of unmotivated monster vacuum cleaner that threatens humanity simply because it's plugged in and turned on. I have trouble coming up with genuinely evil characters who are horrible, remorseless, and deserving of everything the hero can dish out. I always want to give them a human side, which puts them in the social misfit category.

In my *Riddle-Master* trilogy, I used various kinds of misfits: the renegade wizard Ohm, who was motivated by an unprincipled desire for magical power; the sea-people, whose intentions and powers seem at first random and obscure, until they finally reveal their origins; and the ambiguous character Deth, who may be good and may be evil—and who keeps my hero offbalance and guessing until the end of the tale.

In *The Sorceress and the Cygnet,* I used much the same kind of device: allowing my hero to define characters as evil until, in the end, they reveal that the evil is not in them, but in my misguided heroine. I do this because evil as a random event, or as the sole motivation for a character, is difficult for me to work with; it seems to belong in another genre—to horror or mystery.

Jung says that all aspects of a dream are actually faces of the dreamer. I believe that in fantasy, the vanquished evil must be an aspect of the hero or heroine, since by tradition, evil is never stronger than the power of the hero to overcome it—which is where, of course, we get the happy endings in high fantasy.

MAGIC

If you put a mage, sorceress, wizard, warlock, witch, or necromancer into fantasy, it's more than likely that, sooner or later, he or she will want to work some magic. Creating a spell can be as simple or as difficult as you want. You can write, "Mpyxl made a love potion. Hormel drank it and fell in love." Or you can do research into herb lore and medieval recipes for spells and write: "Mpyxl stirred five bay leaves, an owl's eye, a parsnip, six of Hormel's fingernails, and some powdered mugwort into some leftover barley soup. Hormel ate it and fell in love."

Or you can consider love itself, and how Mpyxl must desire Hormel, how frustrated and rejected she must feel to be obliged to cast a spell over him, what in Hormel generates such overpowering emotions, why he refuses to fall in love with Mpyxl the usual way, and what causes people to fall in love with each other in the first place. Then you will find that Mpyxl herself is under a spell cast by Hormel, and that she must change before his eyes from someone he doesn't want to someone he desires beyond reason.

The language of such a spell would be far different from fingernails and barley soup. The Magic exists only in the language; the spell exists only in the reader's mind. The words themselves must create something out of nothing. To invent a convincing love potion you must, for a moment, make even the reader fall in love.

WHY?

Why write fantasy? Because it's there. Fantasy is as old as poetry and myth, which are as old as language. The rules of high fantasy are rules of the unconscious and the imagination, where good quests, evil lurks, the two clash, and the victor—and the reader—are rewarded.

Good might be male or female; so might evil. The battle might be fought with swords, with magic, with wits, on a battlefield, in a tower, or in the quester's heart.

At its best, fantasy rewards the reader with a sense of wonder about what lies within the heart of the commonplace world. The greatest tales are told over and over, in many ways, through centuries. Fantasy changes with the changing times, and yet it is still the oldest kind of tale in the world, for it began once upon a time, and we haven't heard the end of it yet.

Dear Pat

Afterword by Peter S. Beagle

Ah, Pat. . . .

I know for certain that you and I met in 1975, because *The Forgotten Beasts of Eld* had very recently been published. I remember hunting through an entire convention, back in 1975, looking for the person who had written that astonishing first novel. I can't count how many Q&A sessions with fans and professionals I've sat through over the years, mentioning you first whenever I'm asked what modern fantasy writers I read.

Then I remember you came to visit me in Santa Cruz and we walked on the beach where the elephant seals are. I know I owe you for dragging me into Brisbane, one night almost forty years ago, to catch a scraggly-looking band called the Prairie Dogs—who turn up, charmingly transmogrified, in your *Fool's Run*—which resulted in a singer-songwriter named George Kincheloe's becoming the nearest thing I've got to a functioning brother. Also for staying for one delightful night with you and your mother in Roxbury, New York, when George Kincheloe's twin brother, John, came over with his wife and toddlers, several of whom grew up to become the band Sister Sparrow and the Dirty Birds.

And the books . . . ah, the *books.* The growth in range and language, the progression in style from the epic Riddle-Master trilogy to *The Book of Atrix Wolfe,* twenty years later, to that bloody breathtaking

The Bell at Sealey Head. Somewhere around there—speaking personally, as another writer, prey to the very mixed bag of genuine professional admiration and raw envy that is our shameful lot—I realized that you were becoming flat-out alarming.

Mind you, even *I* don't know all the books. There's no keeping up with you, but that's cool. I can live with the fact of your output far surpassing mine: prolificacy isn't the same as prolixity. The real problem is that you just keep getting better, more daring, more original. I mean, how long has this got to go on?

Of all the stories amassed in *Dreams of Distant Shores,* "Weird," the first and the shortest, may be the weirdest. I know it's the one I keep coming back to, because of its puzzling central image: two lovers under siege in a bathroom, the woman challenging the man with increasingly strange tales out of her own life . . . while someone beyond the door pounds on it with insane rage and howls in an incomprehensible tongue. The story feels as hauntingly unresolved as a major-seventh chord, left hanging in the twilight air at the end of a song. Except that it *isn't* unresolved at all, and it *is* warmly sad, and distinctly scary as well; and I'm going to read it once again, when I've finished this foreword, to make certain that I understand what I think I understand. Because, in its small, dark way, it's not like anything I know of you or your work.

"Mer" is an easier read, but no less of a knockout for that. The nameless witch who has inhabited, first, a goddess's body, and then a wooden mermaid; then, temporarily, a tall, slightly ungainly, human body, working as a waitress in a coastal Oregon fish-and-tourists town; and *then* finds herself—to her own mild surprise—protecting nestling cormorants against their human predators (the church service at Our Lady of the Cormorants is well worth the price of admission) mostly wants to curl up somewhere comfy and silent and go back to sleep. She's earned it, between one thing and another.

I might not have written "Mer" as well as you've done—you're always quietly setting the bar just a bit higher—but at least I can imagine *thinking* about writing it. That's something, anyway. Its blend of humor and the suggestion of things that, as a major character puts it, "I will never want to know," brings it somehow closer to my side of the street—to "my ain countree," as the old song has it. That being said . . . okay, *maybe*. On a good day, with a following wind.

But then . . . then you follow that with "The Gorgon in the Cupboard." Now it's personal.

Okay, Poul Anderson beat me to the title "A Knight of Ghosts and Shadows." What the hell, it was long ago, and he was a dear man and a wonderful writer, and fair's fair. And there was no way you could have known that I was working on a story called "To Medusa: We Have to Talk." But did your Medusa story have to be so damn good? I can't even tell you exactly why I'm so taken with that story. (Though I *did* know a Jo once, and the name is still a personally evocative one. . . .) I grew up around painters and models—my oldest friend (we met when we were five years old) is a painter; and those parts of the tale that deal with the relationships of painters to their work and their own lives are as believable as if they were set in my uncles' Greenwich Village studios in the 1950s and 1960s instead of late-Victorian London and its environs. Rightly or wrongly, I see your artists as Pre-Raphaelite types—Rossetti, Millais, Burne-Jones, Ford Madox Brown, and the like—all working away on religious allegories and Arthurian landscapes. And you have the desperation and the casually heartless—practically Republican—attitude toward the desperate *down,* without melodrama or billboards. When Jo finally weeps, we know enough—*enough,* never overmuch—to believe that it's been a very long time since her last tears. *Damn,* Patricia!

And Medusa. Your Medusa.

She's dead—she remembers her head being cut off by Perseus, that obnoxious, not especially bright boy who got lucky—but, in common with many fictional ghosts and figments, she has the best one-liners in the story. She's funny, sardonic, wise, dangerous—and, at times, very nearly as touching as Jo herself, even though she's only a painted mouth on a canvas. Immortal, her survival in this time and this world yet depends on a questionably talented young artist, Harry Waterman, whose knowing, raucous Muse she becomes. The painter fancies himself passionately, desperately, hopelessly in love with the wife of another artist, whose unspeakable beauty almost literally turns him to stone. It is the Gorgon who rouses a different awareness in him and teaches him, for the first time, to see. It may not make him a better or more successful painter—but there will be more to his work than there was before.

I couldn't have written that damn story, Pat. I'm old enough and experienced enough to *want* to write it, but I couldn't have done it. This is not the first time that this has happened.

I have a particular soft spot for the understated and deeply touching "Alien." I don't think I'll ever consider a "little-green-guys-abducted-me-and-studied-me" story in the same way again—sorry, *X-Files.* Sorry, so many long-beloved clichés of first contact, from monster invasions to physical or psychic bodysnatching. Absurdly, it reminds me, of all things, of a French song I often sang at a restaurant in Santa Cruz, long ago and properly far away. In "Un Tout Petit Homme Timide," a flying saucer lands in a Paris park, and what emerges is a shy, big-eyed little guy with his helmet under his arm. He regards the Parisians and apologizes: "Oh, forgive me—wrong planet! But I'll come back again—you seem very nice!" And he's gone again, leaving the singer to comment, "Well, he thought we were nice, which definitely shows that he's not from around here! But once he and his people get a good look at us, at what we are, they'll say, 'Sorry, children, we'll come back when you grow up." And perhaps quit shooting toy ray-guns at us. . . .

And then there's "Something Rich and Strange." What the hell does one say about *that* story? I hardly knew where to start reading this one, let alone start thinking about it afterward. It's about human beings and sea gods, and I'm not going to try to describe it, except to say that if there's one thing you realize perfectly in this truly r-and-s story, it's the thoughtless *otherness* of the gods. I think of it, dazed as it left me, as your take on the eternal legend of Tam Lin: the young knight taken hostage by the Queen of the *Shi*, the fairy folk, and the determined woman who has to rescue him from his otherworldly mistress. Except that in your version, the seducers are two: a brother and sister out of the sea, and the valiant heroine is herself beguiled. And very nearly falls victim to the song that lured her longtime lover from her side. And how they will go on together in the mortal world, knowing what they know, having been where they have been, you have—as, of course, you *would* have—sense enough to leave to your readers.

What strikes me more and more about your recent work—apart from the increasing range of your adventurousness—is your obvious determination either to ignore or sidestep the standard tropes of classic fantasy, or to shake them up so as to leave them more than a bit dizzy and disoriented, like Edie and Henry (and, surely, their calmly competent driver, Thompson), when their motoring jaunt takes them down the Road Not Taken and brings them home—or not?—to a familiar world grown promisingly unfamiliar. Or, in your words, to "a world that had shifted, expanded, to let the fantastic in."

When I speak of your work to strangers and students, the majority of them inevitably want to discuss the Riddle-Master books, or the Kyreol and Cygnet duologies—which is perfectly fine with me, always. But lately the stories seem determined in themselves to challenge you yourself more and take you further toward distant shores, if you will. Not that they ever lose the humor and deep humanity that is their ground bass (to elaborate on the earlier musical metaphor); it's more that the melodies, more often than not these days, don't necessarily go where I was expecting them to go, but swing off over the hills and far away. And as always—for full forty years now—I catch my breath and follow, trusting and sure.